THE STORIES WE TELL

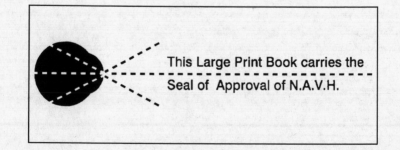

This Large Print Book carries the
Seal of Approval of N.A.V.H.

The Stories We Tell

Patti Callahan Henry

WHEELER PUBLISHING
A part of Gale, Cengage Learning

GALE
CENGAGE Learning®

Farmington Hills, Mich • San Francisco • New York • Waterville, Maine
Meriden, Conn • Mason, Ohio • Chicago

GALE
CENGAGE Learning®

LIBRARY OF CONGRESS CATALOGING-IN-PUBLICATION DATA

Henry, Patti Callahan.
  The stories we tell / by Patti Callahan Henry.
    pages cm. — (Wheeler Publishing Large Print Hardcover)
    ISBN 978-1-4104-7280-9 (hardcover) — ISBN 1-4104-7280-9 (hardcover)
    1. Family life—Fiction. 2. Marriage—Fiction. 3. Domestic fiction. 4. Large type books. I. Title.
PS3608.E578S76 2014b
813'.6—dc23
                                                  2014021452

Published in 2014 by arrangement with St. Martin's Press, LLC

Printed in Mexico
1 2 3 4 5 6 7 18 17 16 15 14

To George Rusk Henry, my son.
His kind, curious, and
creative heart inspires me
to be a better person (and writer)
than I know how to be.

Some things have to be
believed to be seen.

— *Many Waters,* by Madeleine L'Engle

TEN GOOD IDEAS CARD LINE

1. Be Kind
2. Tell Good Stories
3. Always Say Good-bye
4. Search for the True
5. Help Others
6. Create
7. Be Patient
8. Find Adventure
9. Forgive
10. Love

PROLOGUE

My eyes changed color and I didn't even notice. The first clue came when a street vendor in Savannah drew a caricature and painted my eyes green. "This is great," I said, "but my eyes are brown."

"Oh, I'm so sorry," he said with a fake French accent. "I thought they were green."

A few weeks later, a customer in my letterpress studio commented on my earthy-green eyes. I thanked him without correcting him. A polite southern woman does not question a compliment.

It was a full month later, in a hotel with one of those magnifying mirrors — the kind that expose every pore — that I noticed something odd. My eyes were a lichen color, like soft moss between stepping-stones. The color came from underneath the pupil, as if the green of my eyes had been there all along, just waiting for its time. I'd never heard of this happening. Which just goes to show that when I don't think something is possible, I just don't notice. Even if it's happening right before my very eyes. Or in this case, *in* my eyes.

ONE

It was a good day, with all good things. It began with something my daughter and I used to say to each other, until about a year ago, when her eye-rolling adolescent angst took over and she refused our Saturday-morning ritual. But today, when Gwen turned to me and said, "Let's do something fun," I jumped into her request as if it were a languid lake on a summer afternoon. My younger sister, Willa, wasn't far behind.

"What about a pottery class?" I suggested.

"Gross," said Gwen, all of seventeen years old and picking at her nail polish. "Paris. Let's go to Paris."

"Sure," I said. "Why not today?"

When Gwen laughed, I joined in with relief.

"Sailing class," Willa said, jumping into the conversation.

That was it. And the day was the kind of dreamy, laughing suspension of time that we live for. The kind of day when you can believe in anything. There we were: my daughter, my sister, and I, the gray-blue water of the Savannah River, salt water in our eyes and laughter in our throats.

Now it's midnight and I almost regret skipping out on work. Maybe I should've done the responsible thing and forged ahead on the looming deadlines, the orders piling up, and the customers to be courted. Then I remember the look on Gwen's face when she climbed out of the water, sputtering and splashing Willa, who'd tipped the boat, accidentally on purpose, and I know I did the right thing.

This was not a wasted day.

Still, the night feels restless underneath me as a storm rips into Savannah with careless disregard. The rain's coming sideways, clamorous against the window and hard. They usually don't bother me, these storms. In fact, I like the rain in this water-soaked city; it's part of the ocean, part of the rivers, tributaries, and bays that contain the waters that surround us. Storms here are normal, an unassailable part of the water-soaked landscape that I usually find comforting. Not tonight, though.

My husband, Cooper, is out of town on business again, so his side of the bed is empty. Gwen is asleep in her room. Willa is in her cottage a few hundred yards away. No point in my tossing and turning when there's work I can do, work I want to do.

I dress in jeans and a T-shirt to walk down the hallway to my daughter's bedroom. If a watered-down light travels under her door, I'll know she's on the computer. But it's dark. Good, she's asleep, the storm a white noise to her dreams. I think about going in and kissing her on the forehead, looking at her soft face, but she'll bark at me if I wake her. I'm getting used to this new means of communication (sort of), but it still gives a quick stab to my chest.

I understand that girls turning into women are often unsettled and cruel, especially to those they love. As a psychiatrist once told me at a dinner party (aren't there always psychiatrists at dinner parties?), adolescence, by its very definition, is "a disturbance." So there's that. My sweet girl, who once wanted to play American Girl dolls and have me paint her nails a sparkly pink, now rolls her eyes at the way I breathe or chew or walk. It's difficult not to "take it personally," as Cooper says. I'm sure I did the same with my mom; I know I did the same with my mom. But here, with my daughter, I'd hoped it would be different.

15

She's an only child; a decision made when I was so sick from my pregnancy that the doctor put me to bed for three months and Cooper told me he couldn't go through the fear of losing me again. Gwen is our blessing, he said. No need to take another chance. I'd agreed — then.

I tiptoe down the stairs and into the kitchen I redid two years ago to my exact specifications. Everything in this room works for the way I cook and move and reach for spices or pans. White and chrome dominate; an island of Carrera marble squats in the middle of the kitchen, a counter that's alternately cluttered with bowls and food and then homework and mail. The family desk is built into the cabinetry. Framed photos of the family sit on this desk, along with an ancient Remington portable number 3, which was the kind of typewriter Margaret Mitchell used to write *Gone with the Wind.* The typewriter once worked, but, like other things in my life, it's in need of repair.

I make a cup of tea with Tazo Calm, then sit on the window seat, my legs curled underneath me. Growing up, I'd never imagined living in a house this lovely, with a kitchen full of light and chrome, with cabinets full of fine, breakable plates. Now here I am.

The night is a blackout canvas of morphed shapes and moving shadows, yet in my mind's eye I can see everything. The side kitchen door will open and take me down two steps to the brick pathway, which leads to the detached garage and the stone path that leads to the guesthouse, where Willa lives. If I continue, I'll reach the old stables and my letterpress studio, the Fine Line, Ink.

The storm whips louder, and if I believed in portents, I'd think it was nature's morbid warning. That's the problem with having grown up here in Savannah — otherworldly portents and ghosts are everywhere. Or so we're told. Tourists line up to hear about these ghosts, to see the scant evidence of them. There are root doctors and fortune-tellers, stories and legends. There are messages in wind, rain, stars, and tides. And although I don't really believe the storm has some special message for me, the idea that it might gives me a shiver just as a crack of far-off lightning smacks the earth.

I know this about imagination: It needs a place to go. If I don't work at my cards and images and letterpress, if I don't touch the cut metal and carved wood fonts and imagine different patterns as I place letters next to others in a new way, my ideas will turn inward. I'll ruminate about the storm, Gwen's broken curfew, her annoying boyfriend, and her grades, about Cooper's travel schedule and Willa's aimless job search. I'll think about how much I missed Willa while she was gone, and then I'll be afraid that she'll leave again — off to chase a man or a shapeless dream. I'll worry about how she might start drinking again, drinking too, too much. But if I channel my imagination, if I move that energy to the letters and the paper — to this blessed thing called work — I'll be okay.

I finish the tea and slip on my Hunter rain boots before grabbing an umbrella. An industrial flashlight leads the way to my studio with a V-shaped cone of light, and I slosh through the mud. I've done this before.

The Fine Line, Ink nestles itself in the middle of a fallow field that once produced south Georgia cotton and is now filled with grass, wildflowers, and oat stems. The twenty-acre swath was handed down to my husband, Cooper, the fourth generation of Morrison men to own this land.

When I flick on the light, the mismatched furniture and letterpress machines come into view, along with cases of cotton paper piled like children's blocks against the walls. And type fonts — everywhere the cut metal and carved wooden font squares sit on tables, on machines, in drawers, and in boxes waiting to be sorted. The fonts that have been organized are held in California job cases, tall cabinets that flank the walls, like shy girls at a dance.

It's here with my coworkers, Francie and Max, that we tell our stories. *There's a story behind everything* — that's our tagline. We watch tales unfold, unbend, and unwind to form card lines, logos, and images: a poster for a downtown event, a birth announcement, a wedding invitation, or a logo for an interior designer. Each stall, where horses once stamped and whinnied, is now a designated office space. Each of us has his or her own stall, as do the printing presses. In the middle of the barn, on a concrete floor, rests a long pine table, where we convene. When we sit at the project table in this refurbished barn, we create new and handmade worlds.

Some of my best work comes when I'm alone like this. We have ideas and sketches, notes and scraps of paper, scattered on the table. I push these things around to pull together our emerging card line, called Ten Good Ideas. Another collection based on

Greek goddesses, which sounded like a good idea at the time, has been set aside. First things first — finish what we started with Ten Good Ideas.

This card line was inspired by Willa's return to my life, and by one long-ago summer of childhood rebellion.

When she returned a year ago, Willa and I spent hours talking about childhood and our parents, who are both gone now. We pulled out memories of skipping Sunday school to run through the cotton fields and stuff small tufts of their seed-laden softness into our pockets. We remembered getting in trouble for singing too loudly in our bedroom, for laughing at Dad's too-long prayer at supper, for putting our elbows on the table. It was there, in those long talks, that we first reconstructed the summer when my best friend, Caden, and I had decided that the Ten Commandments were way too, oh my God, full of things *not* to do, and wouldn't it be great to make new commandments full of good things *to* do. Every day on the edge of a Savannah River tributary, we made our own list, our own rules for living.

We thought ourselves holy. Every night, I would go home and show Willa our new commandment. With a flashlight under our bunk beds, she'd take out her calligraphy pen and write the commandment Caden and I had added to our list. It was only a piece of lined paper torn from a school composition book, but to us, it was parchment, ancient and glorious.

We were caught, Caden and I, before we finished the Ten Ideas. The list was tacked to the back wall of my closet, warped with South Carolina river moisture. We'd made it to number nine before Mom found it and turned it over to my dad, and to the church elders. Heresy, we were told. There was a Bible verse, one in Revelations, about this very thing we'd done, about adding or subtracting from the Bible: "And if anyone takes away from the words of the book of this prophecy, God will take away his part from the tree of life." We were made to memorize this verse, and for months, maybe years, Willa and I believed we'd been cut off from the tree of life, even if we didn't fully understand what that tree was and where it had been planted.

Then there was the weeklong discussion about sending me to live with a another family, one who could make me understand the gravity of what I'd done. Dad believed they'd failed in Christian parenting, and I'd failed as the dutiful daughter. My defiance, they believed, put our eternity together at risk. They needed someone else, anyone else, to help me see that rebellion was not the way to happiness or a pass through the pearly gates. In the end, I stayed home, and with a stomachache I tolerated the grave silence of my dad's disappointment and my mom's worry.

Eventually, Willa and I exhausted the stories of that summer and turned to the list — our commandments. What had we thought then, as children, were the right ways to live? Could those matter today?

Whenever I think of the list now, I taste the brackish air. I feel like I'm twelve years old again and invincible. Childhood slams into my chest and unfolds its promise of a bigger life.

It was Max who saw the potential for the list to become a card line. "Ten Good Ideas. Come on, it's the best compilation idea we've ever had." And he was right. So one by one, we've been releasing the cards with original artwork. The problem is that Willa and I can't remember number nine, and we still haven't come up with number ten.

This creation, this card line, has been Willa's work with us. In the beginning, I'd thought I was merely giving her something to do, something besides work on her songwriting and find singing gigs in town. But we all soon realized that Ten Good Ideas was the most successful line in our six years of business. Orders tripled by the third idea, and we'd added six new vendors in the South alone.

I feel a wave of intense love for all of it, for all of the ideas and the designs so far finished and for the ones yet to be created.

Number One: Be Kind. An oak tree extends its arms to the heavens, to the earth, and falling off the side of the pages.

Number Two: Tell Good Stories. Books are drawn to appear like leather-bound volumes piled one on top of the other, inviting story-telling, and story reading.

Number Three: Always Say Good-bye. Here Francie sketched human profiles, one facing the other, begging the question of who might be leaving.

Number Four: Search for the True. This design is my favorite so far: The world, blue and floating amid the dark night, stars set as sparkled dents in the Universe.

Number Five: Help Others. Here is the luminescent design, one Max drew, of two hands entwined, fingers knit together.

Number Six: Create. Paint cans of every color are splattered across the page, spilling and dripping into the number six at the bottom of the card.

Number Seven: Be Patient

Number Eight: Find Adventure

I'm scribbling a note about needing more ink for the Vandercook press when I hear the sirens. They sound far off, until they don't. The sirens swell: loud, louder, loudest. Then silence. I stand, staring at the huge barn doors, waiting for them to slide across the track and open, because I know they will. I imagine the three people I love the most in the world. I imagine the news to come.

No, no, no.

A policeman, short, with dark hair, stands in the doorway. The overhead light casts shadows across his face. Rain drips from the eaves onto the plastic-covered bib of his hat.

"Are you Eve Morrison?" he asks.

"Yes." My voice is tight with fear.

"I'm Officer Barker with the Savannah Police Department. Your husband and sister have been involved in a car accident. They're at Savannah Memorial. I'm sorry to be here telling you this. Your husband sent me, as you haven't been answering the phone." He breaks off each sentence with a quick sound: a verbal Morse code.

24

"Cooper? My sister? My God, are they okay?"

"I've been sent to get you. They're at the hospital and your husband is conscious. That's the only information I have at the moment." He sounds robotic, flatlined.

"Wait." I shake my head, relieved that this policeman has the wrong information. "My husband's in Charleston. My sister's at work. She's a singer. I think you've made a mistake."

Officer Barker coughs. "I'm afraid not, ma'am. They were driving in downtown Savannah. That's all the information I have. I've been sent to take you to the hospital."

"Are you sure?"

"Yes, ma'am." He steps into the barn and I see his face clearly. He's young, so young that acne stands in pockmarked relief against his face.

"Take me to them." I back away and bump into a press, the Heidelberg. My hip grazes the sharp edge; it will leave a bruise. I switch off the single light over the table. "First my daughter," I say, panic a rising tide in the back of my throat. "I need to get my daughter."

"Where is she?" he asks.

"Asleep." I point toward the general direction of our house.

25

"I tried there first. No one answered."

"She's asleep." I stop and stare at him. "How did you know where to find me?"

"Your husband."

I reach into my back pocket and yank out my cell phone. Eight missed calls. I hit the callback button while motioning to Officer Barker: Keep walking and I'll follow. Cooper doesn't answer, and I follow the policeman. Fear begins as a firestorm in my belly, moving along my arms and legs as electricity. No. Not my sister. Not my husband. I climb into Officer Barker's backseat and he drives up the muddy path to the house. His car will bear the splash stains as the mark of our rain-drenched driveway.

Officer Barker has barely pulled to a stop, and I'm running up the steps onto the wide front porch. In the moonlight, the white floorboards glow almost blue, reflecting the painted ceiling. I open the door and holler, "Gwen, Gwen."

No answer.

I run through the front hall and upstairs to her bedroom. Damp air washes over me as pink linen curtains flutter around her open window.

"Shit," I say to the empty room. "Not now."

I plod down the back stairs and into the

kitchen, just to be sure she isn't there. The tea bag dangles over the empty cup. I sipped that tea, thinking Gwen was asleep in bed and Cooper was in Charleston. Such naïve peace. My head feels too full, overblown and crowded with fear. In what feels like a slow-motion bad dream, one where I can't run or scream, I dial Gwen's number and hear her voice say, "Leave a message." I tell her to meet me at the hospital. I then dial Dylan — the boyfriend, the lacrosse player, the boy I can't stand — and get his ridiculous voice mail. "Yo, I can't answer, obviously. So leave a message, or don't."

"Dylan, this is Gwen's mother. Her father and aunt have been in an accident and I need you to take Gwen to Savannah Memorial immediately. Thank you very much."

God, I sound like my mom — so polite, so cold, when what I really want to do is scream. I grab car keys from the counter, then burst into the rain again.

Officer Barker stands outside his car with his hands behind his back.

The rain batters against my T-shirt and I'm soaked to the skin. "I forgot she spent the night at a friend's house."

He knows I'm lying, but he nods.

"I'll drive," I say.

"I'd prefer you let me take you."

27

"I'm fine. I can follow you." I jog toward the garage and punch the keypad code to open it.

Thunder joins the grinding rise of the garage door, as if to say, Told you so.

Two

It makes no sense. Willa and Cooper barely get along. The tension between them is mostly unbearable, unless Cooper's on his second bourbon. I'm not sure they've ever been in a car without me.

Willa — my beautiful, wounded sister, the tiny girl with the round green eyes. She moved to Colorado after high school and returned to Savannah just last year after a terrible breakup. She showed up, asking for a place to crash until she could "get her shit together." "Of course," we said, "we'd love to have you here."

Cooper and I stopped talking about it, but I know he doesn't like having Willa only a few hundred yards away. My work and my sister are the two things he believes take my attention away from him, and in his worst moments, he reminds me of this.

I follow the police car through the Savannah streets, gripping the steering wheel with tight hands. Streetlamps flicker dimly, as if sorry they don't have enough power to penetrate the fog. The river is swollen as it pulses against the banks and shoves cargo ships against the docks. My heart rolls around inside my chest, a fast-paced somersaulting instead of a steady beat. Skidding on the wet pavement, I follow the police car under the awning over the entrance to the emergency room. The double glass doors open automatically and I run to the front desk, ask for Cooper, for Willa. The nurse stares at a computer screen for a moment before holding up a finger and turning to me. "Head down the hall. You'll find them in the second and third cubicles on the right." She points like a flight attendant.

The ER cubicle is all silver and glaring, bright enough to make me squint. I can't feel my lips; my hands shake as I push aside the curtain. I look in the bed for Cooper, but what I see is a mash of blond curls against the pillow — Willa. Beeping machines surround her where she lies on the narrow bed with rails high on either side. An IV tube hangs from a metal pole and is taped to the top of her right hand. A small white bandage is next to her right eye, which is swollen shut. A drop of blood seeps through the gauze, leaving what looks like a drop of red ink.

Near the bed is a nurse with dark cropped hair and a name tag that says BILL STANFORD, RN. A doctor, short and brunette, wearing a white lab coat with one large iodine stain on her right lapel, stands beside him. Crumpled bandage packaging and discarded needles sit on top of a stainless-steel tray.

I walk to Willa's bedside and look down into her face. Her eyes are closed. "I'm her sister, Eve," I say without looking at the doctor or nurse. "Tell me everything." I take Willa's free hand and wind my fingers through hers. "Where's my husband? Is he here, too?" I turn to look at the doctor. Finally, the chaos inside me stills for a moment, my mind expectant.

"I'm Dr. Lewis," the woman says. "Your husband is in the next cubicle, behind this curtain. And your sister here . . ." She pauses before saying, "She's stable. Her vital signs are good. She wasn't wearing her seat belt and she flew sideways, crashing into the passenger-side window. She seems to have sustained a mild traumatic brain injury. We're waiting on the last MRI, and we're monitoring the pressure on her brain. There's a slight bleed in the temporal area, which we will drain if need be, but right now it seems to be okay. We're keeping her sedated while we monitor her situation."

"This?" I touch the edge of the bandage.

"She has a small cut next to her right eye. It has a single stitch in it. Her brain injury is the most pressing matter."

"Temporal area. Brain swelling. Traumatic injury," I say. "None of that means anything real to me. Can you explain, please?" My voice holds steady, but my body shakes.

Dr. Lewis points to the side of her own head, above her ear. "This is the temporal lobe, and it's where Willa slammed into the window. There's swelling, what we can also call a concussion, but more severe. More like what we call a mild TBI — mild traumatic brain injury."

"What's the difference between a TBI and a concussion?" I ask.

Dr. Lewis places her hand on my forearm and then withdraws it.

"We can have the neuro practitioner talk to you soon, but for now I can tell you that the difference has to do with how long she was unconscious, which we estimate to be about ten minutes. We should know more soon."

I point to Willa. "But she's still unconscious."

"No. She's asleep and sedated."

"Will she be . . . the same?" I whisper.

"That is the thing with TBIs — we don't know. I understand it's difficult to hear me be so vague, but only time will tell with these kinds of injuries. She'll probably be confused at first, but slowly we'll understand more about how severely her thought processes and memory are affected. It's not like a broken bone that we can see on an X-ray. I wish it were."

I touch Willa's forehead lightly, so lightly. "She'll be fine. She has to be fine."

Willa's curls are mashed against her head and black mascara rims her eyes in a melted mess. "What happened?" I lean closer, my voice in her ear, my hand squeezing hers.

"She grabbed the wheel." My husband's voice.

I turn so quickly that I knock into Willa's IV pole and need to grab it to keep it from falling. The curtain is open. "Cooper." I rush to his bedside in two quick steps.

"You didn't want to come check on me?" he asks in a garbled voice.

I stare at him, stunned into silence, knowing this is Cooper because of the eyes and voice, but everything is distorted in a globulelike mash of blood, bandages, and bloated flesh. I try to say his name but only a groan on an exhaled breath comes out.

Then I find my voice. "I'm here. Right here."

He closes his eyes. "God, it hurts like hell." His voice is full of swollen pain. He raises his hand to touch his head but then drops it again, as if it weighs too much.

I bend over my husband, reaching for him, scanning his body for injury or missing parts. I kiss him once on the forehead. "What happened?"

Dr. Lewis appears at my side. "Broken glass cut your husband's face and scalp," she states, as if this is the most obvious thing in all the world.

"Are you okay?" A stupid question if ever there was one.

"Other than this?" Cooper lifts his hand to his head one more time, a single finger pointing at the bandages.

"No other injuries?" I ask softly, hopefully.

"No," Dr. Lewis says. "All else is clear."

"Clear?" Cooper tries to sit, but he falls back down. "I'm missing half my face."

"You are not missing half your face," I say. I don't know if this fact is true, because a bandage soaked in blood covers the left side of his face, and the tape yanks the skin tight up and around his head. I don't want to, but I look away, turning to Dr. Lewis. "Is he missing half his face?"

"No." She readjusts the tape at his scalp. "But it is a severe gash." She motions to his cheek. "This will require plastic surgery later. There's also a shearing injury on his scalp."

"A bald spot," Cooper says, and his voice is slow, slurred.

"Pain medicine?" I ask Dr. Lewis, referring to his speech.

She nods.

I kiss Cooper's right cheek, which gives no indication of an accident or injury of any kind. "His eye?" I ask her.

"It's fine."

"What happened?" I ask again.

His right eye flashes open, murky and faded. "Is Willa okay?"

"It's her brain," I say. "It's swollen . . . bleeding." My hand rests at the base of my throat, where the grief and panic form a cotton-clogging lump.

"She wasn't wearing her seat belt," he says, as if this one fact explains everything.

"Cooper." I lean close, uttering gentle words. "Who was driving?"

"I was," he says. And then, as if everything is normal, he asks, "Where's Gwen?"

"She should be on her way."

"Where is she, Eve?"

"She sneaked out again. I think she's with Dylan."

"This has to stop," he whispers, his eyes shut.

"I know."

He brushes his hand through the air. "Were you at the studio?" This question an accusation.

"Yes."

I think he's slipping into painkiller oblivion, when he speaks again. "I'm sorry I couldn't help your sister. I wanted to help, Eve. All we've done is try to help her, and it only gets worse." Angry furrows on his forehead smooth, and then he is asleep, snoring softly.

It isn't true, what he's just said. We have helped Willa; she's been doing great — working at the studio with me, writing songs, securing singing gigs downtown. Like I've always wished, my sister and my daughter are close, and they spend every afternoon together. Willa hasn't been getting worse at all. I thought she was getting better and better — until now.

I look to Dr. Lewis. "This is terrible," I say, which is the truth.

The doctor leaves, promising to check in shortly. That's when the tears start. They well up quickly — fat, ugly tears that won't stop. I touch Cooper's cheek, and even in his medicine-induced sleep, he flinches. And just as I sit in the cracked vinyl reclining chair, Gwen bursts through the curtain.

"Gwen." I jump up to hug her, hold her close, as if to make sure that she's safe, that she wasn't in the car with them. "Where have you been?"

"Doesn't matter," she says.

"Yes, it matters." I look past my daughter to the boy standing behind her. "Dylan, you can leave now."

Gwen reaches her hand behind her. "No, stay." Holding Dylan's hand, she walks toward her dad and pulls Dylan along like a towline. "Oh my God, is he okay?" She reaches toward the bloodied bandages but doesn't touch them.

"Yes," I say. "Except for a terrible gash on his face."

Gwen stands next to her dad in too-short cutoff jeans, cowboy boots, and a white tank top.

I step forward and place my hand on Dylan's arm. "You need to leave."

He drops Gwen's hand and nods. "Okay, Mrs. Morrison." He holds his palms up in mock surrender. "Okay, whatever."

Gwen glares at me. "God, Mom, relax."

"Relax?" I ask as the curtain sways shut

37

with Dylan's exit.

"It's no big deal, Mom. We were just at his house, watching movies." She takes a breath and then sees her chance. "Seriously . . . I mean, Dad and Aunt Willa are in the hospital and you're worried about what *I've* been doing?" Her nose stud — a tiny sparkle — glints in the harsh overhead lights. "Can you at least tell me what happened?"

"I don't know yet. All I know is that they were in a wreck."

"Can I see her?"

"Yes," I say. "She's asleep right there." I motion to the half-open curtain at our left.

Together, we walk to Willa's bedside and I repeat the information I was given from Dr. Lewis. Gwen drops into the chair next to Willa, taking her hand. "If something happens to her, I'll die," she says, all melodrama and raw emotion.

I touch the top of Gwen's soft hair. "I'll go sit with your dad until he wakes up."

Gwen looks up at me. "Can I stay here?" she asks.

"Yes."

I return to Cooper and lean back in the chair, closing my eyes for a moment. Just one moment.

■ ■ ■ ■

The raw light needles its way through my eyelids, penetrating my deep sleep. I open one eye — my left one — and for a thin sliver of a minute, I don't know where I am. Somewhere far off, there's a beeping noise, and it's this sound, this monotonous rhythm, that awakens me fully, and I know. I don't want to remember, but I do, one by one: Cooper, Willa, Gwen. I stand up to stretch, rub at my face, and drink from the lukewarm glass of water at Cooper's bedside. A clock on the back wall reads 6:00 A.M.

"Eve." Cooper's voice cracks my name in half, and I look back to him, take his hand. "Where is Gwen?" he asks.

"With Willa, right here." I open the curtain.

Gwen is awake, brushing Willa's hair across the pillow with her fingers. She turns to us, and I motion for her to come to me. Cooper flinches when he looks up at us with his one eye, and he reaches his hand up to take his daughter's hand.

Gwen repeats my plea from hours before. "What happened, Dad?"

Cooper looks directly at me. "Please tell

39

the nurse I need another pain pill."

I push the buzzer on the wall and speak into an intercom to inform the bodyless voice that Cooper Morrison needs a nurse and meds.

"I was coming home from Charleston," he says as I finish my request. "But the clients wanted to stop for a drink at the Bohemian. They'd heard about the rooftop bar, and we stopped there for a late dinner."

He pauses to touch the uninjured side of his face. "Willa was there, at the bar. Drunk as crazy. Bobbing around. She fell off the bar stool. I was praying she wouldn't see me, but she did, and then started to walk toward us. I was with the Berns, clients I've been courting for months. They run a charter business called the Anglers. Willa had that look, that weird look she gets when you know she will say or do something embarrassing. I got nervous, so I went to her before she could get to us."

"No way," Gwen interjects. "She doesn't drink like that anymore."

"That's what I thought at first, too, darling. I thought no way was she messing up now, when she'd just started to get it together. But it was obvious."

I don't realize I'm crying until I taste salt

at the corner of my lips.

"So," Cooper continues, "I talked her into going outside, and then getting into my car. But she was angry as hell. We were driving in that torrential rain behind Martin Luther King Boulevard and then up Twenty-fourth Street to Preston. She grabbed the wheel to make me turn around. The brakes seized up, we slid sideways, and the car slammed into a tree — a huge oak. She wasn't wearing a seat belt. OnStar called nine one one." His voice breaks. "That's it."

"I'm sorry," I say.

"What for?" Gwen asks, shooting me a terrible look, her eyebrows drawn down, her mouth pouted into a scowl.

"For everyone." I take Cooper's hand and wind my fingers through his as if knitting us together. "You didn't have to do that. You didn't have to take her home. You aren't responsible for her."

"It seems I am," he says.

"I'm sorry," I say. "I really am. I'm sorry I let her stay. I'm sorry she's been such a . . ."

"God, Mom, whatever," Gwen says, and plops onto a metal chair. "She's the one who's hurt so bad. I mean, is she in a coma? What *is* going on?" Panic pushes at Gwen's voice, giving it a strangled sound. "Is she going to be okay or not?"

Gwen loves her aunt. She loves walking down to the cottage and sitting on the porch with her, loves hearing about Colorado and camping and mountain climbing. She clings to Willa as the only person who "understands what it's like to be a grown-up without being a jerk" — Gwen's words, of course.

"Someone answer me. Is she going to be okay?" Gwen holds out her hands for an answer.

"If you mean will she live, yes," I say. "Her injuries aren't on the outside. . . . It's what's inside her head they're worried about." I walk behind Gwen and touch her hair, which is pulled back into a messy ponytail at the base of her neck, riding down her back in tangles. She leans back into my hand, a gesture of childhood. I rest my head on top of hers.

"This sucks," Gwen says.

"Yes, it does."

THREE

It was only a month ago that we were featured in *The South Magazine.* Cooper and Eve Morrison, Savannah's power couple. The beautiful people. The lucky ones. Cooper is from an old Savannah family. Cooper Morrison IV, the fourth generation of Morrison men to live on the family property with his wife and daughter. The article talked of how he broke free of the family business that built the family fortune to start out on his own creative project. Cooper launched *Southern Tastes,* an e-magazine featuring all things southern gentlemen. There's the section on guns and hunting dogs, one on handcrafted lodge furniture, another on vintage accouterments. Each month, there's a short story by a southern author. Of course there's the obligatory cooking section, usually featuring a grill and large tools. Oh, and how lovely that his wife, meanwhile, owns and operates a letterpress studio specializing in the handmade. A juxtaposition that the journalist described as "romantic and interesting."

That day of the photo shoot, I learned this: Magazine articles are part fact, part fiction. And they are oh so carefully calibrated. One shot, one picture, takes hours of adjusting and reframing. For every casual moment the reader sees, there are hours of posing. Cooper was thrilled that his schmoozing had resulted in a four-page article about *Southern Tastes,* about our family and the Morrison history in the city. He was out to prove that starting an e-magazine in 2009 had been a brilliant idea. I tried, by deflecting and disappearing, to keep the Fine Line, Ink out of the article. I didn't need the publicity; I didn't want it. This needed to be all about Cooper, about how successful the magazine was and could be. But the final product ended up missing Cooper's target.

The Fine Line, Ink has far surpassed even my wishes for its success. The magazine editor picked up on this and had me talk about the specifics. So I told him how last month both Barneys and Neiman Marcus requested a first look at our next card line. I told him that we were voted the best letterpress in Georgia two years in a row. He asked more questions. Yes, we were thinking of hiring another employee. And, yes, we had thought of using satellite printers to get the orders finished. I stopped there. I didn't tell him that we have money stashed in our back account, ready to make use of when we know exactly what we're going to do. And I didn't mention our plans for teaching, printing, expanding, and creating.

The magazine spread portrayed our family on the front porch: Eve, Cooper, and Gwen Morrison. I'm wearing jeans and a white button-down shirt with my favorite Golden Goose leather boots. My brown hair, the hair I can't get to bend or curl, falls straight to my shoulders, and the sun offers a lopsided halo. Cooper wears khakis and a dark blue sweater. He smiles and has one arm on my shoulder and the other curved around his daughter's waist. His blond hair is turning gray at the temples — a dignified southern gentlemen for sure. Gwen is as fashionable as she is pretty, her jeans disappearing into cowboy boots, and her black shirt absorbing the light. Off-camera, Willa stands behind the photographer, trying to make a sullen Gwen laugh, and she succeeds.

Cooper had the article framed, in dark wood and a cream mat, to present to his parents. Averitt nodded and offered the perfunctory "I'm proud of you, son." Louise quietly asked how I had possibly thought it was a good idea to be photographed wearing jeans.

Louise and Averitt were the parents I wanted. Well, that's what I thought the first time I met them, that they were the parents I had somehow been denied in the cosmic joke that was my life at nineteen. I was living at home in my adolescent bedroom, working more hours a week than most do in two. I hardly slept, and when I did, it was fitful and worried. My parents, Willa, and I were cramped in the small house we'd lived in our entire lives, all of us growing out of it, or maybe into it, becoming one with its slanted floors and peeling shingles.

I didn't think of us as poor. We had enough. Our house was tiny, with walls made of Sheetrock and spit, it seemed. If my parents needed a private conversation in our one-story home, they went outside or took a ride in the car. But the size of the house wasn't the real problem. It was the space occupied by my parents' expectations.

Then there they were — the Morrisons — living in a house big enough to grow any family larger than life. Theirs was a home full of activity and noise and the aroma of pot roast, a house where Cooper had grown from the boy I saw at school into the man who had asked me to marry him. Music (Sinatra and Tony Bennett, mostly) was always playing on their stereo. Louise made her husband a whiskey sour neat at exactly 5:00 P.M. The holidays were steeped in secular traditions, with no interruption in the form of church services.

I wanted this family. I wanted them to be mine. I wanted to be theirs.

Louise was quiet and kind, smiling at me like you would greet a new and sun-filled day. Averitt was distant but benevolent, like a lowercase god smiling down on me with warmth. I'd believed the shimmering image I'd seen, and it wasn't until our wedding day that I realized the truth.

Standing in the back of the vestibule, holding my lace gloves in my right hand while Willa held my bouquet, we waited for the organ music to start for the seating of the parents. I idled slowly out of the bride's room, ready. Willa and I hid, hushing each other, behind a pillar. Mom had already been seated. Louise stood erect behind the closed double doors, waiting for them to open. Averitt was already at the altar as Cooper's best man.

Louise wore a gold lamé dress that day. Her hair was piled high in a Q-tip imitation. Her red lipstick had bled into the lines around her mouth, and I saw this as she turned to the wedding coordinator — her best friend, Lina, whom she'd hired to make sure I did everything right — and said in a clipped but firm tone, "So he's going through with this, isn't he?"

Lina nodded, her hand on the door handle ready to open it.

"My only son, and this is what I get for loving him so much. He goes and marries a girl way beneath him." She dabbed at her eyes. "I swear, I thought he'd back out at the last minute." She stood taller and exhaled through pursed lips as Lina opened the door. Organ music flowed down the aisle.

Willa grabbed my hand. "Witch."

"It's okay," I said. "I get it. They wanted someone different. But it'll be okay. Cooper loves me."

"They have no idea, no idea at all, that they are the luckiest people in the world. Cooper could never have, at any time, in any way, found a woman like you. *He's* not the catch; you are."

I smiled at Willa and pulled on my gloves before reaching for the bouquet. "Let's go."

Cooper's home now, deep in his Percocet sleep. I need to call both Averitt and Louise. If someone else tells them about the accident before I do, it will be another thing to add to the list of my great blunders. I push number three on my speed dial.

"Hello, Eve." It's Louise who answers, and she greets me with the soft voice I once took to mean she loved me but now think of as the whitewash on disdain.

"Louise," I say. "How are you this morning?"

"I'm fine, darling. How are you?"

"I'm okay, but I need to tell you that Cooper was in a car accident. He's okay, Louise. He has some deep cuts and bruises, but he's okay."

"Oh. Oh, my baby."

"He's okay, Louise. Awake and home."

"How is he hurt? Where is he hurt?" Her voice cracks.

"His face," I say quietly.

"No. Not his face." Her pause is long enough that I think she might have hung up, until she says, "I'm coming now."

"I know you want to. I know you want to help, but right now he's finally asleep. I promise I'll call as soon as he wakes up."

"But he's . . . okay, right?" I can hear she's on the edge of crying.

"He is. Just a lot of stitches and pain. There will be more surgeries. But that comes later. . . ."

"Were you in the accident? What about Gwen? . . . Oh dear God. Gwen!" She is almost screaming, but only almost.

"No." Deep breath in. Deep breath out. "I wasn't with him. Neither was Gwen. He was coming home from Charleston." I proceed to give my mother-in-law the facts, one after the other, and yet I leave out the part about Willa. It feels like a lie of omission, but I can't bring my sister into the conversation.

We hang up, with promises that I'll call the minute Cooper wakes up. The last day and night have been a blur — Willa moving to a private room, Cooper coming home with bandages, medicines, and wound care instructions. I called Max and Francie to explain my absence yesterday, and now I walk toward the studio and wonder how to tell them about the accident; I haven't practiced enough, I think.

The coffeepot is always my first priority when I get to the studio, and today's no different. I turn the pot on immediately and then the music. The Civil Wars sing "The

One You Should've Let Go." I attempt to unravel my tangled thoughts and focus on work. I hope Max ordered the dead bar we need for the press. I wonder if Francie has started the photopolymer plate for the baby shower invites. E-mails have piled up, with urgent subject lines like "Need Immediately" or "Typo Problem" or "Order Late," and there are the mundane ones with exclamation points and inspirational quotes. No matter the subject, the in-box blinks at me with too many blue dots signaling "unread." The chalkboard with our schedule is full to the very edges with appointments, design meetings, and print runs. It will be a long day.

On the project table I see brainstorming notes and random stacks of sketches from yesterday, and I'm unable to focus. Even sorting through fonts — my go-to method of procrastination — isn't helping. Last month, I bought a box of antique cut-wood fonts at a craft show, and I'm sifting through them, forming piles across the table. Sorting this way, losing myself in the vernacular of typefaces, I'm able to forget for a moment about the outside world. There's always a low-hum hope that I'll find the letter *t* for our vintage Paragon wooden font set, which Max and I paid too much for at auction.

Francie is the first to arrive this morning. The youngest of our group at thirty-four years old, she's unaware of her beauty and influence. Our best ideas and images come from this smiling, tiny girl who doubts her own brilliance. She walks into the barn, earphone in and talking on the phone. "No way." She laughs and drops keys on her desk. Her long brown curls fall in tangles over her shoulder and her blue eyes are bright behind tortoiseshell glasses. She waves at me. "Hey, gotta go. I'm at work. I'll call you later." She drops her phone into her oversized purse. "Hey, boss."

"Morning, Francie." I smile at her.

Francie is our artist and, outside these barn walls, a singer/songwriter. The music is what drew her to Willa, and their friendship formed as quickly as a clap of thunder.

When Max comes in, he walks straight to the coffee, pouring it into his oversized mug with SAND GNATS BASEBALL on one side and a chubby sand gnat throwing a baseball on the other. He turns to Francie, picking up on a discussion they'd had yesterday, as if they'd never stopped. "By the way, I looked it up, and Elegy was designed by Jim Waseo. So again, you're right." He lifts his mug in salute.

"Of course I'm right. That's my way." She bows to Max.

I look at my coworkers, my dearest friends. Francie squints at me. "You okay? You look like hell."

"Thanks." I toss a wad of crumpled paper at her. "It's been a rough night."

"What happened?" Max walks to the table and sits across from me.

I take in a deep breath. "Cooper and Willa were in a car accident. Cooper's face is all . . . cut up. Willa has a concussion, or brain swelling." I state only the most important facts.

"How? What?" Francie asks on exhaled breath.

I repeat Cooper's story as best I can — Willa's drunken wobbling, the rain, the wheel being grabbed, and then the tree, the obdurate, unmoving tree.

"No." Francie shakes her head. "No."

"It's awful," I say, and then the tears come — the ones I've suppressed for hours, the ones that I didn't want Cooper or Gwen to see. I drop my face into my hands.

Francie comes to me and places her hand on the back of my neck, a warm, calm presence. "Go home, Eve. Get some sleep. We got it here. . . ."

I look up and wipe at the tears, betrayers

of emotion. "Cooper is sleeping with the help of pain pills," I say. "Gwen is home, too. Willa is sedated and they're calling me when she wakes up. This is where I want to be and this is what I want to be doing."

"Can I go see her?" Francie asks.

"Of course. She's at Savannah Memorial."

Francie grabs her purse and glances up at the chalkboard. "I have an afternoon appointment with a wedding photographer. I'll be back by then." And she's gone.

Max sits next to me. "That's a crazy story. I'm so sorry."

The story. Max always wants "the story," always wants to know "What happens next?" Max Winder, our writer and graphic designer, who would be our CFO if we had a CFO, runs the business, does the PR and marketing, pays the bills, and maintains our letterpress machines in top shape. There is no real title for someone who is everything. He's single, forty years old, and as intrigued with vintage fonts and their stories as I am. And I love him. I hope I love him the way I love Francie, the way I love antique fonts or the Vandercook, which I fell for some twenty years before. I've mostly convinced myself this is true. (It's the *not mostly* that's causing some problems.) His smile reaches all the way up to and then across his eyes to his ears.

I think this, too, will pass.

That was my mom's second-favorite quote from a Bible verse from only (of course only) the King James Version.

Yes, this feeling for Max will pass. Everything does. Everything will.

I look to Max then. "I can't seem to work it all out in my head yet," I say. "But it's what happened."

Max reaches for my hand and squeezes it before rising to go to his own stall, his own desk. Now the Civil Wars sing "If I Didn't Know Better." The large overhead fan whirs on high with a pleasant whisper. We sit at our individual desks. Each work space, each stall, is as different as our personalities. My space holds a desk cut from an oak that fell in the back field. Pictures of my family hang on the plank cedar walls next to posters showcasing our designs. I keep a large burlap bulletin board, where inspirational quotes, photos, and random ideas are pinned above my desk.

Francie's work spot contains an old teacher's desk, which she salvaged from a torn-down elementary school. Sheet music and poems are tacked in crooked patterns on her walls. A guitar case is propped in the corner on a circular flowered rug.

Max's place is dominated with an ancient bar, scarred and still covered in shellac, which he'd found in an alleyway downtown. Next to this desk, he keeps an wooden storage unit, where he meticulously files his personal assortment of type fonts. His CD collection fills an entire metal bookshelf, so his books — so many books — are piled on the floor.

An hour later, the day turns brutally hot, one of those blistering afternoons when people visit the Low Country and say, "God, how could you ever live here? It's so blankety-blank hot." Hot as hell, air thick as syrup, humidity stifling as steam. On the most brutal days, the barn smells like hay and horses, as if the heat awakens ghosts of the past. The tin roof is a musical instrument on a rainy day, but on a blankety-blank hot day like this one, it turns into a frying pan.

Max and I work quietly, and the only sound is the music and then the groan of the press as he begins to print a run of birth announcements — a bunny image deeply pressed into handmade cotton paper and the name Beatrice underneath in pink foil. The particulars of her birth — date, time, and full name — scroll underneath in a custom-designed font with daisies at the edge of the letters. A pile begins to form at the edge of the press. When he takes a break, he comes around the corner and rubs his hands on a towel, where grease stains make Rorschach images on the white cotton.

"We need a new gear pedal for the Heidelberg," he says.

"I know." I look up from my desk, and he's already walking away. I check my cell phone again, afraid that I won't hear it ring or beep. I review notes from an interview with an interior designer who needs a new logo. Usually, I can escape with the designs and visuals, but all I can think of is my damaged family.

Oh, Willa, I think.

Ours is a relationship of opposites — complex and simple. We're eleven months apart; "Irish twins," we'd be called if we were Irish. But we're English through and through, Mom always bragged. Puritans all the way back to the *Mayflower,* if you believe her stories.

Dad was a sales rep for small electronic parts Company, but his pride and all his attention went to his position as lay minister at Calvary Independent Church. He wasn't the head pastor, and he didn't get paid at all for his devotion, but he took his position as seriously as if he were in charge of the universe itself. A reverend, a minister, an elder — all of the above. For my parents life was good and bad, black and white, heaven and hell. Anything in between was of the devil, foggy and destructive. My parents moved to Savannah from New York when they were eighteen-year-old newlyweds and Dad had been assigned to the southern parts office.

Willa and I can always claim to be southerners, as we were born in Savannah. We swam in the muck and flotsam of the Savannah River and ran barefoot through dormant cotton fields. Outside, our childhood was soaked with the joy of freedom. Inside, it was constrained by the board and batten walls of the church.

I was six years old when Willa and I stopped fighting with each other and turned our frustration toward a common goal: the church. We sneaked out of services and covered for each other. We ripped up our Sunday school homework and said we'd lost it. We pretended to sing the hymns while saying "watermelon" over and over, smiling at Mom as if in rapture. They may have been small rebellions, but they gave us a sense of power in our powerless lives. And now, alone in the studio, I desperately want to go to the hospital and heal my sister as the elders once claimed they could do with some oil on the forehead and a prayer in babbling tongue.

"So what do you think happened?" Max asks, startling me.

"What?" I spin my chair around.

He laughs. "Didn't mean to wake you."

I rub my eyes. "I'm not going to get a damn thing done today, am I?"

"Why should you? Stop pushing it. Go see your sister."

I stare at him, at his brown eyes edged in blue. There's always a first thing you notice about a person. If I look back, I can tell you what it is about almost anybody I know. For Max, it was his eyes and the way a band of deep navy surrounds the dark brown.

"You asked something." I sit straighter. "What did you just ask me?"

"What do you think happened last night?"

"Cooper was at the Bohemian bar. He saw my drunk-as-hell sister. He made her leave. She was mad and grabbed the wheel and made him crash into a tree. That's what I think happened."

He nods.

"You don't believe it?" I ask.

He looks away from me and his gaze settles on a photo of Gwen tacked to the

59

wall. In this picture, she's twelve years old, laughing and holding a melting Popsicle, her mouth red with its juice.

"What do *you* think happened?" I ask.

He looks back to me. "I don't know. I couldn't even begin to know."

"My sister," I say. "I've seen her drunk, of course. I've seen her embarrassing and slobbering and giddy. I've known nights when I had to fill in her blackouts. I've had to sit with her while she got sick. But that was a long, long time ago, and I've never, in all those long-ago drunken sloshes, seen her angry or belligerent enough to grab a wheel. She was an emotional drunk, a crier. I can't believe she'd do this."

Max doesn't answer, but I know he's listening. With Cooper, I've learned to say what needs saying in bite-size pieces.

"She's always been the more sensitive of the two of us," I say to Max. "When we were growing up, she was sad; I was mad. Hardly ever the other way around." I stare off at the barn doors, closed tight in a feeble attempt to keep the cool air inside. A poster hangs on the back wall, announcing our opening six years before. "Like the time I got in trouble for making up these ten ideas. I was mad, but Willa cried for days. She felt responsible because she'd helped me, which she had, but not that much."

The playlist changes and Johnny Cash's voice cracks open, saturating the air with "I Still Miss Someone." As he sings those lyrics, the barn doors swoosh open. Francie tosses her purse in the general direction of her chair but misses, and it falls on the floor. She slumps into the same chair. "She's still asleep."

"They said they'll call me the minute she wakes up," I say.

"I can't stand to see her like that."

"I know. But it's just swelling. It will get better." Emotion flares inside me, but I can't label it, pin it to an exact word. I don't know how to be both angry with Willa for causing the accident and worried about her recovery. They seem opposite emotions. They *are* opposite emotions.

The door opens again and a woman steps into the barn. The three of us look at her as if she's an apparition, when really it's just the wedding planner, who needs a new logo, a client with an appointment.

Francie stands up to greet her and Max leans close to me. "Go see your sister."

I nod but then hesitate as I reach the door. It's always difficult to leave.

FOUR

The first thing I noticed about Cooper was his walk. He had this way of moving that only those comfortable in their skin can pull off. The other high school boys were tentative and clumsy — all pointy elbows and awkward knees. But not Cooper. He was tall and good-looking, with a touch of the aristocrat about him. You could say that he had the sort of confidence that comes with money. But it wasn't just that. There was something else that marked him as special. He walked as if his limbs were made of liquid, and his smile — well, it settled on everyone he passed. And everyone made room for him. We moved aside in the cramped hallways so he could get to his locker. We bunched up to make room for him on the bleachers or in the cafeteria. We all saw it. We all did it. We all made room for Cooper.

No doubt about it, I made room for

Cooper, too. He was a junior at Tulane when we met again. I was eighteen years old and working at the local print shop. Cooper's single-minded pursuit of me was flattering — and confusing. I mean, he hadn't noticed me in high school. So why now? More to the point, why me?

I was scraggly then, with long tangled hair. I was also painfully thin. But not because I dieted or went to aerobics with the girls in hot-pink leotards. I was thin because I missed dinner at home most nights, because I survived on peanut butter sandwiches. My eyes were almost too big for my face, and this made me appear curious, I guess, and prompted others to confess their life stories to someone they thought was safe. A girl-friend would tell me about how she'd cheated on her boyfriend, another would confess how she stole lipstick, always just lipstick, from the five-and-dime. I gathered the stories and kept them safe. Maybe that's what Cooper saw in me: safety.

I was wary when we first started dating, and then I wasn't, and then I was in love.

And that was that. We were struck down with the kind of love that believes it was meant to be, the kind of love that makes you sure that all the world is in collusion to make sure you find each other. Cooper and

I may not have known each other in high school, or been each other's first love, but we promised to be each other's last love.

We married two years after our first date. That was twenty-one years ago. Cooper's always said that no matter how many choices he had, I would still and always be his *only* choice. But lately, the frustration and bickering, the underlying anger and pushing back — and by lately, I mean the past eight years — makes me wonder if he's not regretting his choice. It's my fault, I'm sure. I stopped making so much room for him. I stopped moving aside.

After high school, I couldn't afford college. Savannah College of Art and Design (SCAD), to be precise, which was where I wanted to go. So my job at Soapbox Press was my education. But as Cooper moved into my life, that thing I recognized as creativity seemed less necessary. But then a few years into our marriage, I found a Vandercook press in the back of a cathedral where I was attending a christening. When I touched the tap lever and stepped onto the gripper pedal, my days at the print shop came back to me in a rush.

I bargained with the priest (probably some kind of sin) and had the machine delivered to our empty barn. While two-year-old

Gwen napped, I lovingly put the press back together. Then I started printing again. At first, I crafted small things like notecards for a friend, a birthday party invite, or a poster for one of Cooper's colleagues. I made coasters as gifts and business cards as favors.

It wasn't a studio in the beginning. At first, it was just me, the empty barn, and a printing press, together in a private rendez-vous, a quiet time that belonged to imagination. As I started getting paid for invitations, for personal stationery or business cards, I named the company the Fine Line, Ink and incorporated. Cooper was ambivalent about this business endeavor, and yet with a smile he said, "Sure, it'll be nice for you to have a hobby as Gwen gets older. And really, we'll never have horses, so why not use the empty barn?"

A hobby. Yep. His magazine was a business; my printing press was a hobby. I hired Francie first, then Max. The Fine Line, Ink found its place in the barn. Then Willa found her way to our guesthouse. Now she's in a hospital bed and pulling me from Cooper once again.

It's been two days since the accident and I've memorized the labyrinth of hallways to my sister's room and come to know the nurses on every shift by name. I'm on my way to the hospital again, and I'm so damn tired, it's as if I'm on autopilot. I'm going around in the kind of daze that only fatigue can offer — a special gift of misery and floating dissociation. The calm after the storm. It's funny, that, because the storm that blew through the night of the accident hasn't spent itself yet, and it spills through the Spanish moss and thick-leaved magnolias with hand smacks of water on the windshield.

It's easy to love Savannah. I've lived here my entire life and yet I still stumble across a building or door I've never noticed, usually one thing that had once been something else: a hotel that was once a convent, a studio that was once an elementary school, a coffee shop that was once a home. No waste here. One thing is turned into another, until the original is long forgotten, a ghost within the existing structure. I'm tied to the city with tight knots, and yet Willa always wanted to escape. Now she's here, unaware and unconscious in its oldest hospital.

I need to compose myself, so I take a seat in the hospital waiting room. Hospital waiting rooms are interminable places of wasted time, and this one is no exception. People are texting on cell phones, holding cold cups of coffee, and staring at framed artwork declaring the winners of the elementary school's art contest. If Willa were here with me, she would likely make a joke to break the tension — maybe something about the toddler who's going through her mother's huge bright blue bag and tossing its contents onto the floor. Or something about the old man whose head has dropped to his chest, displaying a shiny bald pate under the fluorescent lights. She wouldn't be cruel (she's never cruel, my sister), but she would say something funny and sweet; she would find a way to break the tension.

I'm just getting settled in a cracked red vinyl chair in the corner when my phone pings with a text from the hospital: *Your sister is awake. She's asking for you.*

No more waiting.

I try not to run as I wind my way through the sterile hallways with their identical doors. The room numbers are posted in black, and I recognize the font: Cambria. Even here, my mind searches for clues, as if the font will someday offer up some secret.

Number 426.

There's a hushed swish of the door I enter Willa's room. The single bed is positioned underneath a tangled mass of medical equipment that beeps and hisses. A mound of hospital blankets rise from the bed, and at the sides of that mound, small, pale hands rest, palms up, an IV in the left arm. The bandage has been removed and there's only the tiniest cut next to Willa's eye, with a single black stitch that looks like a fallen eyelash. It's the bruised swelling that morphs the right side of her eye and temple.

"Willa," I whisper, my voice cracking. She opens her eyes to see me. I rush to her side. "Should I call the nurse?"

She shakes her head in a tiny movement and says, "No. I'm just glad you're here."

I take her hand. I don't know what to say or where to start. How do you feel? Does it hurt? Why did you do that to Cooper? What happened? What happened? But she asks me first.

"What happened?" she says.

"A car accident," I say. "With Cooper."

Her face doesn't register emotion. Her lips are blanched, and cracked. She bites the bottom left side and speaks clearly. "No. I wouldn't be in a car with Cooper."

"You were," I say.

"Why?" she asks.

"He said you were . . . He said you were drunk and he tried to take you home." I release her hand and sit in the chair, staring at the IV pole, unable to look any longer at the damage.

"Where?" she asks, as if that's the important thing.

"The Bohemian."

"No," she says, and sits up, holding the IV tube stable. "I wouldn't do that. I sing there. I work there."

So I tell her the story — the part about Cooper's Charleston clients and how she fought him about leaving the bar. I tell her about the rain and the live oak. She denies it with a single word: "No."

"The doctor said you probably wouldn't remember anything."

She doesn't answer, because if there's one thing a drunk can't argue, it's what they did or didn't do while drunk. We've been here before and the familiarity makes me prickly. It's been years — ten or more — but it still feels too close.

Dr. Lewis enters the room. "Good afternoon," she says.

"You don't sleep?" I ask.

"Sometimes," she says, smiling. She walks to Willa's bedside. "How do you feel?"

Amid the talk between patient and doctor, I meander to the window, pushing aside the vertical blinds to view the parking lot. I spot my car and then gaze past it to ever-present church spires reaching high, higher. Dr. Lewis and Willa talk about her pain level and her injuries, about how lucky she is that nothing is broken.

"But my head and eye," Willa says. "They feel broken."

"Yes," Dr. Lewis says. "That's the part we have to watch. You have a mild TBI — traumatic brain injury — and some swelling in the temporal lobe. We don't know exactly what this will mean in the long or even short term. But usually it's your memory that will be affected. It might return in little bits or not at all. Sometimes, though, nothing is affected. I'm sorry I can't be more specific. This isn't like a broken bone or an infection that an antibiotic will cure."

I turn from the window. "Long-term damage?"

"This is something that only time will tell."

"My eye?" Willa asks quietly, reaching up with her free hand to touch the very edges of the swelling.

"When the swelling goes down, I expect your sight will be fine. You're lucky; even though I hate to use that word, you are. You took quite a smack to the head, but your blood work is normal. Toxicology clean and hematocrit strong."

She continues in a foreign language about healing and injury, until these words jump out as if they were scrubbed to a high sheen, like foil stamping on paper. *Toxicology Clean.* I don't know a temporal lobe from a hematocrit, but toxicology? This I know. I spin around. "What do you mean by 'toxicology clean'?"

"Meaning no drugs, no alcohol," Dr. Lewis says.

Willa makes a noise much like a deep breath mixed with a sob. "See?"

"No alcohol?" I ask. "When did you take this blood sample?"

"We always take it on admission after a car accident."

"I'm confused," I say.

"Why?" The doctor squints at me as if I'm the one with the traumatic brain injury — a term I was unfamiliar with only days ago.

"Because my husband said she was drunk. Not just drunk but drunk as hell. And that he had to get her out of —"

"No," the doctor says. "She was not drunk. I don't have any idea what happened before the wreck, but not alcohol."

I turn to Willa. Tears run across the bridge of her nose. "Then why can't I remember anything?"

Dr. Lewis moves closer to the bed, placing her hand on Willa's matted hair as if just touching her head is the only answer. It isn't, of course. And now the questions will begin.

FIVE

I'm not ready to ask Cooper the questions about what *really* happened. I need to know more about traumatic brain injury. I need to know how to defend Willa's sobriety when her memory of the night has been as good as erased. I need something to stand on.

It's late evening and I've been home for only an hour. I open my laptop and search the internet for TBI, for concussion and symptoms. I read quickly, scanning for only the most important parts, wanting to be able to ask Dr. Lewis real questions. I absorb facts and statistics that mean nothing in real life. It seems to me that the only cure for a mild TBI is prevention. And we are days too late for that. I read terms like *Glasgow Coma Scale* and initials like MTBI. One Web site calls it "broken brain," which is the best description I can find before I hear my name.

"Eve!" Cooper's voice.

"Oh . . . Coop." I shut the laptop. "What are you doing? Why are you out of bed?" I rise to hug my husband and I soften, tenderly touching his pale face. The bandage is tight against his head, shifting his face. In his right profile, I can't see the damage.

"I can't sleep forever."

"You shouldn't be out of bed."

"My parents are on the way." He glances toward the back door and I hear the car then, an engine's purr coming closer.

"Your parents? They're here?" I point outside. "You called them?"

"No, my mom called me. Ten times, actually. So I finally got up." He takes a breath and then asks quietly, in almost a whisper, "How's Willa?"

"Cooper." My words rush out, unrehearsed, desperate. "She wasn't drunk."

"Sure, Eve. She wasn't drunk. What else is she going to say?"

"She didn't say it; her blood report said it."

"The what?"

"The thing that tells what's in your blood or not in your blood. That thing."

He looks directly at me now, squinting, so the lines around his one good eye dig deeper. "Then she was on something else.

74

Something that made her seem drunk. Some drug probably." His voice is a hiss.

I don't answer; I can't. We stare at each another, and then our gaze is broken as Louise and Averitt come through the back door without knocking. They never knock, and deep down I understand this impulse to enter a house that was once theirs, the home where their son lives. But I'm annoyed and it's this feeling that rises up with its bitter taste.

I greet them both with a kiss on the cheek. Louise releases her husband's elbow and takes my hands in hers. "You said you'd call when he woke up."

"Looks like you woke him for me." I attempt to smile.

Louise rushes to Cooper's side and takes his face in her hands, one palm on each cheek, softly. "My baby. Are you okay? How bad is it?"

"It hurts, Mom. But I'm okay. Really, I am."

Averitt looks to me. "His mother couldn't stand to think of him hurt and alone. We thought you weren't home."

The disapproval comes in such cordial context, with soft voices and sweet smiles, and yet I feel it, the sinking-stomach, sweaty-palm feeling of inadequacy. "I'm

75

sorry," I say. And I am sorry, for everything, for all the things that have led us to this moment. I try for explanations and reasons, which I know won't matter, but I offer them anyway. "I went to check on my sister; I had to meet with the doctors. But I'm home now."

Averitt clears his throat and turns his attention to Cooper. "I'm glad you're okay, son. I spoke to Chief Overman. It was a car wreck; we know that part. And you were driving." It's not a question.

"Yes, I was driving, but it wasn't my fault." Cooper is fifteen years old, defending his report card.

"Well then, what happened?" Averitt asks.

"That's what we're trying to figure out," I say.

"Well, surely you know." Averitt doesn't even look at me; he jabs his inquiry toward Cooper.

"Dad, it was pouring rain. I was driving Willa home from a singing gig and the car slid. When I tried to right it, she grabbed the wheel in panic and we hit a tree."

Louise glances around the kitchen. "Where's Gwen?"

"Upstairs, I think," I say.

"No." Cooper holds out his hand to touch

my elbow. "She wanted to see Willa. I let her go."

"Oh . . ."

Louise smiles, but her lips rise only on one side — a smirk, I'd call it. "You didn't know Gwen was gone?" she asks.

"No." I reach back to grab the edge of the counter. "But I'm so glad she's visiting Willa. I can't stand to think of my sister there alone."

The pause is long and quiet. The wind outside whistles around the edges of the house, the edges of our conversation. Louise takes her husband's hand and leans into him. Cooper takes one step toward me and then stops.

"How *is* your sister?" Averitt asks.

"She's not doing so great. It's a head injury. A bruised brain."

"Nothing broken or cut?" Louise asks.

"Just her eye. She has a small cut above her eye." I point to the same location on my eyebrow.

Louise looks to her son as if comparing the damage. She opens her mouth and then places her hand over her lips. A small sigh escapes.

"So," I say. "Let's all sit down in the living room. I'll make us some coffee."

Averitt looks to me. "I'd like a scotch,

please." He nods his chin at Louise. "And I'm sure she'd like a Chardonnay."

"Okay. Ya'll go sit down. I'll be right there. Cooper shouldn't be up like this anyway."

The three Morrisons, the original Morrisons, stare at me blankly before they move toward the living room. Louise holds her hand on the small of Cooper's back and Averitt walks ahead with long strides. Exhaustion is working its way underneath my skin. "Coffee," I say out loud to the empty kitchen. "I'm going to need more of that."

While Averitt and Louise watch the news with Cooper, I return to the hospital, where my daughter and sister are waiting. I enter Willa's room, where Gwen sits at the bedside. Willa sleeps, her free hand flung over her chest, open and palm down, as if she is covering her heart; her other hand is flat at her side, with the IV fluid moving with invisible force into her vein.

"Hi, Pea." I hug my daughter and use her childhood nickname, which she's asked me to "please stop using because I am not four years old."

Gwen looks up at me, and there she is: the little girl. "She won't wake up. Is she going to be okay?" she asks. Leftover mascara clumps around her blue eyes. Her face is clean and unwaveringly beautiful. I am overcome with love, the kind that steps in front of a bullet; the type of love that cracks open a life. It's the kind of love that drives you crazy. I lean down and kiss my daughter on her forehead. "Willa is going to be okay. After something like this, nothing is ever exactly the same, but she'll be fine."

"What is that for?" Gwen asks, pointing to the bag of fluid dripping into Willa's vein.

"To keep the swelling down."

"What swelling?"

"Her brain," I say.

"Her brain is swollen. What the hell? That can't be good, Mom."

"No, it's not good, but it's not terrible, Gwen. Just sit here with her, okay? When she wakes up, she will be so happy to see you."

Gwen nods, closing her eyes in the tight-squint motion she's done since she was aware enough to stay her own crying. "Sure." Then she opens her eyes. "I'm sorry about sneaking out."

"I know," I say. "We can talk about that later. I'm going to run to the cafeteria and get something to drink. You want anything?"

"A Coke." She answers me, but her gaze is on Willa, her hands on the bed rails, gripping them tightly, as if she can keep Willa from sinking further into oblivion.

When I return, Willa is awake. She smiles when she sees me, points to Gwen. "Your daughter. She's funny."

I nod, nearing the bedside just as the IV pump begins to sound. *Beep. Beep.*

"I had a terrible dream and Gwen turned it around," Willa says. "Always making something bad into something funny, just like you do."

"Like mother like —"

"Don't say it," Gwen says. "Don't."

Beep Beep.

I want to push a button to make that damn pump stop. Or unplug it. Or shatter it. My eyes are raw and dry; my muscles ache with the need for rest.

Willa speaks in an almost-whisper, her voice not fully awake. "I was telling her about this bad dream I just had where a man was running after me. I tried to hide in an old beat-up car, but he ran on top of the car and started jumping up and down on the roof."

I make a groaning sound and swish my hand across the room. "Go, bad dreams, go."

"Gwen said it sounded like one of those old ghost stories girls tell one another at slumber parties. You know, 'The call is coming from inside the house.' "

We all laugh, but it is a weak and watered-down sound. "Who knows what crazy stuff our subconscious digs up," I say, and try to smile.

Beep. Beep. Beep.

"You're right," Willa says. "That's probably where it came from."

"That or the drugs dripping into your vein," Gwen says, lifting the plastic tube.

"Or the hit on the head," Willa says, touching her scalp next to her right ear.

"Or it was just a dream." I reach for the intercom, needing someone to make the beeping stop.

"It's never just a dream," Willa says.

That's what she believes — that dreams are messages, lyrics to a song she needs to write or memorize.

I push the call button, and when a voice comes over the speaker, I inform the disembodied voice that the machine is beeping.

Beep. Beep. Beep.

I want to slam my hands over my ears.

The nurse comes into the room and enters a complicated sequence of numbers into the machine. She changes the IV fluid bag and pushes gently on Willa's needle site. "All good," she says.

"Can I ask something?" I say to the nurse, and she turns to me.

"Not sure I can answer, but I'll try."

"I need to get the toxicology reports for both Willa and my husband, Cooper."

She smiles and I see her name tag: LULA. Seems like a name for a singer or dancer, not a nurse. "I can't give you those, ma'am. They are confidential, for the patient only."

"But the doctor —"

"You can ask her, then," Lula says, and exits the room.

"I'll get my report," Willa says, quietly, sinking back onto the pillow. "You don't believe me, do you?"

"I do believe you; that's why I want it," I say.

She nods, an almost imperceptible movement. She closes her eyes as the medicine drips into her vein and she drifts off again, into dreams and lyrics.

Six

Two people came by to say hello to Willa: Francie and a man whose name I've heard but whom I've never met — Benson. He works at the Bohemian and arranges Willa's open-mike nights.

Their voices are a chorus of overlapping laugher.

"Remember that singer from last month with the dreadlocks?" Bensons asks.

"Carlton or something like that." Francie looks up in the air, as if the name might be there.

"No," Willa says. "Charleston. He was named after the city and he was so proud."

"I wanted to flirt with him," Francie says. "But I didn't have on enough mascara."

Willa's laughter is loud and raucous. "Dumbest excuse ever."

"You two are nuts," Benson says. "His name was Clay and he just got a music deal in Nashville for that song we didn't even like."

"The one about his mama?" Francie asks. "Ugh. It was sappy and ridiculous."

"Well, some music muckety-muck liked it. I'm only telling you so you two don't give up. Keep at it."

In their conversation and lyric lingo, I listen for hints of what happened the night of the accident. Finally, I ask Benson. "Were you there that night?"

"Yep," he says. "I was. But I have no idea what happened. One minute she was practicing in the back room and then she was gone."

Before I can respond, Gwen calls for me from the hospital hallway. She needs me to convince her dad to let her meet Dylan for dinner. I shake my head. "No way, Gwen. Go home, and I'll meet you there. We'll have a family dinner."

"Family dinner," she says in a tone that suggests I've asked her to eat garbage. "Can't wait." She walks down the hall, her long legs swinging out, trying to get ahead of her, as if she can't get away from me fast enough.

In the car on the way home, I try to stop thinking about Willa and her swollen temporal lobe, her memory and that night, about Cooper driving into a tree while Willa grabbed the wheel. I turn on the radio, cranking the volume to adolescent level — meaning LOUD. Lucinda Williams sings at a "Kiss Like Your Kiss," and my mind wanders to the last time Cooper kissed me. Not the kind at the door on his way out, or the respectable sort of kiss he'll use to acknowledge me in public. I mean the kind of kiss that pulls the body closer, that makes time come undone and the heart slow. When was the last time? I come up blank. I remember our first kiss, but I can't remember the last.

Before going home, I drive into the parking lot at Cameron's Print Shop to buy ink. This is how it goes with me: A disturbing thought, a hint of something amiss, and I'm buying ink, wandering through aisles of antique fonts, holding Italian cotton paper up to the light. I know every ink shop, print shop, and stationery store in the city.

The store is low-lit; a seductive barroom. Cameron, the owner, sits on a stool behind the counter, reading a magazine, raising his fingers to turn the pages and humming under his breath. "Hey, Cam," I say.

He glances up at me. "Hi there, Eve. How's it flying?"

"Been better flights than today." I smile. "I need to order some more of that Twinrocker handmade paper and I'm almost out of magenta base color."

"Got it," Cam says. "But what's going on in your world that could be anything but superior?" He rises from his stool.

Cam has never told me his age, but then again, I've never asked. I've estimated anywhere from sixty to ninety. Today I give him a seventy-five. He moves with ease, but slowly, and his wild gray hair is combed back with pomade. His rimless glasses are perched on his wrinkled nose.

"Not all days can be superior," I reply.

"Well, all your days should be." He peers at me directly. "Is Gwen okay?"

"Yes," I say. "But things aren't great for my family, Cameron. My sister and husband were in a car wreck."

"Over on Preston?" he asks.

I nod.

"Heard about that."

"Really?" I lift my eyebrows, and I'm so tired, even that seems to hurt.

"I live a block away. They okay?"

"Cooper's face is cut up pretty bad. Willa has something like a concussion." I'm practicing this sentence, one I know I'll say over and over again.

"I'm sorry, Eve."

I'm quiet as I follow Cam through the aisles, as if the flywheels, levers, and pedals deserve a reverential silence. Shelves are filled with boxes of leftover metal fonts. Flywheels like shrunken Ferris wheels sit discarded on a lower shelf. A Vandercook and a Heidelberg lean against each another for support while wishing for an owner to clean them up, make them useful again. After we find what I need, I tell Cam to put the items on the company tab and I leave with a hug.

I make one more stop at the market for dinner. I buy Gwen's favorite — sea bass — and Cooper's favorite — sweet potatoes. Family dinner: It was my parents' cure-all for any ailment. I'm repeating patterns, but something has to be done, and a family dinner seems as good an option as any.

I turn off the radio and roll down the driver's window, allowing the muggy air to fill my car. I return home and instead of going straight into the garages, I turn on the gravel drive toward the barn. Francie is at the hospital and Max will be long gone, but I want to check on things.

If the printing rollers aren't cleaned every night, they'll gum up, rending themselves useless. If that happens (which it has), an entire day of printing is lost. It's the last thing we do every day before locking the barn doors — insuring that the rollers are clean and stored properly.

I slide the barn doors open and flick on the overhead lights. New customers often walk in and say, "Oh, it smells so good in here. What is that?" And we shrug. "Candles and machine cleaner."

Through the years, we've burned so many fragrant candles, they've soaked into the hardwood floors, the cedar pillars reaching to the loft above, and the cobwebs we sometimes remember to clean so high above us.

A single light burns over Max's desk and I hope to see him bent over a piece of machinery, but his stall is empty. I drop the ink and trip lever he ordered onto his desk and then walk over to the project table. An empty coffee cup, a napkin with the remains of Francie's afternoon cookie, and papers are scattered across the table. I bend over to see what they worked on while I was gone.

Francie's sketches are easy to recognize; her pictures tip to the right. When I tell her that her pictures are "tipsy" she says that is what graphic art computer programs are for — "to fix tipsy." I'm looking at a card's design that isn't any different: A drunken dense-limbed tree is perched on the left, reaching toward the corner of the paper. Francie drew a live oak tree, its branches spread wide and high, until the leaves and arms disappear off the deckled edge of paper. At the roots are the number 1 and the words *Be Kind.* I stare at this rendering of my first commandment, of the first idea. I run my finger across the tree, the number, and the words. This card has sold more units than any we've ever made.

Max's handwriting is on another sheet of paper, a mix of script and block that is his alone. Then on smaller scrap papers there are other sketches: a heart, two hands reaching out, a man and a woman kissing — half-formed ideas discarded in a pile. I look at Max's handwriting, and I feel the same way I did when I first met him: my stomach upside down, a slow-crawling ache along my ribs, a need without name.

Max and I were so young when we worked together at the print shop in Savannah. He was a student at SCAD, but my parents couldn't afford the tuition. Oral Roberts University in Oklahoma had offered me a full ride, in deference to my dad, which I'd quickly turned down, and that transformed our house into a battlefield with a months-long war. "It's an education," Dad said over and over.

"What I'm doing right now is more of an education than anything I'll learn there" was my counterattack. This verbal dead zone continued until Willa came home drunk one night and the family drama turned to her. I actually thanked her the next day. And I continued my job and preoccupation with printing presses.

We worked together for a year — Max and I — learning how to dance together with the verbal and visual elements of imagery. It's a complicated choreography.

Max had a girlfriend then. Amanda was her name. Adorable was her game. They lived together for ten years before she finally decided that she was "living the wrong life." By then, I was married and had a four-year-old daughter. I told myself I wasn't in love with Max, only with what we did together, what we created.

Typography and letterpress, design and branding take place in a social world, when listening to coworkers, clients, and their narrative. It comes from working together, from storytelling. Once the story is finally told, the typeface is chosen, and this is where I excel. All those years ago, we'd lived, worked, read, talked, and thrived on design in a small ink-stained studio on Bull Street.

Francie joined us a month into the job, and through late nights, hangovers and laughter, we'd become close.

"Why do you do this craziness?" Francie asked late one night while lying flat on the hardwood floor of the Soapbox studio.

We then went around the room, the three of us exhausted at the end of a long project, satisfied with our results, and gave our reasons for wanting to pursue the art and craft of design, letterpress, logos, and bookmaking. We talked about our dreams and where this typography life might take us — "this type of life," Max said.

It was my turn, and I said, "You know that feeling when you go to the mailbox?"

"Which one?" Max asked. "When you know there are bills you can't pay?"

We laughed. "No," I said. "That feeling when you go to the mailbox and there's a letter, and it's on cotton paper and someone has handwritten a note *to you*? Someone bought the card, wrote on it, and sent it to you. They didn't e-mail or call or leave a voice message. That's good mail. I do this for good mail," I said.

With that, our company began in utero, yet the Fine Line, Ink wasn't born until many years later, after I'd married and Gwen was eleven years old. I ran it by myself and then approached Francie and Max for help. They started at one day a week, and the company has grown so rapidly that now it is a full-time job — for all of us. It is Max and Francie who create the success; I know this. Their creative powers forge something new, and I'm mostly along for the ride.

I sit at the project table and gaze at the results of the brainstorming session that went on without me, the one about Good Ideas numbers seven and eight. I feel a wave of intense love for all of it, for all the ideas and the designs so far finished and for the ones yet to be created.

A pad of paper, smooth cotton paper without lines, sits across the project table. I pull it toward me, writing the commandments quickly and crookedly in my rushed handwriting. I do this hoping that some visceral memory will kick in and number nine will appear under my fingers.

Nothing appears but this singular thought: The groceries.

Damn. It's hot as hell outside and the fish I bought for dinner is probably turning into a science experiment in my backseat. I haven't cleaned the rollers yet, and it's my turn.

I'm looking for the Putz Pomade and

cleaning apron when I see that Max has already done it all. The rollers are hanging in their storage units, waiting for a new day. I shut off the lights in the studio and run outside to the car to get home.

The kitchen is brightly lit. A cereal bowl crusted with Raisin Bran sits in the sink. Muffled music comes from upstairs, a thumping rapper rhythm. I unpack the market bags and open the fish package, touching it gently to see if it has retained any of its refrigeration. Nope. Warm and toasty. There are many things I'm willing to take chances on, but not spoiled fish. That happens only once.

I reach for the phone and call for order-in Chinese, setting the table for three. At the kitchen desk, I glance down at the Remington, remembering when it had worked, when the ribbon was damp with ink. The letter *p* is now missing. The carriage is thick with dust and the ribbon cracked dry earth. Not one note has been typed in at least ten years. I write myself a reminder to order a ribbon and *p* key from Cameron.

The Remington was the first thing I brought with me to this house when we moved in. The house was empty, echoing with only the past Morrison ghosts, a handed-down china cabinet, and dangling

93

wires from the walls and ceilings where Mrs. Morrison had removed her favorite antique light fixtures to take to their new "downtown home."

I'd come to the house alone to measure the rooms for furniture and curtains, carrying my typewriter in a hard black case. I went straight to the kitchen and its 1970s avocado-colored appliances and green Corian counters, craving clean and sleek, not colorful and trendy. I set the typewriter on the built-in kitchen desk and patted it like a child. Then I said "Welcome home" to this inanimate object.

Cooper and I had been married a full year when Louise and Averitt told us that it was time they moved. The land had become too much for them to care for and they'd asked Cooper to take over the family home, to buy it from them so that they wouldn't have to sell to outsiders. I agreed under one condition: that his parents knew that it was *our* home. I couldn't feel as if I was staying at my in-laws house without building our own family, our own home. It was a frank and uncomfortable discussion, but it ended well. At least until our first Christmas, when I put the tree in the wrong corner.

The typewriter's placement was my meager way of settling into the house. I claimed my stake. This, the Remington said, is where we live. This is home.

During our first few years of living in the house, I typed love notes to Cooper and left them on the kitchen counter for him to see when he woke or left for work — private jokes, intimate thoughts. Then slowly — who knows when anything turns from one thing to another — notes became a vehicle for fact communication: *Home by 6 after yoga. Gwen has chorus practice until 7; please pick her up on your way home.*

Changing again, the typed notes became text messages, until the useless typewriter now sits as a reminder of my first stake claimed.

My hand is still resting on the typewriter when Cooper comes downstairs in his pajama bottoms and a T-shirt to drop a magazine on the counter. I startle. The bandages are clean and white, new. "You changed the bandages again," I say. "I could have done that for you."

"Yes." He reaches his hand up to touch the gauze. "You don't need to see what's under there."

I go to him, placing my hand on his chest. "I don't care what it looks like."

"You will when you see it," he says. "My

face is mangled. A mess." He looks away from me.

"As if I love you for what you look like." I hug him and place my head on his shoulder, inhaling the scent of pine soap.

"It's bad," he says into my hair. "I can't see how it's ever going to look the same. I also have a bald spot as big as an egg." He squeezes me and then pulls back.

"So we shave your head and you can go with the macho bald look." I touch his cheek.

"Bruce Willis in *Die Hard*? Like that?"

"Exactly." I rub at the top of his headful of hair. "I'm sorry. I just don't know what to say. Dr. Lewis said plastic surgery will fix — I'm just glad you're alive and okay." My lips feel shaky, the way they do when I try not to cry.

"My work, my clients, my travel — it's all screwed up now."

"I'm so sorry, Cooper."

He stares at me through that one opaque blue eye and then in slow motion he reaches up and peels off his bandage. An angry red slash screams from underneath his left eye and extends upward along the side of his face. Black stitches crawl like spiders and pull his skin tight to close the wound, yanking at his face and causing his cheek to slant upward. An oval of sheared skin shines from behind his ear.

I hold my face still, taking in a long breath and walking closer to him. "It's an injury. It will heal."

He replaces the tape and bandage just as Gwen enters the kitchen. The doorbell rings — delivery guy with the Chinese food — and I pay, carrying the brown paper bags to the table, where we all sit together.

"Does it hurt?" Gwen asks her dad, sidling up to the table.

"Yes," he says. "Like hell. It has its own heartbeat."

"I'm sorry, Dad."

And there we sit at the table, the three of us, my family, silently eating fried rice and kung pao chicken.

"Great home-cooked meal for *family dinner* night," Gwen finally says, scraping her fork across her plate.

"Thanks," I say. "I worked hard at it."

Gwen smiles, grateful, I believe, for a sarcastic reply instead of a reprimand.

"I bought sea bass and then left it in the car too long."

"Sea bass?" Cooper stops eating.

There's a thing in marriage — a secret code used in front of kids and others. Words can be said and only the spouse knows the true meaning. So if the sentence was dictated and put on paper, the utterings would be harmless, unless of course you knew what the spouse was *really* saying. And this is what Cooper is really saying: You bought expensive fish from the best market in town and let it go bad?

Then I get to choose: Do I answer the asked question or the real question? I choose the asked. "Yes, sea bass."

"My favorite," Gwen says.

"I know. That's why I got it. Sorry, Pea."

She shrugs. "It's okay." She hesitates, her fork in the air. "Can I please go back to see Aunt Willa tonight? I can hardly stand thinking about her alone in the hospital. . . ."

I look to Cooper. "What do you think?"

"No," Cooper says. "You're grounded for sneaking out." He glances from Gwen to me and then again at Gwen. "Does anyone remember that part of the night? Sneaked out with her boyfriend? Am I the only one who thinks she shouldn't go out?"

"It's my sister in the hospital," I say. "That's not going out."

"Then you take her," he says. "Because I don't trust her with the car."

Gwen stifles a cry and stands quickly, so her chair falls backward, hitting the ground with a crack. "You hate me."

"No, I don't. I love you and want to keep you safe." Cooper's voice is low and tired, an admission and an accusation combined. "And while we're talking about this, I need you to hand over the credit card. You've abused its purpose, which was only for emergencies."

"What do you mean?" Gwen asks.

"The shopping. The clothes. Restaurants and movies. If you want to spend that kind of money, you need to get a job."

"What is going on?" Gwen covers her face. "Aunt Willa is, like, totally unconscious or something and you're worried about me going to too many movies? This is insane."

I want to step into the conversation, to ease the tension and clear the air. But the lost sleep finally catches me and is wrestling me to the ground. I stand also. "Let's all just get a good night's sleep and start over tomorrow."

" 'Start over'?" Gwen asks. "As if Aunt Willa can start over tomorrow?"

I reach for my daughter and place my hand on her arm. "I mean us, baby. I mean us."

"Will you please take me to see her?" Gwen asks. "Or please let me take the car."

"If I drive now," I say, "it would be about as good as driving drunk. So you can take

99

my car. But to the hospital and home. That's it."

"I promise," she says.

Cooper gathers the dishes and I place them into the sink, the clanging and ringing of porcelain our only statement. He walks out of the room without a word. Gwen looks at me. "He hates me."

"Of course not."

"Well, I hate him."

"Of course not," I say, repeating myself.

"As if you know how I feel. You're not me."

Gwen takes the keys and leaves the house, slamming the door on the way out. I stand alone in the kitchen and sink into a chair when Cooper reappears in the doorway from the family room. "I need you to support me." His voice is deep enough to reach the center of the earth.

"What's that?"

"You can't negate me in front of Gwen. It's not fair to me," he says, using the palm of his hand to punctuate every word, as if pressing against an unseen wall.

"She's just going to see Willa."

Cooper comes toward me. "You really think she's going to see Willa?"

"Yes," I say. "I do."

And then, sounding as if he's absorbed the adolescent lingo, he says, "Whatever," and walks away.

I rest on my half of the bed with my eyes wide open. Cooper is lying next to me. I'm on my side and I stare at the silver frame on my bedside table, which glints in the slight moonlight. The room is too dark to see the photo inside the frame, but I know what's there: Cooper holding Gwen on the day she was born. He looks impossibly young to have a baby, although at the time he was twenty-seven years old. I was twenty-four.

"Baby," he says.

I roll over and place my hand on his forehead, gently, so as to avoid the bandage. "How are you feeling?" I ask.

"Percocet says I feel fine." He smiles, and in the dark his teeth and the whites of his eyes shine through.

The house creaks in the way it does when it's left alone, and I try to find some words of solace. "I'm so sorry this happened. I know it was my sister's fault, which makes me feel like it's also my fault. I just don't understand any of it."

"What don't you understand?" He wraps an arm around me and pulls me closer, so my body runs along his, skin on skin.

Yes, I think, my husband, I can ask anything. "Why did you make her leave the bar?

I mean, what was she really doing? She wasn't drunk. I'm trying to figure out what it . . . could be."

"All I can tell you is that she seemed drunk. Other than that, I don't know what to say. I didn't ask her if she'd taken anything. Honestly, all I wanted to do was get her out of there because I'd been working so long with these clients that the last thing I wanted was to be embarrassed in front of them."

"Wasn't leaving them alone at the restaurant embarrassing?"

"Dinner was over. I was about to go anyway. . . ." He brushes his hand through my hair. "You know I don't blame you. So you can stop saying sorry."

"I know."

His hand slips from my head and his eyes close. The pain meds are doing their job and my husband slips into sleep. I set my alarm so I can get up in four hours to give him another pill. "Stay ahead of the pain," the doctor told me. Yes, stay ahead of the pain. I wish there was a way in the real world to do the very same damn thing.

Seven

Now, days after the accident, there are brief moments when I'll forget what happened to Willa and Cooper. I'll cook dinner or roll cotton paper under the press and I'll sense a deep heaviness before I remember: *The accident.* In the middle of the night, I'll sense something terrible is about to happen before I realize that it already has.

Willa is still in the hospital and is improving, thank God. In the next day or so, she'll be allowed to come home. The swelling is subsiding, and today I'll meet with the neuro practitioner and try to understand her medical babble. Thank God for the handouts; I can read them over and over without having to pretend I understand.

Willa weeps over the hospital bills. "I've become exactly what I promised myself I wouldn't be when I came here — a burden," she says over and over, forgetting that she's already told me.

Cooper is trying to return to his before-the-accident life; he's back at work, but only part-time. The stitches won't come out for another week, and he hides the damage beneath tightly taped bandages. Soon, the doctors tell us, it will be time to plan and discuss plastic surgery. Cooper doesn't talk about embarrassment or his need to cover the scars, but I've seen him in the bathroom, staring into the mirror, with his thumb and forefinger pinched around the threads of a stitch, as if any moment he is going to pull at the black thread and undo it all. But then he shaves and dresses, has a cup of coffee and a single egg on wheat toast. He leaves for work as if the day at hand is like all the days before the wreck.

This is one of the things I love about him — his ability to keep going, his tenacity, his drive to get things done no matter the circumstances.

When Cooper started *Southern Tastes*, digital magazines were the next big thing. His affinity for all things male and southern — hunting, fishing, bourbon . . . all the accouterments of a well-bred gentleman — filled the pages of the publication. It seemed the perfect fit: a man from the South with all the right personal contacts and a business degree. Robert Redford in *Butch Cassidy and the Sundance Kid* relocated to Savannah.

Last year, when the first article came out about how tablet magazines were failing — how the "platform that would redefine consumer consumption" had turned into a lukewarm business venture — Cooper went into overdrive. He turned everything to high gear: his charm, his frustration, his creativity, and his travel. But success seems to be slipping away in incremental shifts, in decreased subscriptions and advertising money. He'll gain an advertiser and then lose two. He'll add a new creative section — "Home Place" for example, a section devoted to small towns — and then find that the readers don't resonate with the idea.

I watch him at night, his brow furrowed, his face jaundiced by the light of the computer, and I wonder what he thinks and feels. It's easy to take his moods personally, but *I* know how worried he is about this business he started, the one that separated him from his dad's business. He clicks away on the keys, writes notes on a yellow legal pad. When I ask, "Can I help?" or "Is there anything I can do?" he'll shake his head no. "I got this," he'll say. Cooper has used that phrase since our first date. And it's been true. He's got it — always. There's a certain relief in partnership when a task is handed over, when the weight of something is lifted and carried. For me, this was the family finances. He pays the bills, chooses the investments, and leaves the paperwork for me to review. I'm perfectly capable of handling money, but it's still one less thing to do in an endless and vast list of things I'm responsible for.

In a world I know Cooper never thought he'd see, the balance of success has tipped — the Fine Line, Ink is faring far better than *Southern Tastes,* and yet we've not once discussed the situation. This silence is a private pact, some marital contract that I don't remember signing. But I understand. I keep my business accounts separate and put my assigned salary into the family account. Cooper does the same.

He's got it, he says. He always does. It's true — he's always taken care of us.

In any marriage, there are times that the thrill of falling in love leaks into everyday life, into what has become mundane. And that's what happened last month when I remembered the sweet spot of our romance, when I again saw him as I'd seen him in the beginning.

Cooper had organized a baseball game to

raise money for his philanthropy — Home Run, a foundation that manages inner-city baseball teams for young kids. Businessmen from the community jumped at the chance to play in Savannah's historic 1926 Grayson Stadium. (More to the point, they opened their wallets to be a part of what Cooper had offered as a "big scene.") The Sand Gnats — a local-class A baseball team — donated their time by offering team members to play in the game with the kids. It was there that I watched Cooper on the field and remembered how I fell in love: hard and fast with a man who made a girl feel she needed to be along for the ride.

At the studio this morning, music plays, as usual, from Max's iPod speakers. Emmylou Harris sings "Boulder to Birmingham" softly, as it should be. Max and Francie sit with me at the long table and we talk over one another, as we often do, somehow hearing everything, until we simultaneously fall quiet. Max scribbles at the edge of the paper.

We work on the Ten Good Ideas line and it feels like a magic potion, a palliative cure to Willa's healing. We brainstorm about number seven — *Be Patient* — when Francie leans forward. "Don't be mad, boss, but

I have to ask. Did you ever find out exactly what happened?"

"With?"

"The accident."

"I already told you what happened."

"But it's not what happened," Francie says. "She wasn't drunk. She just wasn't."

I don't know how many times I can have this conversation — with Francie, with Cooper . . . with myself. "Look, Francie," I say. I sound angry, but that's not how I feel. "It's just —"

Max interrupts with a light touch on my shoulder. "It'll all come together. These things take time."

Platitudes. I hate platitudes. They were everywhere in my childhood: small statements made to ease the uneasiness, make certain the uncertainty in an unpredictable world. Clichés, placebos: "All things work together for the good." "Patience is a virtue." "Love is all you need." "God is enough."

"A dingle," I say.

"What?" Max looks up.

"That's what Willa and I call those bullshit statements like 'These things take time.' "

He laughs beautifully. "Tell me about this."

It's such a Max thing to say, and I forge

108

ahead. "Well, Willa and I had a name for platitudes, because, of course, as children we didn't know the word *platitude*. We called them 'dingles.' We still do."

"Go on," he says.

"It happened one Saturday afternoon on a youth group camping trip. The boys were being crude, talking about taking dumps in the woods and how girls wouldn't do it because dingles would get stuck on their butts unless they wiped with leaves, which we were all too prissy to do.

"Poor Willa was the girl who innocently asked, 'Exactly what is a dingle?' The boys laughed, and she was crazy-red-faced embarrased. Then they told her, 'It's the little leftover poop that sticks to your butt.' "

Max and Francie burst out laughing and Francie tosses a wad of paper across the table at me. "No way. God, I can see Willa as red as blood at that answer."

"She was," I say. "That night when we got home, hiding again under the bed, Willa was wallowing in the shame. I told her to forget it because the boys were crude and disgusting and had no idea what they were saying. 'They'll forget about it by tomorrow,' I told her. 'And if they tease you again, you tell them that they're a dingle.' Then — just like my mother would have said — I said, 'This too will pass.' And Willa's perfect answer was, 'Now that's a dingle.' And the name was reborn."

"Okay, you're right," Max says. "Those platitudes are dingles. It's just what you say when you don't know what to say."

"Exactly. So I guess sometimes nothing is better than dingles."

"True." Max touched my hand, and quietly we all returned to our work.

Halfway through the hour, Francie asks, "Did you ever think about making Number Four A 'Search for the Truth' instead of 'Search for the True'?"

I shake my head. "Nope. We wanted it to be for everything that is true, not just one truth."

"How apropos," Max says.

"You and your highfalutin Latin words." Francie grins at him.

"Actually, I think it's French," he says.

"Maybe if you spent less time with your printing presses and books, and more time out chasing girls, you'd talk normal." Francie ducks as he pretends to throw a pencil at her.

"You can use the word in one of your songs and then you can thank me later."

Across the room, Francie's cell rings with the sound of cowbells. "Be right back."

Max stands. "I need to pick up a quoin key from Cameron. I'll be back in a few."

"I'm headed to the hospital," I tell him. "I'll stop on my way and get it for you."

"Really? That'd be great."

I walk back to my work space and Max follows me, points to an invitation tacked to my bulletin board. "Don't forget about the party this weekend."

I groan and drop my hand on top of my head. "Shit, I totally forgot."

I take the invitation from the board and read it again.

Eve and Cooper Morrison
& Mayor Stanton
Invite You to Celebrate
Savannah's Philanthropist of the Year
Averitt Cooper Morrison IV
Benefiting
HOME RUN
Music, Small Bites and Libations

This is followed by the date and time.

Max takes it from me. " 'Small bites and libations.' " He doesn't even try to hide his laughter.

"Shush," I say. "I know this is not your kind of party."

"You should probably cancel, Eve. You

111

can't have a hundred people at your house in a couple days."

"I can't cancel," I say. "It's too late. The quartet. The caterer. God, what a mess."

"The quartet. I could definitely jam with them. Maybe Francie could join them."

I scrunch up my nose and shoot him a sideways glance.

"Sorry," he says. "I couldn't resist. Seriously, though — can I do anything?"

"Come to it?" I ask.

He shakes his head. "Anything else?"

I grab the invite from him. "Thanks for reminding me. I've got to make some calls and then . . ." My voice trails off and I drop the paper on my desk.

"I'm sorry, Eve."

"It's just life," I say. "It gets so tospy-turvy, so wiggly and squiggly and . . ."

"I know."

"That's what Gwen says when I say 'I love you.' "

He gives me a smile, but I can feel its sadness under my ribs like a heavy weight.

"Don't look at me that way," I say.

"What way?"

"Like you feel sorry for me."

"Eve . . ." He touches my cheek but quickly pulls his hand away. "I never feel sorry for you. I just wish there was some-

112

thing I could do for you."

I turn away because I feel the need to bury my head in his shoulder, to wrap myself around this man and let him hold me until everything is gone — all the problems, all the pain, all the unknowing. Instead, I wave my hand over my shoulder. "Go to work."

I open a file for my meeting with a caterer later in the week. She's sent some of her recipes and menus so we can get a sense of her style. Outside the studio, the wind picks up and rattles the barn door against the track. Thunder echoes far away and my phone buzzes. It's Savannah Memorial, and Willa is asking for me.

I put the caterer's folder aside and stand. "I'm going to see Willa," I announce, and my voice cracks.

"Oh." Francie spins around in her chair. "Want me to go with you?"

"No," I say. "I got this."

Willa's room is crowded with the paraphernalia of hospitalization: balloons, cards, and flowers. There's a tray with uneaten food — a yellow mess that must have been scrambled eggs hours earlier, and an unpeeled orange. Her bed is cluttered with blankets, as if Willa kept asking for more and the hospital staff just heaped them on one after the other. Her guitar is propped against the bed rails. Willa sits, but her eyes are closed. The TV is on with a *Friday Night Lights* rerun, where Coach Taylor is hollering at a hungover Tim Riggins.

I stare at her and then touch her shoulder. Her eyes are open, green and clouded with sleep. She smiles. "Hey, sis," she says. Her gaze is slow and lazy, wandering up. "Damn, how does a girl sleep through Tim Riggins?"

"Codeine, most likely," I say. "Can't really see any other way to ignore him."

She laughs, and the sound, though weak, is lovely, like one of her softer songs. I sit on the chair next to her bed and move the guitar over. "Who brought this?"

"Benson dropped it by," she says, rearranging her body on the bed, twisting her head to one side to look at me.

"You planning on entertaining the troops in Savannah Memorial?" I ask.

"Yep. Me and Bob Hope."

"For sure you were hit on the head. This is 2014. I'm sorry to tell you that Bob Hope is dead."

She smiles, but no laughter. "No, Benson brought it because he said I'd left it that night." Willa exhales. "I've been trying so hard to remember, Eve — everything — but I can't. My mind is empty, like nothing happened between Wednesday morning and Friday morning. I can't find anything."

"Anything? Getting dressed that night? Being at the bar?"

She shakes her head and closes her eyes tightly. "Benson said he asked everyone at the bar if they saw me leave or get upset or anything. One bartender said it was my turn to sing, but I walked toward a corner booth. Then I was gone."

This was Cooper's story, minus the drunk wobbling.

"But Margot said I hadn't had a single drink. She'd know."

"Who's Margot?"

"The bartender."

"Well, we already know you didn't. Your blood was clear."

Willa stares at me for such a long while that I think she's lost her train of thought, wandering off into some other land. The neuro practitioner has warned me of possible TBI syptoms — agitation, combativeness, slurred speech, loss of coordination, and, worst of all, convulsions. I watch her so closely. Is she combative? Is her speech sloppy? I'm alert and on edge, as if I'm the one with side effects from the accident.

Then she speaks. "I do remember something, though."

"What?" I ask, moving closer with anxious curiosity.

"I thought I'd died," she says simply.

"What?"

"That's all I remember."

"Tell me."

She speaks in the quietest whisper, so I lean in to hear her. "I thought the streets would be gold, but they weren't; they were made of South Carolina mud, thick and wet, no different from the path to the river, really. I was lighter, though, and I could fly. That was the best part — when I realized I could fly. I wasn't sure who I wanted to see first: Mom, Dad, Granddad, or old Uncle Mike and his snake tattoo. But I didn't see anyone and I was alone and I didn't mind it so much at all.

"The river was bluer and bubblier. The fish, God, the fish were huge. I looked for Jesus. He should have been there, in his white robes. But then the sky broke open with these blazing red patches. The sky was something solid and it broke into pieces. Blue scabs fell away and the red part stayed, and it was too bright to look at. I closed my eyes, but even then, even with my eyes shut tighter and tighter, it hurt. And the whole time I was flying, and because I was dead, there was nothing that could kill me, so I flew higher and higher . . . and . . . higher." Willa closes her eyes, as if the telling is too much. "That's all I remember."

I sit, stunned for a moment, as if I have entered her dream and am soaring with her, higher, lighter. I'm inside the red sky, flying. These rushing words — this is how she sings and how her lyrics sound, but not how she normally speaks, so poetic.

"Oh, Willa," I say. "You told that so beautifully. Your words are not mixed up."

"Don't tell anyone about it, because they'll think I'm crazy. The scary part is that my trip to this heaven was more real than the night of the accident. It's like this memory took the place of what *really* happened."

"Things will be mixed up for a while. That's what the doctor told us."

"This is way past mixed up. . . ."

Just then, the door opens. It's Gwen with the leftover Chinese food. "I brought gifts," she says.

"Real food," Willa exclaims. "Thank God."

"No," Gwen said. "Thank Gwen."

As they dig into the food, Gwen tells Willa about a girl who tried to kiss Dylan at a party. I excuse myself and wander to the cafeteria, feeling left out, as if I'm intruding on a private interlude.

Sitting at a table alone in the far corner of the cafeteria, I hold a lukewarm cup of coffee and wonder about the accident, about my sister and my husband, about the tree and the car and how they came together in a mangled mess. Sometimes I just get it all wrong — what I think, what I believe. Confusion is twisted metal, convoluted in my mind.

"Eve."

I look up when I hear Max's voice and feel a warm spread. "Hey."

His hands are shoved into his jean's pockets and he looks down at me. He pulls out a plastic chair with a screech across the linoleum floor. "I went to see Willa, but Gwen's in there and I felt like I was intruding. They told me you were here." He sits.

"I'm glad you found me."

"So what are the docs saying?"

"She'll probably go home tomorrow. Physically, there's nothing wrong with her. It's all in her head."

"You mean like she's making it up?"

"No, like her injury is inside her head, her brain. It's all this terrible wait and see game."

"Wait and see?"

"How the concussion or brain swelling will affect her. It might be nothing. It might be everything."

"Big difference between everything and nothing."

"I know, I know." I rub at my eyes. "So, how was the studio this afternoon? On the way here, I stopped at Cam's to pick up that part for you. He's ordering it."

"Thanks, and yes, all was fine at the studio. I have set up an appointment for you to meet with a new client. She's an accountant who asked specifically for you. She wouldn't meet with anyone but you. Mary Jo something or other. She wants a new logo, posters, and business cards. I can change it if you need time."

"No, that's fine," I say.

"I know this is bad," he says, and waves his hand upward. "I want to do what I can to help."

I rotate the Styrofoam cup in my hand, watching the coffee swish around the insides.

"Her head was hit and hit hard. The whole story, it's so confusing — all of it. I want to make sense of everything and I can't make sense of one thing."

My palm is splayed open on the table and Max places his hand in mine. A wave of warm shame washes over me: I'm confiding in Max about Cooper and Willa, and surely this is a betrayal of some kind. But here he is, in the hospital cafeteria, with his kind eyes and his wrinkled shirt and his soft voice. Cooper is out with coworkers. Willa is in a hospital bed with dreams of heaven. Gwen is laughing with my sister about Dylan. And here I am, alone in the hospital cafeteria with cold coffee and Max.

"I need to go home." I stand.

He stands with me, smiles sadly. "Hey, let's go get something decent to eat. I'll treat. Come on."

"I can't, Max."

"Come eat with me. You need food."

There are things I don't say out loud because speaking makes the thoughts real, like pulling a dream from the subconscious dark night into the brightest day. And here, now, I don't say this: If I go with you, I will rest on you. I will find a way to place my head on your shoulder; I will need that kiss and your eyes open during that kiss so I can see you.

We can't help the first thought; it's the second I can stop. And I do. "No, I can't. I need to go home. . . ."

"I know," he says. "Get some rest. I'll see you tomorrow."

We've kissed only once, and it was a long, long time ago — before my marriage, before

Gwen. In seconds like this, when Max walks away after a tender conversation, I wonder if he ever remembers that one kiss or if it is lost in all the other ones he's had since then.

EIGHT

The hallway leading to Willa's room smells like a school bus that's just been cleaned — an antiseptic odor covering a sour smell. She can go home now. I met with the neuro practioner yesterday and I'm learning a new language, a foreign vernacular, which includes words like *memory impairment, bed rest,* and *postconcussion.*

I've found a spark of hope for Willa in some new research the practitioner has told me about: Scientists have identified a portion of the brain that acts like a digital camera by placing a geotag on episodic memories. Memory and place are fused together here. Remember the hug good-bye with your childhood best friend and you can conjure up the longing, and then the image will be united with the dock on the summer camp's lake in Vermont, the dock where you said your farewell. Just like photos on social media that are tagged with a town or restaurant, a bar or concert: Here, the tag says, here is where you were; this is the location where the photo's image is indelibly printed. The brain, I learned, does the same in the hippocampus, that small sea horse–shaped portion of the brain located in the temporal lobe. And this is exactly where Willa's brain damage pulses with mangled neurons. This is where memories are mapped in time and place. "If only," I said to the practitioner, "we could access Willa's memory as easily as a digital camera card, as simply as turning on a computer." She told me it could happen. Willa might remember because image and location are ultimately entwined.

I've also talked to the social worker about the bills and payments. Willa doesn't have insurance — nothing. How can she possibly afford the care she'll need? No matter the outcome, or how Willa grabbed the wheel, or if she was stoned or drunk; the truth of the truth is that Cooper drove. He admitted to driving. We are responsible.

Willa stands fully dressed in the outfit I brought her the day before: a pair of jeans and a bright blue cotton tie-dyed T-shirt. Her curls, tangled and wet, fall onto her shoulders. Willa holds me close and then backs up, and when she smiles, she's there, fully Willa. "Ready?" I ask.

"More than," she says.

"Well, let's go, then. Can I carry anything?"

"All I have is my purse," she says. "I told them to throw away the clothes from that night."

"Do we have to talk to anyone or sign anything before we go?" I ask.

"I already did all that. I have a pile of papers we have to go through. All kinds of instructions and . . ."

"I'll read it all with you," I say, taking her hand. "I've met with the neuro practitioner, and together we'll have lots more meetings."

"I know." She exhales in some kind of resignation.

We walk down the hallway, and Willa thanks her nurses. She doesn't speak to me again until we're in the car and I reach a stoplight at Bull Street. Turning in her seat, twisting against the seat belt's restraint, she says. "I don't expect you to take care of me or anything, Eve. I want you to know that. This isn't your problem. I'll figure it out. This is all my fault and I'm not going to take you away from your family and job and life. I'm not."

It's obviously a well-rehearsed speech, until the end, when her voice breaks and she covers her mouth with her hand, as if to stop further unpracticed sentences.

"Stop," I tell her. "Just stop. You're not taking me away from anything more important than you. I want to be here with you."

The car behind me honks, and I look up and see the light is green. I drive straight ahead and pull into the parking lot at Cameron's shop. Willa places her hand on my arm. "This is different. I'll understand if you can't . . . help."

"Why is this different?"

"Because it involves your husband, and I refuse to mess up anyone else's life but my own. I don't want this to affect Cooper or Gwen or your marriage. I don't want to . . . be the cause of anything even more terrible. I've thought a lot about this in that hospital room."

"Did you write that speech in your head while you stared at the ceiling?"

"Yep. But my head doesn't seem to be working all the way right yet. I think things and then they fall out. I have a thought and then it fades and then comes clear again. It's scary. It's freaking me out." Her voice is uneven, bumping along the fears.

I take her hand. "I've been reading a lot about this," I say. "And it will be fine. There are all kinds of therapies and exercises."

"That's what they say." She doesn't sound like she believes anything *they say.*

"I have to run in here" — I motion to the print shop — "and grab a part. Want to come in or wait in the car?"

"I'll come."

Cameron sits in his same spot he always does, reading the paper, as if I'd last been there only a moment ago. He looks up when the bell over the door announces our entrance. "Look at you two, like a breath of fresh air coming through my door."

"I'm not sure 'fresh air' is exactly the right description," Willa says. "But I'll take what I can get."

Cameron comes over to Willa and takes her hands in his. "I'm so glad you're okay, my dear. If I'd have known it was you in the accident that night, I'd have run down there."

"Run down there?" she asks.

"I live on that block," he says. "I heard all the sirens and hullabaloo, but I had no idea it was you."

"Oh . . ." She looks at me.

"Been the quietest neighborhood all these years, and now we've been in the paper twice in a week." He rubs his hand along the scruff of his chin. "So you here to pick up Max's part?"

"Yes, sir," I say. "Glad you got it in so fast."

"You're lucky to have Max. Don't know anyone who understands presses like he does. Better hold on to him."

"I'm planning on it," I say, following Cameron through the crowded aisles to the back room.

Willa follows and says, "Why was your street in the paper two times?"

"Oh, that homeless man they found." Cameron reaches up and pulls down a small box and hands it to me.

"What man?" I ask.

"Don't you read the papers?" His grin is lopsided and teasing.

"I've been a little preoccupied," I say. "Tell me."

Willa is still as a tree — Firm, rooted.

"Some kids found this poor guy in the alley between two houses. You know the kind of skinny no-man's-land where the houses are so close that you can barely walk between them? Like that, except he was squeezed into there. Like he'd gone to get out of the rain or something, which doesn't make sense to me, because there wasn't any cover. But anyways, he died in there and —"

"He died?" I envision this man stuck

between buildings . . . dying. I shiver. "Poor guy. Did he die because he got stuck?

"Don't think so. Something about getting beat up," Cameron says, walking out of the storage room when the front door rings, announcing an incoming customer. "Don't know nothing about him except they took him away." He stops and turns to me. "The saddest part is that no one knows who he is. In this world, how can someone not know? It's terrible." He shudders and moves on as he says, "Go on. I'll put it on the tab."

I follow Cameron, and it isn't until I reach the front door that I notice Willa isn't with me. I walk back to the rear of the store and into the storage room, where I find her staring into space. "Willa!"

She doesn't startle, just slowly looks up at me, her gaze traveling in its sleepy-time way. "That is the most horrible story." Tears glaze her eyes. "Some guy crawled between houses and died? Poor, poor man." She covers her face; racking sobs rise from her throat. Her body shakes with the released force.

I wrap my arms around my sister, pulling her close. Emotional lability, this is called. The neuro practitioner told me to expect these displays of "mood-incongruent" behavior. I was warned that Willa might laugh at something sad, or cry fiercely at something mild. The emotion might not match the circumstance. But being warned about a behavior and experiencing it are not the same thing. Besides, this doesn't seem so incongruent as completely excessive. What did the practitioner say to do? I can't remember. At the time, I didn't believe I needed to know. My sister wouldn't have this weird emotional reaction with the initials PBA, which stands for something I will never be able to pronounce. Now I don't know what to do, or how to act. I hold her. "It's okay,' I say, as though she's a child.

"No, it's not okay." She pulls from my embrace and rubs at her eyes, grimacing as she swipes the stitch. "It is just *not* okay."

"What can I do?" I ask, helpless.

"I don't know." She shakes her head. "I don't know . . . anything."

"Let's get home," I say. "Tea and macaroons. How does that sound?"

She nods and turns, walking the wrong way, toward another closet.

"This way," I say, pointing to the doorway.

Willa stares at me; obvious frightened. "What if I stay this way?"

"You won't," I say, flinging these words at the universe in defiance, in earnest.

I decorated the cottage years before Willa came to stay, and yet it looks as if I knew that one day she'd arrive. The walls are painted a dove gray over board and batten walls. The artwork is eclectic and scattered: a painting of an old circus tent I bought at an arts festival; multiple framed posters and sketches of the Fine Line, Ink work; black-and-white photos of my parents' younger years. There's one photo of Willa and me as youngsters, standing on top of a rock with our arms looped together. We are smiling in the photo, happy and free — all of life ahead of us.

The kitchen is bright and painted white. The table is round and wooden. I found it in the barn and painted it with Gwen one summer afternoon. A multicolored glass chandelier dangles above the table like a discarded necklace. This space was fun to decorate, and now Willa adds her own style. Mismatched painted pottery plates are piled on open shelves around the room, most of which she found at flea markets. Linen napkins of every pattern spill from a wire basket. Music sheets and handwritten lyrics are piled in an old milk crate in the corner.

At the table, I unwrap the day's newspaper, spread it out, and flip through the pages, looking for the article Cameron mentioned. The story is buried in the last page of the "Metro" section.

The man's death is summarized in one paragraph, and I have the horrible thought that if Willa or Cooper died on that same street during the accident, they would have garnered more than a few sentences in the back section. The man was an African-American and obviously homeless. It appeared that he'd been in a fight and then crawled between houses, where he died of internal injuries.

Willa enters the kitchen. "I forgot where the bathroom was." Her voice shakes.

"What?" I look up.

"You know how sometimes you have a really bad hangover and you can't find your words, or a thought escapes, or you can't remember where you are?"

"Sadly, yes."

She slumps into a chair and drops her face into her palms. "Well, it's just like that, but a billion times worse. It took me way too long to remember where the bathroom was." She looks up at me, her eyes red-rimmed. "In this house where I've lived for a year."

I close the newspaper and busy myself making two cups of tea, placing the macaroons on a pink plate. I sit next to my sister. "Maybe working with us again will help. You think you're up for it?"

"Of course." She leans her head back to stare at the ceiling. "You know, while I was in the hospital, I had a ton of weird memories. It was like mud from the bottom of my life all stirred up. But I thought of Caden and how you two made up those commandments. How could I forget him?" Then she laughs again, but this time it has a more manic, high-pitched sound, and for a moment I think it's the emotional lability hitting. "I guess right now that is the wrong question to ask."

"Huh?" I ask, confused.

"*How could I forget?* That was the wrong thing to say." She shakes her head. "Anyway, I remembered so much about that time — you getting in trouble. Big, big trouble. Willa closes her eyes. "I wish *that* memory had been hit right out of my head."

"Me, too."

"I wonder what ever happened to Caden." She closes her eyes, as if the answer is behind her eyelids. "He had those green eyes, and he always carried a baseball."

Maybe this is one of those times when the

past is clearer than the present — another symptom. Willa can't remember the bathroom location, but she remembers Caden's eyes.

"Yes," I say. "The last I heard about him, he'd married and moved to Seattle, as far away from the South as he possibly could."

"I was madly in love with him. As much as an eleven-year-old can be in love. But he loved you."

"He was my best friend," I say.

"Um, yeah. Sure thing, Eve."

"I don't want to talk about this. It was a long, long time ago."

"Have you remembered number nine yet?" she asks, wiggling nine fingers in the air.

"No, I was hoping you'd help."

"Great idea, sis. Get the brain-injured girl to help you remember." She laughs and leans toward me.

"Shush."

"But, yes." She nods and sips her tea. "Absolutely I want to keep helping with this."

I take a lavender macaroon and pop it into my mouth. Willa picks up the other one, vanilla, and takes a tiny nibble from its corner, so hers lasts longer.

I stand. "I need to go. I have to check in

on the studio. If you want to come over for dinner tonight, I'm making lasagna. Just walk over in a couple hours."

"Thanks, but I'll probably just stay here. I want to get into my bed and sleep on a real pillow. I want to go all night without something beeping or someone poking me."

"Call me if you need anything at all. *Anything.* When Marci came to clean, I had her put groceries in your fridge, so you have the basics."

She takes another sip of her tea. "I will pay you back. Someday I will make up for this."

NINE

There is a story behind everything. Those are the words Cooper uses at the beginning of his keynote speeches, or his fund-raising talks, or his retelling of how he started his e-magazine publishing company. That's also the tagline under the Fine Line, Ink's logo. I'd never thought much of the fact that he took that sentiment from my letterpress company. It's a compliment when your husband uses something of yours, when he admires your work enough to emulate it.

Tonight, when he begins his speech, I will be able to mouth the words: *There's a story behind everything.* He will then launch into his own story of how baseball changed his life, how he once believed he'd play college ball, until he threw out his shoulder. His talk will end on a high note, but for now, it's three in the afternoon and I'm checking on every last detail for the party.

It hasn't always been this way — with me

trying to prove my worth to Cooper. But it's this way now and I can feel the push of the idea behind me: Show him and maybe he won't be so upset about everything else — my sister, our daughter, my time at the studio. A hundred people will be here soon. I left the caterer in the kitchen, placing canapés on silver trays. The string quartet arrived an hour ago and they are deciding where to set up. Along the driveway, strings of twinkle lights cast a starlight glow from the trees, the heavens closer to earth. Nice, it's all looking exactly as I planned.

The party has a theme — baseball — but the theme for me is all about getting through the evening.

I amble up the long driveway. One string of lights has come unhinged and hangs like a soft hammock of stars. "Brian," I call out to the workman who hung the lights, but there's no answer. Against the tree, the ladder rests with its pegged feet digging into the earth. I'm on the top step, tucking the string back into the branches, when I hear Max's laughter, and I wonder if he is talking to Francie or Willa, and what is so funny. I lean my forehead against the tree. The bark is rough, a calloused hand on my skin, and I close my eyes. Then I hear my name.

"Eve," Max says, and I look down, startled he is below me.

"Oh," I say, and grip the ladder. "What are you doing?"

"What are *you* doing?" He squints against the evening sun.

"A string fell loose." I climb down to face him. "And I couldn't find Brian."

We're facing each other and he's holding the ladder, so when my feet touch the grass, we're so close.

"Why isn't anyone helping you?" he asks.

"I'm fine," I say. "I got it."

He smiles at me. "I'm *so* very sorry I can't be at this party tonight."

I smile in return, but my face almost doesn't know how to do this; I seem to be out of practice. "I know you wish you could come, because you love to put on a tuxedo and eat small bites and have libations."

"You are so right," he says. "And I wish I could smile and shake hands and talk about the state of South Carolina politics while holding a tiny martini."

"You'd have a blast with all the small talk — it's your very favorite."

"Small talk *is* my favorite," he says. "I much prefer it to big talk." His laughter rises into the oak leaves and settles there with the evening sunlight. "Maybe I could just hang out in the kitchen and eat all the small bites before they can be served."

"Get out of here." I laugh and gently nudge his shoulder.

"I will." He picks something from the edges of my hair. "Moss," he states simply, and then hands me a wisp of it.

I take the tangle of spindly plant and then drop it onto the soft earth. We both look down to where it lands and then glance back up together. Our eyes meet and he smiles. "Have a libation for me." And with that, he walks back across the field toward the barn.

The evening sun plays catch me if you can with the Spanish moss hanging from the oak trees. Slivers of light stab and then retreat through the screen on the porch, where Gwen and Cooper are sitting on lounge chairs, each absorbed in their own reading. I can't see the novel Gwen's reading, but I'm sure it has something to do with true love or vampires, probably both. Cooper flips through a stack of papers with charts and graphs. I'm propped on the arm of a living room chair, watching them. They can't see me but I can see them. And I can't resist eavesdropping.

Dad and daughter.

Cooper loves his daughter. He's devoted

to her. But deep down, in the honest places, I've always considered Gwen to be mine. She grew inside me. She was nursed by me, rocked by me. I took her to every doctor and teacher and tutor. I shuttled her to dance class and horseback-riding lessons and camps. I sat up with her the nights she was sick. I've let her cry and made her laugh. Maybe I didn't give Cooper any space to do these things, but he's never tried and I've never blamed him. He wants to be close to her, and he tries with words of love, always telling her how much he loves her, how proud he is of her, at least until lately. I've watched and cringed with frustration at Gwen's attempts to get closer to her dad on those occasions when Cooper hasn't been able to sit still long enough, listen long enough to hear what she's *really* trying to say.

Now that he wants to be more involved, to dictate the discipline and rules, I find myself defensive and annoyed. He didn't stay up all night when she had a fever or sit through a slew of teacher conferences, so why does he want to slam his hand down on her life now? I think it must have something to do with her fading childhood, about her becoming a woman with her own opinions and needs. But who can know anyone's

139

motivation?

They need to understand each other better and I need to step back and not interfere. I've placed myself between them in some meager attempt to stop Cooper from hurting Gwen and to stop Gwen from infuriating Cooper, and I've been about as effective as Willa was when she grabbed the steering wheel.

"What are you reading?" Cooper asks her.

"The Fault in Our Stars."

"What's it about?" Cooper asks.

"Two best friends with cancer who fall in love. It's really sad and really great. Want to hear my favorite line?"

"Sure."

" 'I fell in love the way you fall asleep: slowly, and then all at once.' " She exhales the last part of the sentence, a sigh. "Isn't that perfect?" she asks her dad.

There is a lull, a silent pause, a breath, before he speaks.

"You coming to the party tonight?"

My fists grip and my jaw clenches. Can't he hear her? Can't he hear the need for response, for something, anything, that doesn't have to do with him? I hold back; I stand still, but my heart rate speeds up, as if I'm running for Gwen.

Then she answers, quietly, almost defeated. "Yes, of course I'll be at the party. I mean, like, it's totally here in our house, so how could I not?"

"Good. I want you there. It's a big night and I'm a little nervous."

"You?" Gwen laughs and places her book on the coffee table.

"Yes, me." He leans toward her. "I haven't really been in a crowd since the accident and . . ."

Gwen nods. "You're back at work, though."

"Yes," he says. "But this is different."

She's thoughtful for a moment. "Right. It is. I get it."

"I'm sorry I've been so tense with you, Pea. I've been . . . stressed with work and I worry that you might make a mistake you'll regret, one that will hurt you. If I've made a mistake in how I talk to you, it's because I'm clumsy. I don't know what to do to keep you safe. But I *will* keep you safe. It's my job."

Gwen is silent but leaning forward, taking in these words.

"You understand, right?" Cooper asks.

"Not really, but I guess so."

"Whatever you do or don't understand, you know I love you, right?"

"Um, yeah, I do. But I don't understand

what happened with Aunt Willa."

"Neither do I, Pea. Neither do I. Well, I guess it's time for us to get all dressed up for the night. Ready to face the crowd."

"Are you glad you won this award?" Gwen reaches toward her dad with words, with kindness.

"Yes. It's a really big deal and it will help with fund-raising. I'm thrilled, actually. Just bad timing on the party."

"Yep." Gwen stands. "Doesn't really seem like a night for a party."

I move quietly toward the kitchen, away from the porch, away from their intimate conversation and their raw needs. Sometimes it seems so simple. Cooper needs to be respected in the family, but his clumsiness is creating a rift. Gwen needs to be close to him, but in her teenaged confusion, she's creating a distance.

If there was one thing I could do — any one thing to mend our hearts and disparate needs — I would. Instead, I pull out silver trays from the kitchen cabinets and prepare for the caterers. What else is there to do?

I stand at the front door, ready to meet the guests. My dress is simple, cream linen with satin piping running along the seams' edges. It flares out at the bottom and I if twirled around, which of course I won't, it would swing in a circle like those cute girls in the commercial for the lipstick that will change your life. I've worn the dress before, but only once, and from what I can remember, it was for a school function, which means no one here will remember. The shoes, though, are new and pinching my toes in a death squeeze.

Men arrive in tuxedos, women in cocktail dresses made of sequins and chiffon. I hug the women and shake the men's hands. "Thanks so much for coming," I say to Bill, to Carter, to Sally and Mark. Names come easily and they, too, greet me, Cooper's wife, with wide smiles and then a furrowed brow, all with the same question, phrased differently but always meaning this: "Are *you* okay?" For a half hour now, I've fielded this question, until everyone has arrived and we shut the front door.

The quartet plays something soft and elegant — music to fund-raise by. I scan the scene. Overhead lighting is off, so there is only the soft glow of lamplight and candles; trays on the dining room table are full of bite-size food; the bartender stands in his black suit behind the table covered in white cloth, where liquor bottles are lined up; bottles of white wine sink inside a silver ice bucket. Everything is in place.

Louise and Averitt wait on the far side of the den. I wonder what it must be like for Louise to stand in her house, one that is no longer hers anymore. Does she see the red plaid couch that once sat there? Does she abhor the painting of the sailboat that hangs where her portrait once did? Her lips are coiled into the pout of annoyance I have become accustomed to but still avoid. I approach my in-laws with a smile.

"I'm so glad you are here." I hug them both and they hug me.

"You are beautiful tonight," Averitt says, and nods with a single tilt of his head.

"Thanks, Averitt."

Cooper is at our side now, hugging his mother, shaking hands with his father. "Hey, Dad. Glad you came."

"We are so proud of you, son. Look at what you've done with the family name. It only gets better with you."

Cooper beams at his Father's praise. He takes my hand and squeezes it. "It's been a great ride, knowing that I can do something good with the sport you taught me."

"You know," Louise says, and places her hand on her son's arm, "Dad was so upset when you didn't go into the family business. But you've proved us wrong. You've made a name for yourself. We are so proud."

I wander into the living room, where I've cleared all the furniture out to create a gathering space to view the inspirational video that is designed to bring tears and get everyone to donate to Home Run. Cooper's plaque — the one he received as Philanthropist of the Year for this very cause — is prominently displayed on an easel over the fireplace.

Fritz Webb is the only man in the room wearing a suit and bow tie instead of a tuxedo. His hair is mussed, a word my mom once used when I didn't brush my hair. I've always liked him; he speaks efficiently, quick remarks with explanation points seeming to hide at the end of every sentence.

"Hi, Eve," he hollers across the room, and moves toward me.

"Hey there, Fritz. I'm so glad you came tonight."

"Me, too. Yep."

"How have you been?" I ask, while in my peripheral vision I see Cooper heading toward us.

"Good. Except for that harebrained scheme we all fell into. That was bad." He shakes his head and a flock of hair falls across his forehead; he swipes at it. "Bad."

"Huh?" I grab champagne from a passing

145

tray and take a sip. "We fell into?"

"The oil rigs in the gulf."

For once, I am annoyed with his short explanations and minimal word count. "Oil rigs?"

I try to laugh. "Okay, Fritz, you're going to have to be a little more specific. Less obtuse this time."

"Okay. The investment we all made in that company doing prospective oil drilling off the coast. It was a joint venture thing. I'm pissed we put so much into it. Sure, if it had panned out, we'd be having a different discussion. But since it didn't, I'm trying to figure out how to pay my son's fall college tuition."

"Oh, yes, that." I glance at Cooper, who has now reached our side. "That investment, right, Cooper?"

I feel his muscles tense, although I'm not touching him. "Hey there, Fritz. How are you?" Cooper shakes Fritz's hand and leads him across the room without once glancing back at me.

It's happening again: One casual comment and I feel the ground shifting under me. I glance around at the crowd and wonder again how I could not know these things that are part of my life, inside my life.

My heart is sluggish, like it doesn't want

to pump enough blood to get me through this night. It would be lovely to climb upstairs and get in the bathtub, and then into bed. I wonder how long it will be before someone needs something.

"Eve." Cooper calls my name and that answers my question: one second.

I turn around and smile at him. He looks so handsome; even his bandage against his face seems to be part of his tuxedo, white and tight. "Yes?" I ask.

"Where are the gluten-free foods?"

"The what?"

"I told you — our largest donor is on a gluten-free diet and I needed at least two types of gluten-free appetizers."

I shake my head.

"I did. I told you."

"I didn't remember." I cringe. Did he really tell me this and I let it fall out of my head completely?

"Shit." He turns and stalks into the kitchen.

My stomach plummets. It's like a roller coaster I don't know I'm riding and the drop comes without warning. Had I forgotten? Had he told me? I exhale and turn, bumping into Mark Langdon, one of Cooper's childhood friends. "Hey, Eve," he says, and hugs me. "How are you?"

"Fine, thanks, Mark. And you?"

"Good. But I know these have been rough days. Just want you to know I'm thinking about you and praying for all of you."

"Praying?"

"For healing." He pats my shoulder, then reaches over to grab a glass of wine off a passing tray. The server pauses and asks if I'd like one. I shake my head and thank Mark for his prayers before walking away.

I hear Willa's voice from somewhere behind me, high from what I hope is laughter. I can't distinguish the words, and I rush toward the arched entryway to the kitchen. She's talking with the caterer, a friend she's known from her rounds singing at restaurants. Willa looks beautiful, wearing a thin blue sundress that hangs off her shoulders, loose and lovely. Her hair is pulled into a ponytail, yet strands have come loose. Dangling silver earrings hang low and catch the light. She sees me. "Hey, sis."

I hug her. "I am so glad you're here," I say. "So glad you decided to come."

"Gwen begged me," she says, and looks around the room. "You know where she is?"

"Probably still upstairs."

Willa is moving toward the back of the house to look for Gwen when we both hear Cooper's voice. "Yes, it was Willa. You know

148

her, right? Eve's sister."

We stop, listen.

"Well, I'll pray for peace and healing." Mark Langdon, again with the prayers.

Cooper answers in that low, polite voice he uses in business. "Thank you."

"But my God, what *really* happened?"

"Crazy pants sister-in-law grabbed the wheel and took us into a tree. That's exactly what happened."

Willa looks at me, and her face is white parchment with red lips. The blood inside me rushes away from my head. I'm dizzy. I grab Willa's hand.

A bell clangs from the front room — Mayor Stanton attempting to gather the crowd for Cooper's speech. Willa releases my hand and moves toward Cooper and Mark. "Not now," I say. "Please."

Willa snatches a champagne glass from the counter. I want to stop her, want to stop the world from spinning for a moment, just long enough to know what to do, what to say, how to say it. But I don't have that time, and Willa slugs back the champagne, then grabs another. "Don't," I say.

She waves her free hand toward the living room. "I think they might need you in there more than I need you in here."

Her dress flares out as she turns away

from me and heads toward the back door, her hand reaching for the knob. The music stops and every sound in the house is amplified: the clanging of the dishes as the caterers move around the kitchen; the murmur of voices quieting for the speech; the slip-slap of the screen door as Willa leaves. It's Gwen who breaks my frozen stare when she comes into the kitchen.

"Mom. Hello? Dad is looking for you." If sarcasm can really drip off words, it just did so now.

Gwen wears a sequined orange dress she wore to homecoming the previous year, but she's cut the bottom off, taking it from a long gown to a short cocktail dress — too short. Her hair, so long now, is up on top of her head, a squatting bun falling loosely to the left. "You look beautiful," I say. "Let's go hear Dad." I walk slowly toward her and feel as if my head is too large, too heavy and lopsided on my neck.

"Where's Aunt Willa?" she asks.

"I think she went back to the cottage."

Gwen's mouth screws into a circle, as if she's just put an invisible pacifier in her mouth. "Oh."

I enter the room where Cooper is standing in front of the fireplace. His speech is one I've heard before, many times before.

He looks the part: the man who started his own company from scratch; the man from a legendary Savannah family; the father and husband. Injured but strong.

"Baseball." He smiles and pauses for the flavor of the word, the sport, the sacred religion of it all. "I believe it is a game that changes a young boy's soul. It teaches character, patience, and losing with grace. The game offers focus and goals in a world that doesn't give them either."

The crowd claps, a polite echoing of palm on palm.

He continues, but I don't hear another word. I learned how to do this in childhood — appear to pay rapt attention without really listening. Sermons at our church could go on for over an hour as the preacher repeated the essential message that we were unworthy, so unworthy. And yet, luckily, we were also chosen and saved. It was in the pews that I learned that the mind can be an escape more powerful than any getaway car.

Long ago, I taught myself how to be present and absent at the same time. Sometimes I'd leave a two-hour church service and never remember having been there at all, my special and inventive kind of blackout. But I've never done this with Cooper, and I'm startled when his speech is over.

Cooper shakes hands with the mayor and I peek over Gwen's shoulder. Her text to Dylan reads *Finally over.*

"Don't leave," I whisper to her.

"Creepy, Mom. Don't read my text."

The crowd moves toward Cooper, shaking his hand, taking out their phones for photos.

The absence of music is a gaping hole: I need something to fill the quiet. I walk to the foyer to greet the quartet. "Can we start back up?" I ask the violinist in the tuxedo.

"Sure thing," he says.

I stand there as they begin, first the violinist and then the woman in the black dress with the cello. She stares past me and into the crowded room; I follow her gaze. There they are: Cooper and Willa, standing in the dining room. He is backed against the antique buffet table. The candle's flame quivers as Willa's mouth opens and she leans toward him.

Cooper glances left and right, as if making sure no one hears or sees them. Willa steps closer and jabs her finger into his chest.

My feet come loose and I rush to them both. I grab Willa's arm and pull her away. I know it looks like I want to save Cooper but it's Willa I want to protect. She allows me to guide her out of the room, and the crowd blurs. We enter the kitchen. Willa sinks to a bar stool and her face reddens; tears fall and her face contorts. "Oh my God, I thought I was whispering," she says.

"You were. I just saw what was coming."

Cooper enters the kitchen and stands before us with his hands spread out. "Do not come in here and ruin this party." He looks directly at Willa, as if I'm not there at all.

"Stop," I say, but I might as well be talking to a tornado already in motion.

"Crazy pants? That is really how you want to explain that night?" Willa stands, defiant.

"Not here," he says. "Not now."

"You didn't quite seem to think that 'not here, not now' was a good idea when you just told your praying friend that I was crazy. That I was drunk. That I grabbed the wheel." Her voice is strong and loud. The catering crew is watching and I know that Cooper is worried that the spectacle will move beyond the kitchen and into the living room where the guests are gathered. I'm a little ashamed to admit it, but I am too.

Willa moves closer to Cooper as if to whisper, but her voice comes louder. "We both know you're lying. I was *not* drunk. So you can make up whatever else you want about that night, but not that, Averitt Cooper Morrison the Fourth. Not that. You

153

can take your awards and charm your guests and lie about any damn thing you please. But I was not drunk."

"Calm down, Willa. You'll be okay," he says, as if soothing a child, a tantrum-throwing child.

"Okay?" she asks too loudly, too sharply.

"Shhhh," I say, shackled to my spot and desperate to stop them.

"I have to get out of here." Willa glances around the kitchen, confused, as if the room has no doors.

Cooper spins on his heels, leaving the kitchen with a parting comment. "I'm joining our guests."

Gwen bursts into the kitchen, hopping on one foot as she attempts to remove her high heels to run toward us. She has her arms around Willa before I can react. "Are you okay?" she asks.

Willa's face is smashed into Gwen's shoulder, like a child who has fallen asleep on her mother. "I think I'm going to throw up," Willa says.

I rush to grab a bowl from under the sink, bending over and tripping on Gwen's discarded shoe. I fall into the side of the cabinet and then onto the floor. The back of my head bashes against the corner of the cabinet. My dress, splayed out in its wide-skirted glory, hides my tangled legs.

"Oh my God," a male voice says. "Are you okay?"

I look up to a server with the name tag that says MARTIN. "Yes," I say, and let him help me up. I stand and cover my face with both hands. I'm embarrassed. My ears are ringing.

"Mom," Gwen says.

I uncover my face to look at my daughter and my sister, both of whom are staring at me with wide eyes.

"I'm okay," I say.

"You are anything but okay, Mom."

"Somebody go get Mr. Morrison," a woman says in a high, manic voice.

"No," I say. "No. Let him be. We're fine."

Willa places her arm around Gwen's shoulder. "I think I need to get out of here," she says. "Now."

"I'm coming with you," I say.

Gwen holds up her hand in a motion I know too well, the same one Cooper uses when he wants her to stop arguing with him.

"I am," I say.

"No," Willa replies. "Don't do that, Eve. Don't."

They leave, Gwen and Willa, going out the back door. I stand in the middle of my perfect kitchen, my hand on the back of my

155

head to cover the throbbing center, the caterering staff staring at me. I open the back door and walk into the evening light, the sky darkening. There was a time when I'd believed that if I stared long enough into the clouds, I would be able to fly. I look up now through the scribbled circles of oak branches, tilting my head to find an expanse of sky. I hear someone calling my name, and I turn slowly, my heels digging into the soft earth. It's Cooper and he's in the doorway, framed and backlit.

"Eve, the guests are leaving. Maybe come say good-bye?"

"Sure," I say.

He holds my hand as we make our way through the dispersing crowd. We pass Mark and he touches my shoulder. "You okay, Eve?"

His wife, Linda, stands next to him. Her black hair is short, a pixie cut I know is meant to look like Audrey Hepburn's, because Mark is obsessed with her. Linda takes my hand. "I'm so sorry about everything going on."

"Me, too," I say, and try to release my hand, but she holds tight.

"Is there anything I can do?" she asks.

"No, but thanks so much for coming

tonight." I hear my voice, it, and it's not mine.

"Well, you do look beautiful," she says. "I thought the same thing when I saw you wear that dress to the school fund-raiser."

I wrench my hand from hers and back away slowly. Cooper is gone by now, at the front door, shaking hands and saying good night to our guests. I join him.

TEN

Who knows when anything becomes a routine, but every afternoon there's a crunch of gravel and the ring of the bell as the mailman drops our mail and packages. Bills, catalogs, and supplies stream in daily through the front door. It's Francie's job to grab and sort the mail. Bills are put in Max's box. Supplies in their designated storage. Everything else is dropped on the project table. But this . . . this is a first. I know even before I pick up the envelope and see our logo that this is one of our own cards. Someone sent me a card from my own line. *Cool beans,* as a younger Gwen would have said.

The card, it's number two from the Ten Good Ideas line: *Tell Good Stories.* I open it slowly and a clipped *Savannah News* article falls out — it is the one I've already read about the homeless man's death on Preston. The note inside is cryptic: *Good Stories for you.*

There's no name, no signature or return address.

Good mail, that's why I make these cards; that's my impetus. But this is anything but good. It feels downright sinister.

"Max," I call out.

The air around me has a heartbeat. I hold out the card as he approaches.

"What's that?" he asks.

"Someone sent me our own card."

"Well, that's a first. Nice, right?"

"No, it's not nice. I don't know what it means."

Max takes the card and the clipping from me before he sits at the table. He shoves aside some early sketches for number seven and skims the article before looking up. "Why would someone send this to you?"

"I don't know."

"Ignore it. People are crazy. We know this. Someone is bored and . . . has too much time on their hands."

"No. It feels more than that. Why would someone take the time to do this?"

"I think that you have more than enough to deal with right now. Figuring out why some idiot sent you this article should not be on the list."

I take the article back from Max and place it inside the envelope, as if I can undo the opening, put things back into place as they were. "We can't let Willa see this, okay?"

He agrees. "No. Not now."

It's nice at times like this, the two of us, the silence made of whirring machines and rustling paper. But it never lasts. Not when we both, always, eventually need to be somewhere else.

Hours later with evening drawing near, I stand in the hallway of our house and call out. "Cooper? Gwen?"

It's funny how this goes — here I am shouting out to my family and I'm surrounded by family, too. Well, Cooper's family anyway. Our front hall is adorned with portraits of Great Morrisons. At least that's how I think of them. First are Cooper's grandparents, who stare at the camera wearing tight grins and tighter clothes. Louise and Averitt's wedding photo is framed in gold; Averitt looks at Louise with a beguiling smile while she stares vacuously into the camera. So many photos: Averitt shaking hands with the mayor; Louise at a fundraiser, wearing a red ball gown, her hair in a chignon, posing with Ronald Reagan. Farther down is Gwen's last school portrait, with her insecure pasted-on smile. This ode-to-Morrison wall must be passed through to get to any part of the house and is a not so subtle reminder of all that came before me, what must be matched or exceeded. This wall, this display, existed when I moved into the house and Louise "graciously" let it stay. Photos of my parents, of Willa and me as children are in frames scattered throughout the house, but not here, not on this wall.

I climb the stairs to our bedroom. It's in the far corner of the house, the windows facing east, ready to receive the breezes, if so offered, in the days before central air. When I reach our doorway, I hear Cooper's voice coming, muffled and angry, from the bathroom. The shower is on and its river-rush sound is background music to his voice. I know he can't hear me with the door closed and the water pounding, but I hear him. I step closer.

"I don't give a shit what he thinks. He's a prick."

Then silence.

"He's lying. The press didn't contact him; he's just being nosy and hoping for some kind of an exclusive. Son of a bitch."

My diaphragm tightens under my ribs. I breathe in shallow sips of air. But I listen.

161

"I've told you this story over and over. It was raining. My sister in law, crazy and angry as hell, grabbed the wheel to make me take her back to the bar. I skidded; the car locked up. I hit a tree. The End. There is nothing else to say and I won't talk to some asshole who wants to make me look bad for doing the right thing."

I step back from the anger, which isn't even directed at me. I return to the kitchen, pick out a bottle of Malbec, and open it with a swift twist. I call Gwen's cell and she answers on the first ring as I pour the wine into a glass. "Where are you?" I ask.

"Um . . . at the river with Dylan and some friends. We're out in Pete's boat. We'll be home after dark. Promise."

I hear the slur of her words, the way she talks very slowly, articulating carefully. "You're drinking." I close my eyes against the knowing.

"Nope."

"You sound funny," I say.

"You can test me when I get home. I'm not drinking. Whatever."

"Be careful, okay?"

"Always. Gotta go, Mom." She hangs up.

The wineglass, red and round, is in my hand, and then it isn't. I've smashed it on the hardwood floor. Droplets and splashes of bloodlike liquid are everywhere: on the lower cabinets, on the bar stool cushions, on the hem of my white jeans. And I don't feel any better; only worse. The tears come hot and mean. Furious. Heat rushes into my face, under my eyes.

Cooper's voice: "Eve, what happened?"

He's staring at the floor, wiping his hand back and forth across the air.

"I threw the wineglass," I say.

"Threw?" His forehead lifts and his bandage puckers. His hair is still damp and he wears jeans and a black T-shirt, smelling like the Savannah Bee Company soap I keep in the shower.

"Yes. Threw. Tossed. Hurled."

"Okay." He walks to the storage closet, where he grabs towels, a broom, and floor cleaner. "Want to tell me why?"

"I wish I'd just drank it." I reach into the sink for a dish towel. "I heard you on the phone upstairs. You want to tell me what is going on?"

"So we're switching subjects?" he asks with a broom in one hand and a dish towel in the other.

"Yes, we are."

"It was Matthew, from the *Savannah News.* Thank God we're friends. There's some nosy reporter who wants to write

163

about the things that go down on that street and in that neighborhood. He wants to add our accident to the list and interview me. Hell, no way."

"Why would he want to interview you?"

"I just explained it, Eve."

"What things go down on that street?"

"The drugs. The death of that homeless guy. The shoddy construction. The false 'historic homes.' Those kinds of things."

"I still don't see why your accident should be included."

"Your sister's accident," he says, correcting me.

I close my eyes and wish I could hear the lovely shattering of another glass of wine, see the redness burst onto the floor, watch the slivers of crystal fly into the corners of the kitchen. I didn't pay enough attention the first time to fully enjoy it.

Cooper's voice interrupts my vision. "Want to help me clean this up?"

"I got it," I say.

"Why would you throw this?" He bends over and picks up the stem of the Riedel glass.

"I didn't realize I'd done it until I'd done it."

"What's wrong with you?" He comes

closer, stepping around the broken fragments.

"I'm not sure," I say. "I'm mad. I'm sad.
I'm worried. All of the above."

"So you're taking it out on our stem-
ware?" He smiles, an attempt at unity. I
smile in return.

When the glass is swept up and the wine
wiped clean, I continue cooking lasagna,
and Cooper goes into the living room to
watch the news. I turn on the house music
system, switching from Rihanna (Gwen was
obviously the last to use it) to the Lone
Bellow, singing about the two sides of
lonely. I cook to their lonesome sounds, sipping a new glass of wine, one I will not
throw.

Cooper makes a tentative entrance back
into the kitchen. "You better?"

I nod.

"Do I get a kiss?"

He does this thing where he asks me to
walk to him for a kiss, when he could just
as easily walk over and kiss me. I don't get
it. But I go to him. "So, remind me what
this trip is for tomorrow," I say.

"I'm securing funding for the new 'Home
Place' section. I have a couple of ideas I
think will really work this time." He sits on
a bar stool and watches me place the cooked

noodles on the bottom of the pan. "Tell me, how is Willa since she lost it at the fund-raiser?"

It's been two days since the party and this is the first time Cooper has said her name. "She's getting better. The swelling around her eye is almost gone, but she's . . . confused sometimes. But I'm not even sure *confused* is the right word. Things are all mixed up inside her head."

"Tell me what you mean."

"Like things don't make too much sense to her. She cries over something small. She can't remember where the bathroom is. Things like that."

"Oh, well, that's okay. Those are small things."

"I don't know. Like today, she talked about that old homeless guy and she cried again."

"Willa's always been sentimental," he says. "Always emotional."

"But this is different," I say.

"Different how?"

"I don't know." And I didn't. Not really. "I guess with the accident and all, well, of course Willa is feeling vulnerable. Lucky, but vulnerable."

"Okay." He draws the word out.

"While I was reading about the dead man

in the last page of the "Metro" section, I was thinking that if you or Willa — God forbid — had been injured more seriously in that accident on that same street, you'd have had a front-page spread describing everything about you. But what happened with this poor guy? Barely a mention, and hidden at that."

"Well, he wasn't Willa or me."

"That's maybe what Willa was crying about," I say. "Because it could have been."

"But it wasn't, and I was trying to help. We had nothing to do with that drunk in the alley."

"I know," I say, and then swallow the apology, the one that comes so easily. "Cooper?"

"Yes?"

"We are going to have to figure out what happened that night. It's important to Willa. She wants to talk to you."

"I've already told you everything."

"She wasn't drinking. And it's important to her to know why she was acting that way. She doesn't remember anything. Wouldn't you want to know that about yourself?"

"No," he says, "I wouldn't." He takes a few steps and then turns again. "Do you so badly need her to be right that you want me to be wrong?"

He doesn't stand still long enough to hear

my answer.

He leaves, and then the TV's muffled sound fills an empty space in our home.

Again I feel misplaced, dropped into a life not my own. I'm watching: Oh, look, there I am, cooking. There I am, being wife and mom. There is the lasagna and the preheated oven. "Bloom where you are planted," Mom would say. Okay, okay — I'm alone in the kitchen, trying to bloom.

Go in there and sit with him, a voice inside my head tells me. Be sweet.

Yes, be sweet. The southern epitaph I wanted to put on my mom's gravestone: the catchall phrase meant to solve conflict.

But what was going on with us, between husband and wife, wasn't conflict. It was something much deeper, and more troubling. Conflict is when Gwen wants to wear a skirt so short that I can see the bend where leg meets butt and I tell her to go upstairs to change. Conflict is when I want to go to eat seafood and Cooper wants steak, or when I forget to pick up the dry cleaning.

But this — what we're going through now? I'm not sure what to call it. The changes in personality I catch out of the corner of my eye and ear; the insults called "jokes"; the adamant aversion to my work; the weakness in defending me to his parents; the flash of anger that paralyzes me until slowly Cooper, the kind man, returns and I love him. Waiting for the return of the warm Cooper is a breath-holding time that always pays off. It is worth the wait. Or so I've always thought.

And love conquers all.

Dingle.

"Cooper," I call out.

"Yes?"

"Dinner is ready." I toss chopped tomatoes into a bowl of lettuce for the salad.

He appears in the doorway. "Where's Gwen?"

"I'll call her." I pick up my cell and hit her name on my favorites' list. She answers on the first ring.

"Mom, relax, I'm pulling up the driveway right now. Dylan is joining us."

"Okay, love you."

I set the phone on the counter. "She's pulling up now. Be nice to Dylan."

Cooper rolls his eyes. "Just what I need tonight. We have this delinquent over for dinner, and meanwhile my parents have been asking to come for dinner for a week now."

"I know. I'll call your mom tomorrow. I promise." I pause and a question, a smaller one, below the others, niggles at me. "What investment was Fritz talking about the other night?"

Cooper waves his hand in the air and yawns, turning away from me. "You know, he's always into something nutty."

"Were we? I mean, did we invest also?"

He laughs. "No." He sits at the round kitchen table and cuts into the pan of steaming noodles.

Gwen and Dylan come through the back door, flush with sun, water, and July adolescence. Devouring the food as if she hasn't eaten in weeks, Gwen finally settles back in her seat, a satiated grin on her face. "So, Aunt Willa is home, right?"

I nod.

"But don't go bother her," Cooper says.

"Oh, she won't care if I go see her. She'll be happy." The surety of Gwen.

"Did you hear your mom say not to bother her?" Cooper asks.

"I heard her for sure. If she's asleep, I won't wake her." Gwen looks to Dylan. "Want to go walk with me to Aunt Willa's?"

Dylan's smile spreads across his face and then upward, as if in a slow-motion short called *How to smile*. His dark Elvis hair, whipped by river and wind, is tangled. "Yo, Mrs. Morrison, how is your sister? Gwen won't stop worrying about her, but I told her I've seen lacrosse players knocked unconscious and they've healed quickly."

"It's a little more than that," I say. "But thanks for asking. She's doing better. A little better every day."

"Well, I looked it all up on the Internet cuz Gwen wouldn't stop talking about it."

Gwen leans over and lightly pops him on the shoulder with her palm. "Stop. You're making me sound OCD, like it's all I talk about."

"It sort of is," he says, and kisses her. Right there at the dinner table in front of her parents, he kisses her on the lips and laughs. "But that's okay. OCD is cute on you."

They seem in their own world — just Gwen and Dylan — in a world where secret code and inside jokes turn into love.

"Anyway," Dylan says, turning to me again. "I'm sorry about your sister. It really sucks."

"Yes," I say. "It does."

Cooper is silent, twisting noodles around his fork and staring at Gwen, who is looking only at Dylan. It occurs to me, in the silence of this stare standoff, that Dylan has asked more about Willa, and researched more about head injuries than my husband has.

It's Cooper who stands up and speaks. "I think it's time for you to leave, Dylan. These have been long days for all of us."

"No way, Dad." Gwen stands, too. "We're going to see Aunt Willa."

Together, she and Dylan walk to the side door. Dylan turns. "Thanks for the dinner, Mrs. Morrison. It rocked." He gives me a thumbs-up and walks out with Gwen.

Cooper stands and takes his empty plate, places it in the sink. "What are we going to do? You can go after her if you'd like."

Cooper sighs long and loud. "Our daughter seems to be on one long road to a terrible decision. Something life-changing. We have to stop her."

"I know. I think about it every day. I don't know what to do. I'll get drug-test sticks, and we'll keep setting the house alarm at night. I'll try talking to her tonight when she's calm." I list all the solutions I have, the ones I've listed in my own mind already.

Cooper shakes his head at every suggestion. "Talking doesn't do a damn thing. We need to take everything away from her — phone, TV, boyfriend, car. All of it."

"One thing at a time," I say. "Okay?"

"Well, you asked what I'd do, and that's what I'd do."

"I didn't ask what you'd do," I say, turning to face him and wiping my hands on a dish towel. "I told you to go after her if you wanted."

"Do you always have to be so literal?" he asks.

"No, I guess I don't." I drop my gaze.

We stand there in silence, neither of us able to build that bridge created by the word "Sorry" or the touch that means the same. Cooper walks out and the TV voices return. ESPN music is the sound track to the distance between us.

I'm more careful than most about leaving conversations unfinished in moments of anger. And not just because I'd memorized the verse from Ephesians about not going to bed angry, winning a youth group Bible trivia contest in seventh grade, but because my last words to my parents had been in anger and the regret weighs on me with heavy shame.

I drop the dish towel and enter the living room. I sit next to Cooper on the couch. "We have to be a team, Cooper. I can't do all of this alone."

"All of what?"

"Willa, Gwen, the Fine Line, the house, your parents. . . ."

"What do you mean by my parents? Is there something to be done about them?"

"No . . . I just meant . . . I don't know what I meant. I feel like they need something from us, from me, that I'm not giving."

"They always want more time with me than they have. It's not your fault."

He places his arm around me and pulls me close. The sportscaster drones on about a record being set. There is always a record being set. Cooper mumbles into my hair. "It's been a long week. I'm exhausted. And darling, you don't need to do it all."

I relax into his shoulder. This is what I've always wanted: someone at my side, a partner. I rest in this.

Then he speaks again. "Sometimes you just have to pick your priorities. Right now, I think that's at home with Gwen. And me. Then Willa."

The Fine Line hasn't made the list of priorities. I close my eyes and exhale. Maybe he's right.

"I love you," he says. "You know that, right?"

"Yes," I say. "I know."

"Our family, it's the most important thing of all. It's why I do what I do. It's everything. . . ."

"I know," I say, repeating myself.

"Listen, I'm swamped tomorrow. Could

you and Gwen go pick up my car from the body shop? It's ready."

"That was quick," I say.

"We've been good customers through the years. They're prompt with me."

He kisses my forehead and his attention returns to the baseball stats. My attention returns to Gwen and Willa, to the cottage, and then wanders down the dirt road to the studio. But my body remains on the couch, still and quiet.

ELEVEN

Again, there's an envelope on the project table with my name in block letters. There's no return address and the stamp is crooked. It takes me a long time to decide whether to open it, but of course I do, because an unopened letter will eventually have its due. This I know.

What I try to do — what I've always tried to do — is bring something good with my work. Now someone is using this goodness to bring fear. I want to open the envelope. I want to burn it. I'm curious. I'm scared.

Finally, after what seems like ages, I lift the cotton envelope. I rip the flap quickly, like a Band-Aid from skin. There it is, another card from the Ten Good Ideas line. This time, the *Search for the True* card — number four in the series. The design shows the world, blue and floating amid the dark night. Stars are set as sparkled dents in the universe.

I brace myself for the anonymous note, but this time — nothing. There's just blank space where words should be. Something is inside, though. A small business card falls out and lands on the painted concrete floor; it stares up at me with block letters, e-mail and a phone number for the Anglers.

I leave it there, this offensive business card on cheap paper. I stand and use my foot to push the card under the table, toward the trash can on the far side, and I turn away.

If there's a truth to be known or told or written, I want to know. Who wouldn't? But to hint like this is perverse. I wish I had a wineglass to throw again. I wish I had something to smash and hurl and splinter, but I don't.

I've come here to print wedding invitations and I'll focus. We have a huge order — four hundred invites using both a polymer plate of two tiny birds facing each other on a tree branch, which Francie had designed for the bride, and also our carved-wood fonts, which are set and tied into a metal chase. Setting this card took Max and I the better half of a day. I lift the large platen top, placing the first sheet of cotton paper.

A meditative calm comes over me, as it often does when I'm alone and printing.

Four hundred invitations. My God, who invites four hundred people to witness the exchange of vows? Does this make them more binding? Cooper and I married in front of a small crowd in a downtown chapel. My family couldn't pay for a large wedding and Cooper didn't want one, although his mother begged us to please let her have a cathedral wedding and she'd pay for it.

For this invitation's design, I met with the new bride for hours over a month's time. When I asked about her groom, she flushed. She loved him so much and she told me, she couldn't believe her luck. He'd been her best friend, and then love showed up.

My parents claimed to have a great love — one that lasted through thirty-six years of marriage. So tied together that they died together. It was an accidental carbon monoxide death. Usually when you hear about this kind of dying — the slow, in your sleep death — it's suicide. But not my parents. Suicide would have meant an eternal hell, and no matter what they feared here on earth, they feared damning separation from God more so. What I've learned since is that carbon monoxide poisoning is the number-one reason for accidental death.

There are some things you don't want to learn.

They'd gone to bed that night and closed their Bibles — Mom's with the pink quilted cover and Dad's with the leather so cracked, it looked like dried mud. They'd turned off the lights, let Buster, the mutt, jump onto the bed, and together closed their eyes. They were lost in their own worlds, asleep when the ancient furnace, which they'd sworn to replace, started to leak. Sleep, I think, is the only time we can live entirely in our own world. And this time, for my parents, it was an eternal sleep.

The church secretary found them the next day. She had said that the worst part was the way they looked alive, curled in repose, as if they didn't know they were yet dead. Buster, too.

But the worst part for me, the terrible part, isn't that I wasn't the one who found them; it was the *reason* I didn't find them. Two weeks before my parents passed away, we had a disagreement about why I didn't regularly take Gwen to church, why I myself had stopped meeting them at the front steps. I'd tried to explain, but because I didn't fully understand my motivations, I couldn't rightly explain it to them. My decision then was vague and unformed. Dad yelled at me, telling me that I would destroy my family and my life. I said a terrible and hurtful thing when I told him that church hadn't exactly saved his family, that it wasn't the catchall insurance card he'd wanted for us, was it?

I was sick for days after this fight and I'd spent hours forming an apology. But Mom and Dad died before the gap was healed. A simple ending, a terrible ending, and one I couldn't undo.

My dad was an old-fashioned "father knows best" kind of dad. But there was more to it than that. At least for Willa and me. There was this dad, this charming and gregarious man who made people laugh and cry, who enriched their lives. Then there was the man who would only appear at home — the moody, angry man frustrated at the daily goings-on of any life. The rages came from unexplainable sources: a barking dog across the yard; a pair of shoes left in the middle of the kitchen; crumbs in the beanbag chair in the den. And there he'd be, his forehead scrunched up like a wrinkled sheet, his eyebrows drawn together, screaming.

God, the screaming.

The weird part (the part Willa and I would discuss under the bed) was how the scream-

ing usually wasn't prompted by our disobe-
dience or back talk. It would usually be
something random and unpredictable that
would set him off. That's what made it all
so terrifying. There was the night I came
home crying because I'd been excluded
from a club my friends had created. The
Cool Clique, they'd called it, an uninspired
and dull name for a club that didn't invite
me, and I told them so. "Stupidest name
for a club ever." It hadn't gone well, and for
days, until it became boring to them, the
girls shunned me, closed gaps at the lunch
table, refused my phone calls, and turned
away when I approached. I wept at the dinner table, wanting solace or comfort or
anything parents should offer when a child
is hurting. But instead, I was rewarded with
a lecture about "not being of this world"
and how I cared about the wrong, wrong,
wrong things. When Willa piped up and told
Dad to have a heart, he exploded with a
lecture and rant so severe, it rang in my ears
for a week. So, no matter what it was, the
irritating circumstance reminded him,
again, that his daughters were disobedient
and willful. Mostly, we were. Although we
tried very hard not to be.

And yet my favorite phrase had been
"That's my girl." I always wanted to please

my dad, even in my rebellion. If he gave me a compliment, I would repeat in my head over and over like a poem or love song. "You look lovely today, Eve." "Great report card; that's the Wetherburn way. You got the brains in the family, for sure." Then the big smile and "That's my girl."

But that was only part of it. I hated him too. I hated the smell of his aftershave as he came down the stairs; his black hair combed sideways across his head; his loafers left in the exact spot at the front door; his change of voice when he believed other people were listening. I hated it all. Yet I needed him to approve of me.

Oh, and the drinking. I hated the havoc alcohol wreaked upon my family. It wasn't the drink's fault: it was the excess. When Willa started drinking in high school, she didn't drink a beer or two like the rest of us at the bonfire; she drank a six-pack and then a twelve-pack. She didn't get drunk; she got hammered.

By the time Willa met the boy from Colorado on Tybee Island one summer afternoon, she was that other person all the time: alternating from hilarious and witty to sarcastic and sad. She left on a Sunday afternoon after church. We'd come home and she'd walked upstairs to take a nap, she'd said. Later that afternoon, we realized she was gone. A note said that she couldn't live with the hypocrisy and ridiculous faking; she was gone to live a "real life." Sadly, I knew "real" for her mostly rested in a bottle.

I wanted out of the family house as badly as she did, but I'd been biding my time. When she left, she was eighteen years old, had graduated from high school only three weeks earlier. I was working at Soapbox then. Willa's absence throbbed with pain in that small house, like a missing limb taken in a brutal accident.

She "got sober" a few times through the next years, but ten years ago, after a DUI in Boulder, she quit, or so she said. Her abstinence lasted for weeks and then months and now coming up on ten years. Sobriety wasn't so good for a love affair that was based on dependence. When drinking ended, so did his love. That's how she came to live with us.

Dad didn't often drink, but when he did, he drank until he passed out, wherever he happened to be: the shower twice, the garage, the living room couch, the kitchen table. He never took a sip of alcohol outside the house. He kept his vice private, for our enjoyment.

"Eve." Willa's voice startles me. Sunlight surrounds her and forms a halo around her hair and body, a ring of fire as she steps into the studio. I see her as she'd been in those days we hid under the bed during our summer of heresy, a summer that was now being turned into a card line, into something good: one thing again made from another.

"Good morning," I say. "How're you feeling?"

She bites her bottom lip and steps closer, speaking in almost a whisper. "I'm scared."

I set down the pile of thick paper in my hand and wrap my arms around her, hugging her tightly. "It takes time."

She gives me a look. "Dingle."

"Sorry."

She tries to smile. The sliding doors open again, and Francie and Max enter. They see Willa, and loud greetings erupt; hugs are given all around. Max touches Willa's swollen eye and Francie cries a little bit before turning on the music. Johnny Cash sings "Folsom Prison Blues," proving that Max last used the iPod.

Francie tosses a pad of paper on the table. "Welcome back to work, Willa. Today we work on number seven."

"Yes," I say, "but we also have that appointment with the accountant this morning and then I have to finish this wedding run. So let's spend the afternoon with number seven. And I have to pick up Cooper's car."

"Cooper can't pick up his own car?" Francie asks.

I don't need to answer Francie, because the resounding bell that signals a guest outside rings through the studio and Max opens the door for our client.

Framed in the doorway, she appears small. She carries a large satchel, hugging it to her chest like a kid running away from home. She strikes me as nervous and afraid.

"Come in." Max waves her in.

"Thanks," she says, and stops for a moment to listen, and then looks at me. "I love Johnny Cash."

"Good," Max says. "So do we."

"I'm Mary Jo," she adds.

Francie walks toward her. "Nice to meet you. We have some ideas and concept boards to go over with you." She points to the project table.

"Are you Eve?" she asks Francie.

"No." I step forward and hold out my hand for her to shake. "I am."

She stares at me for the longest time — or what seems the longest time, although it might have been only a few seconds. Finally,

185

she holds out her own hand, clutching her satchel, so that her elbow is bent up. "Nice to meet you," she says.

Behind me, there's a small sound like a cat's weak meow or the squeak of the printer before we oil her cog. But it's Willa. She's stepped underneath the overhead hanging work light, so she looks like she's under a stage spotlight. Her bruise is greenish blue against white skin. Her lips are bloodless and thin, pulled across her face in a line. As pretty as Willa is, she looks anything but at this moment.

Mary Jo drops her satchel and it lands with a loud clunk it as it slams onto the floor. "Oh," she says.

Francie calls from the project table. "Over here."

Willa, Mary Jo, and I stare at the satchel on the floor. Finally, I speak. "Sounds like something broke."

Mary Jo grabs her bag, again clutching it to her chest. And she steps backward, so I see her clearly. She is small, and not only because she is thin but because her bones seem made in miniature. Her eyes are round, two stormy worlds floating in her pale face. I've never seen eyes so blue. Does she wear blue contacts? I wonder. Her hair is not quite blond and not quite brown, and it's pulled back in a loose knot that rests on her neck and falls a bit onto her right shoulder. *Cute* would be the right word for her if she didn't look so pathetically nervous.

"It's okay," she says. "Nothing broke." Her voice is lovely, with the sugary southern accent I've tried in vain to master.

We all move to the project table and Max brings the concept board, where our ideas and Francie's sketches are displayed in overlapping squares and rectangles. Mary Jo settles into a chair and squints at the board, staring. "Tell me about this."

Max launches into his normal introductory speech. "We listen to your story about how and why you started your company and then we dig into the symbolism we hear. This is our first concept, and then we move onto concept two after we hear your thoughts."

Francie walks to the board, touching the top right corner. "This is the color palette we chose, since you said that "the numbers tell the real story." We're all about words and image here, so your take on numbers really inspired us. We started with green, but of course that was way too obvious, so we moved on from there and eventually ended up with these shades of blue and gold. Blue because it's expansive and positive. And gold because," and at this Francie laughs, "it's gold!"

Mary Jo's face takes on a new expression; the childish nervousness is disappearing and turning into something more mature. "This is great. Go on."

"Well," Francie says, "you talked about your connection with nature and with Savannah, so we've incorporate sea grass and, here, a wave." She points at her sketch.

Max stands on the other side of the board and continues to talk about their vision for her logo.

Then Mary Jo holds up her hand and looks directly at me. "And what do you do?"

"Excuse me?" I lean my elbows on the table.

"I mean, do you help with the logos or just . . . what is it that you do? Just curious," she says.

Max takes a few steps, until he is standing behind me. "Eve owns and started this studio. She is brilliant with fonts, printing, and layout. *We*" — he points to Francie and then himself — "are the graphic designers and artists. But nothing is complete without Eve. Nothing."

"I was just asking." Mary Jo licks her lips and her eyes move rapidly from one face to the next. "So what font do you think we should use?" she asks me directly.

"I usually wait until I see a more concrete design." I take a deep breath. "Fonts are a language all their own. I can't choose one until I know what we need to say."

"Does that part really matter all that much?" Mary Jo asks.

Max walks away and returns with two poster boards — one for a rock concert and another for a sweet sixteen. "This is why font is important. Imagine if we switched them."

Mary Jo shrugs. "I get it. Whatever. But it's the image that's the most important to me."

Max, Francie, and I glance at one another and smile — another kind of private language — and we continue explaining our process.

"Well, this has been interesting and I can't wait to see the next version. I'll email you my thoughts." Mary Jo gathers her things and stands. "Where did Willa go?"

I search my mind, nudge words and sentences around, trying to remember when we'd introduced Mary Jo to Willa, but it's Max who says it. "Do you know her?"

"No. She was just standing here when I came and now she's gone. I thought maybe she worked here."

"How do you know her name?" Francie asks.

Mary Jo squints, as if Francie were made of sunlight. "Because," Mary Jo says slowly, "you said it."

Willa approaches us now and gazes at Mary Jo. They stare at each other and then Mary Jo turns quickly on her kitten heels and walks out, speaking over her shoulder. "See you in a couple weeks."

When the door closes and then tires crunch on the gravel outside, Francie says, "What a bitch."

"I know her," Willa says quietly. "But I don't know how."

"I think she knew you, too," I say.

Willa shakes her head. It's as if she's trying to loosen memories, to shake them to consciousness. Quick tears come to her eyes. "This is terrible. It's like looking into the dark, like finding your way through a room without lights or windows. There's everything there, but I can't see anything at all. I'm bumping into furniture and walls."

"It'll get better, right?" Francie says. "We'll help you. What do they say helps?" She is desperate for an answer and trips over her need to help Willa.

"Reorienting over and over," I say. "But the problem is that we don't know what

190

only you can know. . . ." I pause. "One of the things I learned is that our brain, your brain," I say to Willa, "holds memories with a little tag of place and time. I mean, I know it's all mixed up now, but somewhere the image is tied to place."

Willa sits on a chair next to Francie. "Nothing is tied to anything. I dig around inside my stomach . . ." She pauses, seeming to know she's used the wrong word, the wrong body part, but still searching. "My head," she finally says. "I dig around in my head and try to find one scrap of something from that night. And what do I find? Nada. I know Cooper's story, but I can't remember it. What scares me the most is that someone can tell me exactly what happened and I have to believe it because I don't know anything at all." She talks so quickly, manically, with her voice rising at the end in a crescendo of frustration.

No one speaks; not one of us knows how to combat or fix this blackout in her memory.

Willa claps her hands together once, a signal, a resounding end. "Here. I know how to explain it. It's like this," she says. "When we were kids, Eve, we heard the creation story, right? Adam and Eve. The garden. The snake."

I nod.

"And part of us knew it couldn't be all the way true, right? It was true that God made the world and a man and then a woman, but the other stuff seemed as real as Narnia, right? Or the myths you loved in high school about Zeus and Hades and that goddess you loved — what was her name?"

"Persephone."

Willa continues. "Then when we were in high school we took that field trip to Atlanta to the museum. Fieldstone . . ." Her voice fades.

"Fernbank," I say, filling in her gaps, writing over the blank spots as if our conversations are fill-in-the-blank tests.

"Yes." She shakes her head again. "Anyway . . . we learned about other theories and the big bang and the dreaded word *evolution* and we discovered that there were other stories about the same event." She is quiet for a while, shuffling the blank memory cards as if we are about to play poker. "That's how this is with the accident. I know I've been told a story I'm supposed to believe. Mostly, I do, I think. But there's another story out there, and I don't think I'm going to find it at Fernbank this time."

We laugh, but it's a weak sound, a sad resonance.

Humiliation, a filling and nauseous feeling, overcomes me. We aren't talking about some version of that night told by a stranger. This was my husband's rendition of the accident, which might or might not be true: a creation story of his own mythology?

"How can we help?" Max asks.

"You can't. . . ." Willa stands, waves her hand, and smiles. "Go back to work."

We are silent, all of us.

"I do need to finish this print run," I say, and then we break free. Tears sting the back of my throat like bees released from a hive under my ribs.

I lift the printer's top, checking the magenta ink level, burying again and again the rising sadness that I just can't fix. I focus on work, on my search for the right shade of green, for the poster for O'Leary's pub. I flip through the Pantone color chart, which is a book of color recipes — an indispensable tool in the printing universe. Our chart is ink-stained and well loved, worn at the edges. Max startles me when he touches my elbow. "Hey, you okay?"

"Looking for that perfect Irish green." I hold up the Pantone chart and then look at him, his eyes, at the circle of blue and then the brown. I close my eyes. "What color are my eyes?" I ask.

He laughs; I feel it as a low rumble under my ribs. "Mostly brown, but lately they've been greener and not so brown anymore."

My lids pop open. "You noticed."

"About a year ago."

"It's weird, right? Why would my eyes change color?"

"I was going to ask you, but . . ."

"But what?"

He looks away. "Eve, I don't know. It seemed personal. And we stay away from those kinds of conversations. . . ."

"We do?"

His gaze wanders back to me, slowly, languid and swimming. "Of course we do."

"Oh, I didn't realize. . . ."

"Here." He takes the Pantone chart from me. "Let's do this later. Francie really wants you to see her new sketch."

"Wait," I say, a fluttering feeling moving under my skin. "Why do we do that?"

"Do what?" He touches the Pantone chart. "Use this?"

"No, of course I know why we use that." I smile. "Why do we stay away from those kinds of conversations? I'd have liked to know that you noticed my eyes, just like I know that you have a blue ring around your brown eyes. Did we somehow agree never to talk about these kinds of things and I don't remember agreeing?"

"Eve." He takes a deep breath. "You've always kept your private thoughts private. You keep your life outside this studio and inside this studio very separate."

My eyes well with tears, but not enough to spill out.

"I'm an ass." He picks up a clean white cloth and hands it to me like an old-fashioned handkerchief. "I wasn't saying it was good or bad. You asked."

"I know." I hold up my hand. "I don't want it that way, though. I didn't realize I was doing that. I want to know how you and Francie feel about things outside these walls. I want to know what you do and think and notice. I do."

He stares at me for a bit, pushes back a strand of hair from his forehead, but doesn't speak.

"Tell me something," I say. "Something that has nothing to do with this life inside these walls. Tell me something, anything about you."

He smiles. "Okay."

I wait and he falters, reaching for something.

"My brother is visiting this week. Yesterday, we kayaked from Savannah to Daufuskie Island and spent the afternoon drinking warm beer on Bloody Point Beach."

"Beau?" I ask.

He nods.

"Sounds amazing." I close my eyes, imagining kayaking across the green-gray water to an island with Max. Just as quickly, feeling danger, I stop the vision in mid-vision, opening my eyes to reality.

Francie and Willa walk toward us and they laugh about something we don't hear. Before they reach us, Max whispers, "I like the green."

I'm fairly sure he isn't talking about the Pantone chart.

TWELVE

The car-repair shop is the kind of place that remains unnoticed until needed. Broken-down and smashed cars litter the parking lot out front, while men in grease-stained overalls mill around as if they're only looking at the cars, not actually doing anything with them. But in the back of Brando's Car Repair there's a larger lot, unseen and busy as a hive. It's there that I find the owner.

I call out his name. "Brando."

He approaches me, and the smell of burned tires comes with him. His dark black hair is a slick, shining helmet. He smiles and his two gold-capped teeth flirt from the left side of his grin. "Hello, Mrs. Morrison. Nice to see you today. The Beemer is all ready for you to take home to its comfy garage."

"Thanks. You made these repairs so quickly. I appreciate it," I say as Willa comes to my side.

He shrugs. "Your hubby said you needed it for a trip tomorrow and so we needed to put a rush on it. Guys were up all night working on it, like it was the president's limo or something." He laughs and this sends him into a spasm of coughs. Bent over, he finishes coughing and then stands up, wiping at the edge of his mouth with a stained towel. "But it's ready for sure."

There is no trip tomorrow, but I don't say this.

Willa stands to the left of me and winds and unwinds her fingers in a nervous gesture I haven't seen since childhood. Her eyes twitch and her gaze moves across the lot and then to the right. Cooper's BMW is parked in the side lot and a bright cloak of sunshine falls on the silver paint. Brando is right: The car is perfect, as if it had never been in an accident at all.

"I wish I could be fixed that easily," she says, quiet and not seeming to know that she'd spoken out loud.

Brando looks to her. "You were in that car, too?"

"Yes."

"You're lucky Mr. Morrison is such a good driver and that Beemers are so safe with the side and front air bags and all; otherwise, you'da been wrapped around that tree yourself."

Willa stares at Brando without moving: an unnerving stillness. "I'm lucky?" she asks.

Brando blushes, diffuse red patches covering his cheeks. "Didn't mean nothing by it. I just heard the story, that's all. . . ."

"What story?" I ask.

"About the wreck and all," he says.

"And?" Willa asks.

I look around for Max but don't see him. It was good of him to drive us here . . . but where did he go?

"Well I don't have no details or anything," Brando says. "All I know is that it must've been one helluva rotten tree, because whatever broke off and smashed into the hood did the most damage."

"Thanks for all your help," I say. "Are the keys in the car?"

"Sure are," he says. "Wanna take her for a spin to make sure it's okay for your trip tomorrow?"

Cooper's tiny lie quivers. It's so easy to tell the small lies — the ones that get the car fixed quickly or get you out of a dinner party. But where do you draw the line? Cooper told Brando I needed the car for a trip; he told me that Willa was drunk and grabbed the wheel. He's not alone. I do it, too — tell people that a job is almost done

199

when I've just started; that I'm fine when I'm not.

Cooper wanted his car back quickly. Big deal.

I smile at Brando. "I'm not going on a trip, but we do so appreciate the rush with the car. Thanks so much."

Willa and I approach the car, and as she reaches the passenger side, she stops. Large sunglasses cover her eyes, and I can't tell where she's looking, but she's bent over, her face to the passenger-side window. "I thought this might help, you know."

"Seeing the car?"

"Yeah. Seeing where I sat." She stands up, and above the sunglasses her eyebrows draw downward. "I thought it might make me remember." She slams her hand on top of the roof. "This is so unbearably frustrating."

"I know."

She removes her sunglasses and rubs under her eyes. "I wish I'd seen the car all banged up. Maybe that would've helped."

"Should we ask if Brando has pictures?"

"Yes," she says, a jump behind her voice. "Can we?" She waves her hand toward the front of the building. "And where'd Max go?"

"Probably back to work."

"I know I've told you before, but you are so lucky to work with him."

"I know." This isn't a convenient lie; it's the truth.

We walk around the half-mangled and partially fixed cars — those that had been in serious accidents and those in fender benders all together. We reach the office and Brando looks up from a pile of papers and credit card receipts, which he stares at as if they are written in another language. "Something wrong?" he asks.

"I'm wondering if you have any photos of the car before you fixed it." I smile the best I can, but fake grinning is not one of my talents.

"Yeah, I got some for the insurance company."

Willa steps forward, touching his hairy forearm. "I need to see them."

Brando looks up at Willa. Even bruised and ragged, she is a presence. Men notice her. I've seen the way they treat her, as if she's fragile. They feel an irresistible need to take care of her. I know what Brando will say, and then he does.

"Sure thing. Be right back."

We wait in the office, which is black with soot and grease that can only be removed by fire. Talk radio drones on somewhere in the rear of the garage and then Max's voice startles us. "Girls, everything okay?"

I turn. "I thought you left."

"Not yet."

"It's all fine," Willa says. "Car is ready, but we just wanted to see the pictures — you know, before and after."

Brando appears with a file folder and slides it across a counter of cracked yellow linoleum. "Here you go."

Willa picks up a pile of Polaroids. She holds them like a fan of tarot cards, gently, carefully, spreading them out in a pattern as if to read our future or a hidden truth.

"As you can see right here" — Brando points to the hood shot — "most of the damage is on the right side, where you sat. Must've hit that tree sideways." Then he points to the top of the hood. "This is what damn near could've killed you if it had gone through the windshield."

Willa stares at the photo, running her finger along the hood. "If what had gone through the windshield?"

"Musta been a branch." He points to a different photo, the one where the car's front right side was mashed up like thin rice paper folded into ugly origami. "This is where you hit the tree, but this is where something fell off the damn tree." He uses his other hand to cover the hood photo, tying the two together in a car-wreck scenario.

Willa nods. "I don't remember any of it."

"Do you have any photos from the wreck site?" Max asks from behind us, moving closer to look over my shoulder.

"Nope," Brando says, gathering the photos in a proprietary move, shielding Max's gaze from the pictures. "I got the car off the tow truck. I wasn't at the wreck site."

"Brando," I say. "Thanks for everything. Especially the quick fix."

"No problem. Hope everything's okay, since your trip got canceled and all."

"Thanks again."

Max walks out the front door, telling us he'll meet us at the studio, and Willa follows him. "Where you going?" I ask.

"I'll ride with him." She stops at the door, her hand on the knob. "I don't think I want to get in that car."

"It might help?"

"No," she says. "It won't. I'm not sure anything ever will."

Then they're gone: Max and Willa. They walk to his truck, where he opens the passenger side door for her before walking to the driver's side and starting the engine. I'm still standing in the dank office when they drive away.

"If you ask me, she's damn lucky," Brando says, judgment as sure in his voice as a god looking down on the stupid.

"Yes," I reply. "She damn sure is."

And I know we aren't talking about the same thing.

THIRTEEN

Best friend isn't really a term you use when you're an adult. It feels a little demeaning, as if you're placing all other friends on a lower scale. Dear friends are dear and there isn't a best. I can say all of that with certitude and yet in the same breath tell anyone this: "Willa is my best friend."

She knows everything there is to know about me and she can detect any falseness on my part, like one of those airport security buzzers that screams when you forget to take off your belt. So this new Willa, the confused, disoriented, and weepy Willa, is a great loss. There are moments she seems present and others when she is as gone as if another has inhabited her bruised brain.

When I stop by her cottage on my way to the studio, I can almost see the cogs in her head trying to churn out my very name, which had once been her first word. Mother was completely inconsolable when Willa's first word was *Eve.* This morning, Willa called me Gwen.

The past three weeks have stretched out interminably, unrolling with moments of healing and then backsliding. The swelling has subsided, and yet often Willa's eyes still appear flat, like matte ink on dull paper. She comes to the studio every day and helps with layouts and fonts and design. We work on the card line and laugh a lot, which is when she seems to be the most Willa-like. There are days when her quick wit shines, and others when she barely speaks a word, smiling at our jokes but with a look, a faraway look, shadowing her eyes. I imagine her inside her mind, searching under and around the broken synapses for a recognizable moment. She'll recall a memory — a night out with Francie; a walk in the woods with me; our day sailing with Gwen — and then ask, "Or did I dream that?"

Benson comes by and they hang out on the cottage porch. I can hear their laughter falling into the air when I walk past. Just yesterday, she found herself lost in lyrics and chords, and wrote five songs in a blur of creativity. But today, she stares at the guitar as if she doesn't know what it is or how to touch it.

Francie, Max, and Willa have started going out together in the evenings so that Willa can hear Francie sing at open-mike nights. Willa still isn't cleared to drive. And she won't be until her doctor does more tests.

As for me, I stay home. I cook dinner, avoid fund-raisers and dinner parties because Cooper wants to "lie low." The bandages are gone now, but he still acts as if the angry slash is a humiliation.

Cooper and Willa avoid being in the same place at the same time and they haven't crossed paths since the dinner party debacle. I only once asked Cooper to go down to the cottage to talk to her, but he refused.

Gwen is grounded and is giving me the silent treatment, unless, of course, she's being sarcastic. Take your pick — sarcasm or silence. I don't like either of them. I want her back; I want my daughter to come home.

With summer's empty days looming ahead, Cooper and I agreed that she should get a job to occupy the hours when she isn't helping me in the studio so she came home a week ago and announced, "I got a job."

"Where?" I stirred the spaghetti and didn't turn around to let her see my smile. I was hopeful; maybe here we would find common ground.

"Savannah Style," she said.

I know the place — it's a local tourist shop on River Street where they sell Savannah trinkets, T-shirts, loose sundresses, mood rings, and — my favorite part — hookah pipes.

"Gwen, really? That's where you want to work?"

"You made me get a job, so I did. You can ground me and take my car and the credit card and make me get a job, but you can't freaking tell me where to work."

"Nice, Gwen."

"Whatever."

There we go again and again to the dead end of "whatever."

On this particular Saturday, Gwen is at work and Cooper is reading the newspaper on the screened porch. I sit with him, propping my feet on the wicker ottoman, silent. After a few minutes, he places the paper on the white-painted hardwood floor. "What's your day like?" he asks.

"Just catching up at home. You?"

"I'm going for a run." He stands to look down at me. "Then catch up on some work."

"Okay."

I sit alone for a few moments, absently leafing through the *Savannah News* until I hear the back door shut. Then, as if this was my plan all along, I go upstairs and enter the forbidden zone: Gwen's room. Marci was here to clean yesterday, but Gwen was asleep and there was a note on her door: DO NOT ENTER.

I gather the dirty clothes and change the sheets. I arrange her six pillows across the headboard. A pale blue hand-painted wooden sign hangs above her bed — a piece of art we chose together at a festival — stating I LOVE YOU TO THE MOON AND BACK. Notebooks and school papers are piled on the floor next to the wastebasket — remnants of her junior year. I bend down to look.

The papers are full edge to edge with her slanted handwriting, which is a combination of script and block. In the margins, multipetal flowers and vines spring from the bottom of words and grow into the margins. I lift one paper to see notes on *The Great Gatsby,* along with Dylan's name scribbled and heart-decorated.

A bulletin board hangs over her desk, and pinned to it are old swim team ribbons, dried flowers from ballet recitals past, and pictures Gwen drew and tore from a notebook. There are also photos of Gwen with her friends, their arms bent and their hands on hips, assuming the same stance, so they all look alike, chins tilted down and big pink-tinted smiles. They seem to be pretending to be older than they are — posing as grown-ups.

I straighten the papers and walk to the closet, opening the door. Given might keep her room askew, but her closet is organized as if for a magazine photo shoot. Shoe boxes are stacked on a shelf at the left of the closet, each labeled with a note card: White Sandals; Black Boots with Tassels; Red Converses. And then there is another box: pink and white, without a label, and covered in yarn and stickers, cut-out hearts, and decoupage words from magazines. I pick up the box and remember the day she and I made it.

One rainy afternoon years before, we went into the craft closet and emptied it. "We'll make wish boxes," I told Gwen. "We can decorate old shoe boxes with everything pretty we can find in this closet and then fill it with wishes."

Hours later, we had our secret wishes. We used a fountain pen on cotton paper, pretending to hide our wishes from each other. "A horse," wrote Gwen. "A new Vandercook," I wrote. "True love," wrote Gwen. "Willa come home," I wrote.

Gwen never did get her horse, and she

quit riding months after she'd expressed the fleeting desire. Now standing alone in her closet, I lift the lid of that wish box, wanting to immerse myself in the sweetness of all that has deserted us. Inside are the following items: Tylenol PM; Cigarettes; a Photo of Gwen and Dylan kissing on the bow of a boat, his hand on her hip, his fingers twisted around the elastic of her bikini bottom, pulling it out to expose a tan line; beer can tops; the butt end of a joint; a can opener shaped like a hand; and three round white pills, which I recognize as Cooper's Percocet.

I slam the lid shut and shove the box onto the shelf, dropping to sit on a pink footstool.

Downstairs, a door slams, and I stand with its impact, wading out of Gwen's room like swimming through an undercurrent. I wait at the top of the stairs when Cooper appears, looking up, sweaty, earbuds still inserted, so he's deaf to anything but the music. He starts to walk up and then sees me, startling and taking the earbuds out. "Hey, darling. You okay?"

I shake my head. "No, I found some stuff in Gwen's room."

"What kind of stuff?"

"Cigarettes, sleep aids, a joint . . ." I should have been crying; I wanted to cry.

He climbs the steps and stands next to me. The physical exercise has awakened the scar like a purple tear. I avoid staring at it, looking into his eyes as he speaks. "Like that's some big surprise?"

"Yes, it is to me. All that was in her childhood wish box," I say, choking on the last words.

"In her what?" He wipes his face with a towel he's tucked into the back of his running shorts.

"And your Percocet. A few of those, too." I grab the base of my throat — I can feel the bile rising.

"It *shouldn't* be a surprise, Eve. She's been insolent, rude, and disrespectful. She's a seventeen-year-old girl who seems to hate us. She's been caught drinking and I'm fairly sure she was stoned the other night. Add all that together . . ."

"I get it. I just don't get how you can talk about her like she's a statistic and not our daughter."

"We have to crack down on her."

"What?" I ask.

"You really want my opinion?"

"Well, yes. We *are* her parents."

"Here's what I think," he says. "You stay on my team. We do this together. Support me."

"Even when I don't agree?" I ask.

"Yes. We have to be a team."

"I can't do that, Cooper. It's too important. This is our daughter, her life, our lives together. I can't support you if I think you're wrong. We have to talk about it to agree."

He stares at me without speaking. "Then don't ask what I think."

"Stop it," I say. "I want to know what you think. God, I do. We *are* a team. I'm drowning here, Cooper. But I seriously don't think you mean for me to support you when I think it's bad for Gwen."

He doesn't answer, just turns away, walking down the hall and into our room. Far off, as if another world away, I hear the rush of water through the house pipes as he turns on the shower.

Late that afternoon, Gwen arrives home from work, tossing her car keys onto the kitchen counter and opening the refrigerator, staring into it. "There's nothing to eat."

I don't answer. Nor do I argue the point that both the refrigerator and the cabinets are stuffed with food. I sit there with the paraphernalia of her wish box scattered on the table. She hasn't noticed, but when I don't defend our food status, she turns around. Her face is full of obstinate teenage superiority, and then it isn't. Her eyes close to shut out the view and she sighs and says one word: "Shit."

"We have to talk," I say.

She stands with her eyes shut, and I imagine her struggle inside, her decision to fight and defend or actually open up. Her eyes open and she sits in the chair next to me. "I'm grounded for life. I know."

"This isn't about being grounded," I say. "What's going on?"

She bites her bottom lip, and my chest aches. "It's not such a big deal. Seriously, relax."

"Relax?" I push my fingers against my eyelids; phosphenes flicker in the darkness.

"Trust me, my friends are doing a lot worse." Gwen's voice makes me open my eyes.

"I don't care what your friends are doing." I hold up the Tylenol PM. "You can't sleep? I didn't know that." My voice cracks. "What else don't I know?"

"Mom," she says in a too-old voice, "I think there is a lot you don't know. Living here is like living . . ." She looks off. "I don't know. Like nothing is what it looks like."

"What does that mean? What looks like what? And what isn't what that is?"

She laughs quietly. "I have no idea what you just said." Sighing, she leans back against the chair; tears gather into a puddle in the hollow below her eyes. She wipes them away with a forefinger on either side, removing the evidence of grief. "I'm miserable. Dylan broke up with me. Dad yells at me twenty-four/seven. My friends are stoned, mostly. I'm the only one who is forced to have a summer job. I'm only allowed to drive to work and back. And no, Mom, I can't sleep worth shit."

"Oh, Gwen." I reach to take her hand, but she refuses me.

"And," she says quietly, "Aunt Willa is all messed up. I love her and everything is screwed up."

"I know."

"You know?"

"Yes, Gwen, I know. She's my sister. My best friend. She's broken. And I can't fix it."

"But it's Dad's fault. Don't you care that it's Dad's fault? You just pretend like nothing ever happened. You just cook dinner and go to work and fold the laundry and go to the studio like nothing, like NOTHING ever happened."

"That's how you see me?"

"Yes, Mom. That's how I see you."

"And you think this is Dad's fault?"

"I do."

"You were there, Gwen. You heard him explain what happened. It doesn't sound like it was all his fault. And there was the storm. It was an accident."

"He made her leave the bar. He didn't have to do that, Mom. Why did he do that? I know what it's like when he's mad or wants you to do something, and I bet Willa didn't have much choice, and then I bet she was mad and —"

"That's a lot of betting about things you don't know."

"Nothing makes sense."

"What happened with Dylan?"

"Like I just said, nothing makes sense. One minute 'I love you' and the next 'I need space.'"

"Sometimes things just don't make sense."

"But you still can't just pretend it's all okay. That's weird."

"I'm not pretending anything, Pea."

"Yes." Gwen stands, staring down at me. "Yes, you are. And stop calling me Pea, I'm not a little girl anymore." She slams her hand on the table, where the cigarette packet shimmies and falls off the edge from the force. "If it looks good, then it is good, right?"

"That's not what I'm doing, Gwen."

"Like that creepy party with the perfect everything." She rolls those blue eyes. "Whatever."

" 'Whatever' is not the way to end a conversation. It's a cop-out." I stand to face her but speak quietly. "And the Percocet. Gwen, those are prescription meds. Did you share those with anyone?"

She blushes. "God, Mom. No. I didn't even take one. I totally thought about it, but I didn't. . . ."

"Thought about it? Stole it also. Can't you see what's wrong with that? You took prescription meds from your dad."

"God, you're so mad at me." She places her hand over her face to cover her eyes.

"Mad? Yep. Also worried like crazy. I want to understand; I do."

"If you're so worried, maybe you could keep Dad off my back — that would be good, too. Just leave me alone."

"Really?" Cooper's yells, as he enters the kitchen, and his voice soaks the kitchen with the vibration of his anger. "You want *me* stay off *your* back?" he asks in a tight voice, a wire that if released would injure anyone close by.

"Yes, I do." Gwen pulls her shoulders back to stand tall, but her voice doesn't match her stance.

"Stop," I cry out. "Both of you, stop. We're a family. Let's act like it."

Cooper steps toward Gwen. "I'm not on your back. You stole my pain pills. This is not to be taken lightly."

"God, Dad, you sound like you're in a courtroom. It's weird." She mimics him. "*Not to be taken lightly.* Please."

"I'm trying to help you; to save you from yourself."

"Like you were doing with Aunt Willa?" she asks.

"Yes."

"That worked out well for you, didn't it?"

Cooper runs his hands through his hair and then waves over the table. "What about this, Gwen? Am I supposed to just ignore it and stay off your back? Let you get in trouble or, worse, get yourself killed?"

"I guess not, Dad. I guess you're supposed to make me feel terrible about myself and then ground me and ruin my life. Sounds good to me."

He sighs, defeated. "Well, I'd rather be the one to ruin your life than for you to ruin your own with a drunk-driving incident or . . ."

Gwen looks back and forth between us. "And what's with all the weird money

218

lectures lately? You're all over me about getting a job and not spending money, and yet you go all over the country playing golf and fishing and hanging out with your buddies."

"That's ridiculous. Comparing my work trips to your credit card extravagance? New bathing suits. Shoes."

"Whatever. Are we done here?"

"For now," I say.

"Okay, I'm going to see Aunt Willa."

She walks out the side door of the house, obviously no longer starving, but only wanting to escape the house and her parents. I drop back into the chair and Cooper sits next to me and takes my hand.

We look at each other, dumbfounded. "Cooper, I have no idea how to handle any of this. But here's the thing: She's hurting and we can't fix that by yelling. I don't know a lot, but I do know that you can't hurt a hurting child. It doesn't help."

"What does help?"

"Maybe we could listen to her instead of threatening her."

"We can listen to her while she's home, grounded." He walks to the refrigerator to drink orange juice straight from the container. "I'm gonna go hit some golf balls with Landry."

"Now?"

"Yes, now."

He's gone, just as Gwen is — out the same door to escape the house and the kitchen, where I remain. The house phone rings and I pick up the wireless handset to look at the caller ID. *Savannah News.* My heart does a quick rollover, a duck and roll, but I answer.

"Mrs. Morrison?" a male voice asks.

"Yes."

"This is Noah Yorker. I'm a journalist and reporter for the *Savannah News.* I am doing an exploratory piece about Preston Street. I'm hoping I can talk to you and your husband."

"I believe he already refused," I say.

"I've talked to your sister and I would love to have his side of the story."

" 'Side of the story'? What does that have to do with Preston Street?"

"Ma'am, this has nothing to do with blame or the accident itself. This article is about that area and its inherent dangers. The road is both pockmarked and dangerous. The accident is a small part of the article; but I want to cover all my bases and talk to your husband."

"I will pass on the message, but I can't guarantee anything."

"Thank you. Let me give you my numbers and e-mail."

"Okay."

I sit at the family desk and pull out a pad of paper, scribbling the information. "Got it," I say.

"One more thing," he says, as if it is an afterthought. "Did you know someone died there that same night?"

My chest opens with a fluttering of fear. This man is not just after anecdotal information about the street; he's after someone.

I hang up before I respond. What did Gwen say only moments before? "Like nothing is what it looks like."

Next to the notepad with Noah's information is my typewriter. The ribbon inside is cracked and dried. Time has gathered underneath the carriage, building sand castles of dust. A few weeks ago, I ordered a new ribbon and new letter *p.* I pick up the oilcloth I've taken from the studio and drop two small drops of blue fluid onto it. I wipe across the larger parts of the keyboard and carriage, cleaning it as carefully as I would a newborn. Then using Q-tips, I flip the machine over and clean the internal bones. While I clean, I think, What to do? What is next? How do I fix any of this?

When I remove the old ribbon, it breaks apart in my hands, disintegrating into chunks of black waste. I rip open the packing for the new one and insert it into the Remington, wrapping it around the spool and slipping it into the type guide below the roller platen. I screw the letter *p* into place, and then when I finish, I step back. It's something at least — I've fixed one small thing.

FOURTEEN

Gwen slept at Willa's cottage. Cooper came home from hitting golf balls at midnight. Apparently, Landry needed to talk and they'd gone out for dinner and drinks. In Gwen's language, this deserved a "whatever."

As for me, it's only 5:00 A.M., but here I am back in the studio. The sun hasn't joined the day. The Ten Good Ideas line now has inspiration boards stretching along the project table. Sketches and notes are scattered; Pantone color charts and font types are placed in strategic squares for each of my commandments.

A thin, long poster board lists the ten ideas as if they are carved on stone. Francie sketched a mock tablet around the list, where the numbers are listed in arabic.

I am sipping coffee and staring at the list when Max shows up.

"What are you doing here so early?" he asks.

"I could ask you the same thing."

"I didn't finish that wedding run last night and the bridezilla will be here by sunlight to pick up the invitations. Apocalyptic consequences are possible if they aren't waiting and wrapped in white tissue with satin silver ribbon. So that's my answer. What's yours?" He leans over to check the coffeepot.

"I don't have an excuse," I say. "Just . . . here."

"Good enough." He fills a large mug with coffee and then joins me at the table. "So what do you think?"

"I think it might be the best thing we've ever done."

"It was your idea," he says.

"No, it really wasn't. It was your idea to turn it into a card line. And I've been so little help since the accident."

"You've had a few things to keep you pre-occupied, Eve. And this wouldn't exist without you anyway. Any of this . . ." He sweeps his hand around the room.

"And we need numbers nine and ten," I say.

"In good time. But right now, I'm going to spend quality time with the printer." He stretches. "Care if I turn on the music?"

"No, go ahead. I'm gonna catch up on e-mails and paperwork," I say.

Max stops and turns around. "Speaking of paperwork, the credit card was declined on the ink order. Any reason?"

"No. The bill is paid automatically through e-banking. I'll call."

My mind is cluttered with the detritus of my family's undoing. I want to pay attention to the financial aspects of our business, but I'm distracted. No surprise there. I've come to a pause since the accident, and yet I knew the money was waiting in the bank account.

I pick up the phone to call the bank before realizing it's only 5:30 A.M. I return to the card line, mumbling the childhood wisdom of each idea out loud. I lose myself in this until the bang of the studio door startles me as Willa and Gwen walk in.

"Morning," Willa says.

"What is this?" Max asks. "Get to Work Before Dawn Day?"

"We heard y'all coming in and we were up anyway," Gwen says.

"Have you been to sleep yet?" I ask.

Willa and Gwen look at each other and smile. "Nope," Willa says. "We've been up talking all night. We didn't realize it was soooo late . . . and then we heard ya'll com-

225

ing to work at five in the morning."

Gwen walks to the table, facing me. "What's all this?"

"Brainstorming the last good ideas," I explain.

Gwen stares at the boards, shifting papers and color charts.

"You okay?" I ask her, but I look at Willa.

"I'm fine, Mom. Totally."

"Go home and get some sleep." I kiss her cheek.

Gwen nods. "Think I will." And she turns to leave, but not before saying hello to Max and teasing him about his ink-stained apron.

When Gwen is gone, I pull Willa aside. "Is she okay? Did she tell you . . . what I found?"

"Yep. She's pretty upset. She feels . . . terrible."

"I'm so worried about her. I need to get her some help." I rub at my eyes, feeling the too much of everything pushing in on me.

"She's confused," Willa says. "And it's not like I'm much help, since 'confused' is my new definition." She attempts to laugh, but it comes out a near cough.

"Confused?"

"Yes. She wants to know what happened that night. She talks in circles about it, as if she's trying to solve the puzzle we can't solve. And she's really sad. I mean, not just teenager sad. But sad. That's why she's doing those stupid things — the drinking, the smoking, the dumb boyfriend. And now wanting to get a tattoo."

I groan. "No. Not on her beautiful skin. She's killing me. I don't know what to do."

"Take her to see someone or something . . . a therapist maybe?"

"You really think?"

"Yes."

"Everything seems to be . . . coming undone."

"It's all my fault," she says quietly. "I would do anything to fix it all. To go back to the one minute that night that might have changed everything. Maybe I decided not to sing. Or I went to the coffee shop instead. Or I didn't see Cooper. Something. Anything."

"It's not your fault. What is coming undone has nothing to do with what you did or did not do that night."

"Yes, it does." Willa stares at the project table as if she's here and far away at the same time, as if we aren't discussing Gwen at all. "Number nine," she says.

"You remember it?" I ask.

She lifts her gaze from the table as if her pupils themselves weigh too much to heft

227

upward. "Remember what?"

"Number nine."

"Number nine of what?" she asks.

"Willa," I say. "Go get some sleep. I can't believe you both stayed up all night." I want to jolt her mind, shake her memories clear. "What did you talk about all that time?"

"Everything and nothing really. Breakups. Blackouts. And my weird dreams. Which is why I don't want to sleep. Which is why I want to stay up all night and talk to Gwen and never close my eyes." Her voice is clear now, changing tone in those quick instants.

"What dreams?" I ask.

"The ones about the car. . . ." Her voice trails off, fading like color at the edges of an ink run. "And the man chasing me."

"You had that dream in the hospital."

"I still have it."

"Have you asked the neuro practitioner about it?"

She shakes her head.

"Why not?"

"They're just dreams. My scrambled brain sending out bullshit messages. I've heard about it. Like when an eye can't see right because of macular degeneration or something, and people hallucinate because the eye *wants* to see something, anything, so it makes something out of fragments to create a new image."

"Yes," I say with my newfound under-standing and need to separate fantasy from truth.

"That didn't make sense, did it?" She places her hands on either side of her scalp and groans a sad, low sound. "I never seem to make sense, even to myself."

"I thought you said the writing and sing-ing were helping. . . ." I am out of things to say.

"They are. But helping is not the same as fixing. I still can't put things in the right order in the right place."

"You will."

She shakes her head. "I have to accept that I might not. That's what they tell me. Ac-cept it — I might not remember entire chunks of my life and I might have trouble finding words and names forever or for a day. Which I guess will be really great when I go crazy, because you won't know I'm crazy, because I'm already a freaking mess."

"You are not a mess."

"But I am, Eve. I am. Memories flirt — I mean flit — in and out of my head. I see something, an image or a word, and then it melts away. Like we learned from that pamphlet, I remember things in a differ-ent . . . formula. No, *format.* The place where I would know a word or a person or anything at all gets shifted to another area and I don't know how to find. I try to follow the thread of something — like that woman's voice — and I get lost, finding threads that aren't tied to her voice at all."

"I wish, God, I wish I knew how to help. But I know this from what we've read and heard — it's not linear. Healing isn't going to go in a straight line and remembering isn't . . . and . . ."

"What is linear in all the world?" she asks with a sly smile.

"Not much," I say.

"Well, I know I'm lucky. In a weird way, I'm really lucky. I've read about other people with these injuries. They can't remember names or they have terrible pain or they can't relate to others at all. I'm just . . . struggling with memories and words."

"Lucky? As if you can compare?" I ask.

"Yes, I can compare. I am comparing. It could be worse."

"Yes."

"But no matter what I read or hear, I know this — everyone says creative expression is key. So I'll keep on. And I want to tell you something weird. So just humor me for a minute."

"Go ahead."

"The man . . . the one in my dreams."

I nod.

"I think it's that homeless man they found in the alley."

My breath rises and I exhale to take in another that tastes like metallic fear. "Go on." I speak quietly, hoping Max can't hear us over the music.

"Well." Her eyes fill with quick tears, clearing the haze of the blue world inside. "I know you're going to think it's insane, so pretend you don't think so."

"What is it?"

"I think we hit him. Or I hit him. Or he hit us. Or he was there that night. He's not haunting my dreams . . . or maybe he is, but I dreamed about him before I heard about him, not after."

"But you may be projecting now. In the hospital, you dreamed about a man chasing you and then Cam told us the story about the homeless man after you left the hospital. So maybe you're confusing them."

"Yes, I may be doing that. Of course . . . but I'm going to ask for a favor. One that is more than what you should do for me, because you've already done too much and this is your husband . . . but . . ." She bit her lower lip.

"You want me to ask Cooper about it?"

"No!" she says, shaking her head, so her hair whips her cheeks.

"We *have* to believe him, Willa. It's all we know, and meanwhile we need to try to heal you, find out what happened to you."

"I was gong to ask you to take me to the morgue or police station or wherever they'd have photos." She closes her eyes. "I know it's the most disgusting request, but I have to know if he's the same guy . . . and then I can let this go."

"Same one?"

She opens her eyes to me. "The same man I see in my dreams."

"Oh." I sit at the table again. "But let me ask you something."

"What?"

"Have you heard from a reporter?"

"Yep. Some guy from the *Savannah News.* He said he's writing on article on the Savannah homeless community."

"He told me he was writing an article on Preston Street and its dangers," I say.

She shrugs. "Maybe that's part of it — the homeless and that street."

"Did you talk to him?"

"I told him it was no use talking to me because I don't remember anything and I'm officially mumbled in the brain." She stops.

"Not mumbled. Scrambled. Anyway, he's stopping by tomorrow."

"You told him he could come here?"

"He's just writing about homeless people. It's not like I asked Charles Manson to stop by for some helter-skelter."

I laughed loudly. "God, Willa. What am I gonna do with you?"

"No idea," she says, and smiles.

Then her eyes snap as if some leftover lightening from that stormy night remains inside her mind. She picks up a pencil and scribbles the word FORGIVE in all capital letters. A quick burst of laughter before she says, "Number Nine. Yep, that just happened."

The day passes quickly with our assignments and appointments, with phone calls and e-mails. Gwen stops by in the late afternoon to tell me she's found a ride to work and that she'll be home by ten, when they close the shop. I kiss her and whisper into her hair, "I love you."

"I know."

The rude accountant, Mary Jo, stops by to see her second concept designs and talks only to Francie. A photographer picks up his stack of new business cards and Max offers the bridezilla her wedding invites with gracious aplomb, as if he hasn't been up since five in the morning.

It's the restaurant owner — Larry Ford — who changes the afternoon when he arrives to pick up his new menu cards. Larry has been our client for years, a loyal customer who has us do his weekly menus along with his logos, posters, and cards. Many restaurants print their menus on cheap paper and in black ink, but not Larry. He likes to change the font, change the color, and print on linen paper. He is a kind man — tall and skinny, which I find humorous, since he owns an Italian restaurant.

"I'm having a party," he announces.

"A party?" I glance up from the table, where I've been sorting through a file.

"Yup. I'm having a party to celebrate my five-year anniversary. And you've all got to come. I found you at the very start of my business and I wouldn't be where I am without you."

"That's a lovely sentiment, Larry, but I think you owe your success to your overflowing plates and cheese-laden pastas."

Max butts in. "What Eve meant to say was 'Brilliant idea.' "

Francie stands. "Yep. planning parties is my favorite procrastination tool. I'm on it."

"Okay," I say, laughing. "Good idea." It's

then that I remember to call the bank. I pick up my cell, and within seconds I hear a deep male voice on the phone. "Mrs. Morrison, how are you? This is Neal Bush."

"Fine, Mr. Bush. Thanks for asking. I'm calling about The Fine Line, Ink account. It seems there was a mix-up in the e-billing and the credit card payment was rejected."

"The payment didn't go through because you were overdrawn at the time. You are fine now, if you'd like to resubmit."

"What?" A cold chill moves underneath my skin.

"When the funds were transferred out for a week, you were overdrawn. Because of your extraordinary credit, I didn't charge you overdraft fees."

"Transferred? I didn't authorize any fund transfers."

"Well, someone did." His voice is losing its surety.

"Will you please check for me?" I ask.

The music playing while I'm on hold butchers the theme song from *The Sound of Music*. I glance toward Max. Would he have withdrawn or moved money? Francie? Had I done it and not remembered?

Max is wearing his apron, stacking paper to place under the platen. His eyes are focused on his work and his dark hair falls across his forehead. And in that moment, I see everyone I love through a different lens — it's a quick and disturbing flash. What are they capable of doing? Do I see them only the way I want to see them, not for who they really are?

Mr. Bush's voice returns. "Mrs. Morrison?"

"Yes, I'm still here."

"Your husband, Averitt. He moved the money from the Fine Line account and then replaced it a week later."

My heart is pushing against my chest. Yes, Cooper has access to our company account. This is a small bank, owned by a friend of my father-in-law. Our family accounts, the philanthropy accounts — everything is there in one place. But Cooper has never touched our company money before.

"No," I say. "That must have been a mistake. He wouldn't move company money."

The uncomfortable pause leaves me holding my breath. "Well then, you need to ask him, because I am looking at the signed transfer slip."

"To where?" I ask. "To what account did he transfer it?"

"If you'd like to discuss this, you can come into the bank, Mrs. Morrison. This is not the kind of information we normally discuss on the phone."

"I will."

I hang up, and Max lifts his head. I imagine he felt me staring at him. "You okay?" he asks.

"I need to get to the bank."

The bank is in an old schoolhouse converted, as is everything, to accommodate the business. It's a bloodred brick structure with curved windows and dark brown trim that mimics the color of rusted iron. The windows, wide-paned and tall, reflect the cloudy afternoon, appearing murky and shadowed. I park on a side street and deposit my quarters into the meter. The afternoon is heavy with threatening rain. I stop for a minute and glance up toward the sky. When I was young and overwhelmed, afraid, I would stare into the sky through the tangle of gnarled branches and imagine the world like a puzzle I could put together. The sky — divided into pieces by oaks — was really whole and complete, and I liked knowing this fact. That no matter how I looked at it, it was still the same sky — always.

I enter the bank and cold air whooshes toward me. The entryway is decorated like a waiting room in a plush doctor's office: muted photos of Savannah framed in white; overstuffed peach-colored couches and a large glass-topped coffee table. A receptionist sits behind a long white desk, where she types into a computer. She looks up as I approach her. "Hello, Mrs. Morrison. How are you?" Her voice could come from a computer, it's so polished and robotic.

"I'm here to see Mr. Bush. He's expecting me."

"Well then, go on. He's waiting." Her gaze returns to her computer as her hand waves me toward the back hallway.

The second door on the right is where I find his office. Mr. Bush is standing behind a long table, and he smiles at me as I enter. He's an intimidating man, his hair gray around the temples and his blue eyes dark. He flashes a grin and points to a chair across from his shining black desk. He then sits and clicks on his keyboard before twisting the computer screen toward me. "These are your family's multiple accounts: family; business, LLC, philanthropy."

"My name is on all of them?" I ask.

"No."

"Can you tell me which ones don't have my name?"

"I can print you a list." He speaks like an

unpracticed ventriloquist, his lips barely moving.

"Great. I'd appreciate that. For now, I'm here to figure out where Cooper put the money when he moved it for a week."

"It was divided up, Mrs. Morrison. If you'd like, I can print you statements of your full accounts, but it will be Mr. Morrison who knows where the installments went and why."

"Was any of it transferred into the family account?"

"No."

"Okay, if you will please print all statements from all accounts, I'd appreciate it."

He clicks his fingers across the keyboard and his mouth is screwed up tight, twisted. Beneath his rimless glasses, his eyes squint. He is quiet; the room is quiet, until the printer groans and spits. Within minutes, he hands me a stack of papers. "I hope this will help. But please know that the exact amount that was transferred was replaced."

"I'd like to change the permitted users on my account, please." There, I've said it.

Mr. Bush raises an eyebrow (only one), and his forehead doesn't wrinkle. Botox on a banker. This makes me want to laugh. "Okay," he finally says. "You're the primary account holder and the LLC is in your name."

I hear the words beneath the words: Your husband is one of our most influential customers; you shouldn't be changing things around. Maybe I'm making this up, but then again, maybe I'm not.

Mr. Bush reaches into a filing cabinet and pulls out some papers. "These must be signed, dated, and notarized before any changes are made."

I take a pen from a tortoiseshell holder on Mr. Bush's desk. When I'm done filling out all the blanks, I look up. "It's just me. I am the only authorized user right now, until we can get this figured out."

"Not your other employees?"

"No. Just me." I stand and hand the papers to Mr. Bush.

"These need to be notarized," he says.

"Then notarize them."

"My notary isn't in today." He stares at me without standing.

"You're kidding, right? I mean, you are a witness standing here watching me. This is my money, my company. Authorize it now."

He takes the papers from my hand, the papers I am waving at him as if fanning him for the heatstroke he looks like he might have. "Thank you, Mrs. Morrison."

I turn to leave, but then at his door I stop to look at him one more time. "Thanks for your time."

The rain starts just as I slam shut my car door and see the fluttering white paper on my windshield: a parking ticket. Five minutes past my meter time. Just perfect.

I've avoided eye contact with anger for most of my life. When I feel it coming, I run or hide into something more appropriate. Gentleness, I was taught, brings the best results. Yet ever since shattering the wineglass on the kitchen floor, something redfaced and boisterous was released in me. I feel it now staring at the wet and fluttering parking ticket, seeing Mr. Bush's righteous eyebrow lifting. I drop the *F* bomb as loudly as I can inside my empty car, then slam my fist onto the steering wheel.

I returned to the studio in less than the twenty minutes it took me to drive to the bank. My heart slows and I calm down. I'll talk to Cooper tonight. There must be a reasonable explanation. He accidentally moved it and then put it back. He bought me a gift. He was planning a surprise and . . . No. None of it makes sense. I run out of *reasonable* quickly.

I walk into the studio, to find Max, and I realize that he's the reason I've driven so fast, the reason I came straight back here. He turns when he hears me, and I reach his side to see what he is looking at with such intent. It's number eight: *Find Adventure.* "What do you see for the design?" he asks.

"Huh?"

"When you think *Find Adventure,* what do you see?"

"This one is tough," I say, sitting to look up at him. His dark hair is a mess; an ink smear runs across his forehead, where he's been brushing his hair all day. My hand reaches across the space between us to wipe off the ink.

He draws back and away when my fingers touch his forehead. Embarrassment flutters through me with sharp-tipped wings.

A long silence grows between us, and I'm not willing to fill it or answer his reaction with my own. He speaks first. "I see something like two people walking through the forest, where anything at all is possible."

I nod and rest my hands one on top of the other in my lap. "That's nice."

Nice — what an inane thing to say.

When I first met him, Max was attending SCAD. In three short years, he had his degree in book arts, with a minor in folklore and mythology. His parents could pay for only three years of college, so he did everything he could to shove four years into three. His love of ancient stories often rises up in imagery. "There's this story," he'll say. Which is exactly what he's saying now.

"And?" I ask, still refusing to look at him, at the ink smear I want to clear.

"There are dreams that are usually called 'the dream of the predator' — you know, when someone is after you, chasing you."

"Willa has one." I look at him now, and he smiles. "She keeps having a dream like that."

"They're really normal dreams. One of the most famous folklore tales is the one about the bride who goes into the woods." He takes a breath and looks off, as if the story is written on the far stall's wall. "There's this bride. It's her wedding night and she gets that thing — that intuition that tells you that something is just not right. She suspects something is wrong with her groom, but she's not sure. Every night, he sneaks into the woods and returns quietly. So the night before her wedding, she goes into the same woods and hides in the high branches of a tree and waits." Max pauses, picking up the charcoal pencil and sketching a tree, naked at first but filling with leaves as continues the story.

"It was dark and the tree hid her well with

its dense leaves. She waited and waited, finally falling asleep in the crook of a branch. But then she was startled and awoke, to see her groom below the tree, digging a hole and singing a song about how he would bury his bride there." He stops and leans back to look at me and then sings in a low voice, not his own. "Good-bye, my love. Good-bye, sweetheart. Sleep well and long. . . ." Max draws out the last word.

"Stop." I say. "You're creeping me out. You've told much better stories." Laughter gathers at the edge of my voice. "That's terrible and sad."

"No, that's a great story," he says. "She went on an adventure and found out the truth and didn't marry him. Otherwise . . ." He pauses and slashes the edge of his palm against his throat and rolls his eyes back into his head, imitating death, but with a smile.

"Got it," I say. "So, yes, a forest is good, but let's not have her hide up in a tree."

"Agreed," he says. "Adventure means going out into something new, right?"

"Something unknown," I say. "And what's more unknown than a forest?"

"Especially a maritime forest, like around here, where you might end up in dense woods or the river, depending which way you turn."

"Yes! Add a river in the background, a hint of water in the middle of the trees and dark."

"This is where we need Francie," he says, loudly enough for her to hear.

"Moi?" she asks, looking over her shoulder.

Francie comes to us. We catch her up with our idea. "Awesome and all that. But I'm late for a gig tonight. I'll start in the morning, okay?"

"What gig?" I ask.

"Playing at the coffee shop. Nothing big." She waves a dismissive hand and gathers her things to leave. "See you tomorrow."

Max and I sit there, again alone with our designs and stories and thoughts. As the studio doors slide shut, he stands, and I think he'll leave, but he walks to the steel cabinet and pulls out a bottle of Jameson and two glasses I bought at an antique show when I meant to buy carved-wood fonts.

He returns to the table and sits, pouring a glass for each of us.

"No way," I say. "I haven't slept in days. I can't drink dark liquor or I'll . . ."

"You'll what?" he asks.

"Regret it."

"Or find adventure," he says, and pours a half inch into my glass.

"Adventure." I lift the whiskey and tilt my

head back, allowing the liquid to burn past my tongue and down my throat, past the ache in my chest. Tears spring to my eyes. "That story you told," I say through a cough. "You didn't just mean it for the card line, right? You meant it about Willa, too."

Max drinks his whiskey. "Yes . . . probably."

"It's not that easy — like hiding in the wood to wait for the answer. Memory isn't like that. It's not some time line like in history class. It's not some fact sheet, and it's certainly not linear. Memory is mixed and messy even in the best minds. I see pictures from my childhood and I think, Oh, I remember that day. But do I only remember it because of the photo? Is it even a *real* memory? Add getting hit in the head and weird dreams and . . . how could she possibly make sense of anything?"

My hand rests on the table and Max places his hand over mine, hiding it completely. "What is a real memory anyway? But we can make some sense of it, right? We can find out the best we can for her," he says.

The Jameson is loosening my thoughts. "All we can know is what we know."

"No," he says softly.

"How, then?"

"There are things I don't know yet. Things you don't know yet."

I stare at my empty shot glass and wonder how many people have drunk from this old glass. How many to celebrate or, like me, forget?

Max speaks first. "For now, though, let's go hear Francie sing. What do you think?"

"That is by far the best idea you've had all day."

"Wow, thanks. Not the forest or the tree or coming to work at five A.M. to avoid full-on warfare with one of our esteemed clients —"

"Not those at all."

"Well, did I tell you my idea for world peace?"

"Yep, right after you told me how you planned to cure the common cold."

"By drowning it?" And with that smart-ass remark, he pours an inch of whiskey into his glass and takes a big swallow. Then he fully grasps my hand underneath his, no longer resting his palm, but surrounding my hand with his. My body relaxes with an exhale of tension and tight control. I look at him and he at me. Then he lifts my hand and brings it to his forehead, to the place I tried only moments before to touch. Using his own hand, he runs my fingers across his forehead, only further smearing the ink: an apology of sorts. Then just as quickly he drops my hand and stands to look down at me. "Ready? Let's go. You'll really like this. Francie is good."

"It's bad that I haven't heard her sing, isn't it?"

"Don't try to find something to feel bad about."

"I'm not."

"Not just a little bit?"

"No comment."

Together, we walk outside. "I'll drive," I say. "You're a shot or two ahead of me."

He locks the studio doors, shaking them for security. Close by, an owl hoots, an echo. We both look toward the trees and then back at each other. "Owls aren't usually out right now," he says.

"Me, neither," I say, suppressing a smile.

"Well then, wonders never cease."

"Dingle," I say, settling into the driver's seat.

He laughs before asking, "Did everything work out okay at the bank?"

"Yes. Sure. Yes. Everything is fine."

FIFTEEN

The coffee shop is a songwriter's haven. A
string of lights dangles from the ceiling,
corner to corner, crisscross; the aroma of
coffee permeates the air, along with the faint
smell of rosemary; a podium and speakers
are set up in the back corner. Chairs and
café tables are scattered in a messy arrangement around the room, and there are only a
few empty places. Couples hold hands and
lean toward one another, while groups of
college kids sit in circles, laughing too
loudly. Max and I find a wiggling corner
table in the back and settle in. "Can I get
you a drink?" he asks over the din of the
crowd.

"Yes, another of what we started."

"Sure thing."

When he's gone, I pull my cell from my
purse, staring at the screen to see missed
calls from Cooper and a text that reads
"Out with clients. They're killing me. Home

late. Love you."

Max returns and sets down the glass filled with brown liquid. I drink it slowly, allowing the sharp taste to stay in my mouth, wash over my tongue. Max has only water. The music begins and I focus on the front of the room. A young boy plays a mandolin and sings about living on a farm. I whisper to Max, "I bet Francie loves this."

"I think she's shy about it. For all her bravado, she gets pretty nervous about performing."

"I think we're all more comfortable behind the scenes. Probably why we hide in a barn all day."

"I know, but I keep telling her that her light is too bright to hide. All those great lines she puts on the cards? Well, they're even better in a song."

"You've heard her often?" I ask.

"Yes."

I feel left out, twelve years old in the middle school cafeteria with nowhere to sit. I know it's ridiculous, but there you have it.

Francie walks out from behind the bar area and moves to the microphone. The guitar strap stretches across her left shoulder. Her long hair is pulled back. "Hey, everyone," she says.

The microphone screeches and she readjusts it, a nervous laugh echoing off the walls. "Technology." She rolls her eyes.

A man in jeans and a baseball hat comes from the side and readjusts the wires, pulling the speaker farther away from Francie. "Go ahead," he says. "You're on, darlin'."

Francie swings her guitar to the front and plucks a few strings before speaking. "Thanks for coming tonight, y'all. I'll play a few songs. The first one is about an old heartbreak, but not mine. I've had plenty of those, but this one is called 'Someone Else's Heartbreak.' "

Max leans forward as Francie's voice rings through the room, a mid-alto with such depth coming from such a tiny girl that the room falls silent, conversations stopped in midsentence.

She sings about wanting a relationship to work out and knowing it won't, about watching it from afar and her desire to fix something for someone else. She sings about trying to find the right thing to say to mend "someone else's heartbreak," but finding herself unable. It's beautiful and full of deep melancholy, and I have the thought that I will one day lose her to this career.

Everyone claps, a few people stand, and Francie gives a quick bow of her head before delving into her next song. Max

251

notices my empty glass and signals a waitress for another; I don't stop him.

Francie sings three more songs — the limit on open-mike night — and then wanders over to our table. "Eve, when did you get here?" she asks, leaning down to hug me.

People work their way across the room to approach Francie and talk to her. "I've been here the whole time. You're amazing," I say. "But don't talk to me. Go talk to your fans."

She looks to Max and then me before turning to speak to the people who've followed her, hoping to meet her. I lean across the table. "We should go?" I ask Max, draining the remains of my drink.

Together, we walk outside. The whiskey slackens my limbs, my mind. I stop in the middle of the brick sidewalk and look up at the sky, leaning backward to see the few visible stars and a waxing three-quarter moon.

"Savannah," I say, speaking to the sky and city. "I think I need to walk around you before I go home."

Max laughs. "Can I join you and Savannah?"

"Hmm . . ." I say. "Let me think about it. Hmm . . . yes, I'd love for you to join us."

Our silence is restful, a place to sink into without the frantic need for filling space and time. Four blocks down Broughton and almost to the riverfront. I say, "My parents always wanted to live down here."

"Why didn't they?"

"They couldn't afford it."

"You miss them."

"I do. And I regret how they left me."

"What do you mean?"

"I'm sure they died believing I was going to burn in an everlasting hell. We got in a terrible argument right before they passed away."

"They didn't really believe that, right? I mean, they were just mad."

I stop on the brick sidewalk, and under a gas lantern, I shake my head. "No. A real hell."

He doesn't try to answer this assertion, or fix it, or manage it with a cliché. He drops his hand onto my left shoulder. "Eve."

It's a simple saying of my name, a soft utterance, kind. I'm falling into this peaceful place with Max and I need to wrest myself from him, from his touch. His shadow falls across my body, stretching behind, as if eradicating my shadow from the sidewalk. I step back and Max's hand falls to his side.

"Had they ever been mad like that before . . . at you?"

"Once. When they found those commandments and threatened to make me live with another family for a little while."

"Who?" he asks quietly.

"A family that was part of the church." I take a breath, stepping sideways so that I can again see my shadow on the sidewalk, feel a separate person. "I've forgotten their names. I wanted to forget their names. I wanted to forget everything about it. I could barely stand the thought of being cut off from my family. If they'd sent me, I would have run away to home. It was Willa who wanted to run away from home."

"If that happened to me, I'd be afraid, for all my life; I'd be afraid of losing my family."

"Well, that didn't happen to me. We got past it."

"And you're still afraid of losing your family," he says, so quietly that I'm not sure he said it at all. But he did. And then a single word: "Again."

"Stop," I say, feeling the groundlessness that comes with his soft voice. "I don't think much about it at all, so stop looking at me so sadly. You tell me a story. Your turn."

"Matchstick girl. You know that one?"

"Probably, but tell me anyway."

"If I ever imagine you as a little girl, it's as the matchstick girl."

254

"Why? Was she usually covered in mud from the river and hiding under her bed with her sister?" I laugh and turn around, walking backward to face Max.

"Something like that."

"Go ahead, tell me."

"It's a Danish story," he says. "About a little girl all alone in the world. It's New Year's Eve and it's freezing outside. The snow is everywhere, and this little girl has only a few matchsticks, just a few. She's trying to sell them, but instead she lights them one by one and watches her fantasies in each tiny little fire."

"Uses them for dreams," I say, and stop walking backward to turn and walk with Max, side by side.

"Exactly."

"At least that story doesn't end as sadly as almost all your folktales do."

He laughs. "That's because that's not the end."

I groan. "Of course it's not. Go ahead. Ruin her life."

"So she burns them, staring into the flames, until she thinks she sees her dead grandmother, the only one who ever loved the little matchstick girl. She stares into the last match flame, the very last one . . . and her grandmother comes to her."

"Great, so she dies alone in the snow. God, Max. Can't anyone be happy in your stories?" I hit his arm lightly.

"Who says she wasn't happy?"

"She was . . . dead." I drag out the last word.

"Maybe her grandmother did come."

"Stop. Now you're lighting your own matches."

He laughs and stops at a corner, turning to face me. "You asked for a story. I've got some happy ones hidden in here." He taps his chest.

"Find one of those for me," I say.

"Will do."

A car turns the corner and then we cross, walking for a long while, quiet and still. I want to talk, to have our usual words and laughter and banter tumble out. But something unalterable has happened between us, a drawing closer, an understanding of history and personal story.

We make our way back to the coffee shop and Max reaches to touch my lower back as I waver with my face toward the sky. I don't know exactly why I do what I do now — the moon so low, the stars like holes in the universe, the fatigue or the Jameson — but I turn and face Max and then drop my head onto his shoulder, resting it there, with my face toward his warm neck.

He stands there, quiet and still, and then slowly lifts both his arms to put them around my waist, supporting me. "You okay?" he asks.

I nod against his shoulder. His body runs along mine and I settle in, placing my forefingers in the belt loops of his jeans. "Thanks."

"For?"

"Letting me rest on you."

He doesn't answer, and I know I've overstepped my boundaries. And yet I can't move. Then finally, he speaks. "You can rest on me anytime."

We are here for a little longer, my weight resting into his, until he finally speaks, his voice hoarse and quiet. "We need to go."

"Yes, we do." I step back and take in a long breath.

He smiles. "Keys?"

"Smart man, you."

"Not always."

We climb into my car and I lean back against the passenger seat's headrest. When we pull to the front of my house, Max slows the car. "I'll walk down to the studio and get my truck," he says.

"Or you can drive down there and I'll walk home. I want to check on Willa anyway.

257

And I could use the fresh air."

He drives to the barn's parking area, where we get out, facing each other. He hands my keys over, dropping them into my open palm. "But you're walking, right?"

"Yep."

"Tell Willa hello for me."

"Will do."

It is only a small step he takes toward me, but it brings us face-to-face. He reaches forward and tucks a piece of my hair behind my ear. "Good night, Eve."

I look up, and there's nothing to be done but what I do: I kiss him. My hand slips behind his head and my fingers wind into the hair at his neck — soft. The memory of the long-ago kiss is awake, easy and soft, and I slip backward, way, way back. I'm nineteen years old. I can decide anything or everything — nothing has yet happened to take away my choices.

Max's hand slips around my waist and he pulls me closer. This is not a chaste kiss, a quick and dry mistake. This is soft and soaked and welcoming. This is something I want to keep. His hand slides between my cotton shirt and my spine, fingers tracing along the skin until he pulls away, quickly and sharply. He leaves me standing with my hands still reaching out, my face upward.

He takes another step back and glances up the drive to my house, my home, and my family.

"I'm sorry." I drop my face into my hands. "I'm . . ."

"Don't be sorry," he says.

And for one glorious moment, I'm not.

SIXTEEN

This isn't the kind of place I'd ever have imagined finding myself. But who imagines these things? I'm sitting across from the neuro practitioner, Becky Moore. The desk is stacked high with papers. Post-it notes with initials and numbers — a secret code — flag each pile.

"Pink notes everywhere. What are those called? Posties?" Willa mumbles.

"Post-its," I say.

"Right," she says, and looks at me. "For other patients who can't find the right words."

I touch her arm and smile; it's all I can think to do.

The office itself is sparse, like it needs to exist in contrast to the cluttered desk. Becky matches her desk more than her office, as if she's borrowed someone else's space and brought the desk with her. She wears a bright blue silk blouse, a loose silk scarf untied, and a blazer that hasn't been pressed in a while. Her long dark hair is pulled back and then yanked to one side, where her ponytail falls over her left shoulder. Her wire-rimmed glasses rest on the bridge of her nose, and yet she still squints to read her notes.

She looks up with what I label the "serious smile." "So Willa Wetherburn, tell me how you're doing in your transition home?"

"Good, I think. I just have trouble bringing things to the surface of my mouth."

"Could you explain further?"

"See? See?" Willa looks to me. "That's the perfect example. I knew exactly what I wanted to say and it all came out in a different way. It's like that inside my head and then in my mouth."

"Frankly, I think that you expressed yourself better than most people who haven't been slammed in the right temporal lobe."

Willa smiles. "The only time I feel like my brain is working right is when I'm singing. But I can't remember the old lyrics, and when I talk, I mix up the words." She exhales through pursed lips. "And I can't remember simple things, but I'll remember the smell of Mom's old house when she cooked pot roast."

"I can explain that." Becky reaches under her desk and pulls out a rolled-up poster, spreading it over the labeled piles, over her desk. This large poster, torn at the edges, a coffee stain on the lower left, is a huge illustration of the brain. The lobes are colored, the sections divided by dark lines, Cambria font labeling each section. "Here" — Becky points to a purple glob of brain tissue — "is the frontal lobe. The cerebral cortex is the gray matter surrounding this portion, and this is where blood gathered in your head like a bruise. This is where your injury is. And this is also" — she taps the illustration again — "where a memory starts and then travels through here, the hippocampus" — she points at a seahorse-looking creature in the middle of the brain — "to become a long-term memory. So you can see that when something happens to this area, it is difficult for your brain to remember."

Willa runs her forefinger around the curves and undulations of the sketched brain. "So memories could be in here and not going to the right place or not coming out at all."

"Or the memory could be all together gone." Becky leans back in her chair. "Even the genius neurologists can't explain it all.

But I'm giving you the Cliffs Notes version. Your MRI today will show how much you've healed, but you'll have to give it some time."

"Is there a way to make myself remember . . . better? Is there a way to make *this* work?" Willa presses the poster paper, denting it into the pile of papers beneath. She lifts her hand to her own head to correspond to the purple-lobed image. "Is there something I can say or do to my head to make it remember?"

"Memory has its own language," Becky says softly. "It doesn't speak simple phonetics. Emotion can bring a memory. Music can dislodge or set one loose, as I'm sure you know. Smell, color, a word. Anything, everything."

"In other words, you don't know."

"If we did know, if the neurological world knew exactly what language your memory spoke, we'd speak it now for you. Teach it to you."

"I play guitar. Will that help?"

"Yes. We found that knitting helped one woman, drawing another, running another. You have to find your language, Willa. And accept that some things are gone. Some images were erased in the injury."

Becky looks away and I follow her gaze to the far wall, where a framed photo of a

263

younger Becky and a small blond child hangs on the wall. She flinches, and I imagine a memory of her own bubbling up, finding its language beneath her skin, before she turns back to Willa and me. "And the alcohol doesn't help, either. All that past drinking you did . . ."

"That was years and years ago," Willa says. "Ten or more."

"I know." Becky nods. "Me, too." She looks to Willa and smiles, knowing that she has something to offer. "Eleven years here, but the damage is there, of course. There are things that don't return."

I fish into my purse for gum. I don't really want gum; I need something to do with my hands. "What can I do?" I ask.

Becky looks at me as if she'd forgotten I was there all along. "Just be understanding and help her when the simplest things won't return."

"Of course." I want to tell this woman all the things I'd do for Willa, all the things I have done. Asking for understanding is too simple; I need something complicated — a road map with markers and to-do lists.

Willa rises to leave, thanking the practitioner, when I blurt out, "I want to fix this."

"I know," Becky says. "I do, too. That's why we're here."

Willa places her hand on my arm and nods to the door. Together, we walk to the car without speaking. Before she opens the passenger door, she looks at me over the top of the car. "So, Miss Fix It, it seems that the ticket is finding the language of my memory."

"Music?" I ask.

"Maybe it is, but so is *feeling* something. I know that doesn't make much sense, but sometimes feeling a particular emotion makes me remember a scene or piece of conversation or . . ." Her voice trails off mid-sentence and she climbs into the car.

We drive in silence as I do my best to be quiet — not my best attribute by a long shot — to allow Willa to find the words she needs to describe her memory. We're on Martin Luther King Boulevard, and I'm steering the car toward the street where the accident occurred. I take in a breath before saying, "Keep talking about *feeling* something. What do you mean?"

"I'll feel a certain way, and then bam!" She claps her hands together. "I'll remember an event that felt that exact same way."

"You have to be more specific." I can see Willa's profile in the side mirror, and the red comma of a scar above her eye.

"I'm alone in the cottage and the rain

comes sideways, not hitting the window, but sideswiping it. The thunder is far away. Then I'll get an empty feeling, an opening in the middle of me, and I remember being ten years old. We were left home alone during that hurricane. But it isn't the rain that makes me remember, because the rain is different; it is the actual *feeling of the rain* that brings the memory." She leans her head against the window, as if this recounting had been exhausting, an emptying in itself.

"I get it."

"Where are we going?"

"Trust me," I say.

It's midafternoon in Savannah. The temperature is above ninety and the humidity the same. The haze of heat may be slowing the city, but the tourists with their paper maps persist in gathering for ghost tours. They're pointing their cameras and cell phones at old houses, trees, and, of course, the bench where Forrest Gump sat. Those who aren't wandering around the streets are perched in horse-drawn carriages. The dark and magnificent animals walk forward with blank round eyes, with their heads down and a slick sheen of sweat on their bodies. I want to stop traffic, untie the horses, and lead them to the nearest fountain. These tourists will never understand

266

the true allure and mystery of this city. The fascinating parts of this city are inside the stories.

I turn the car onto Twenty-fourth Street and slow behind another carriage. Willa makes a small noise in the back of her throat and I stop the car. "There," she says as I turn onto Preston Street.

I was five years old when I heard a tour guide say, "Savannah is the first planned city in the United States," and I thought he'd said, "first *planted* city." For years, I believed that every live oak, magnolia, and camellia bush had been the first planted in the United States, *just* for Savannah. And this street does look as if every tree had been deliberately planted to create an arch of carved branches reaching over the street and then across the spaces between one another: a shield, a wall, a tunnel.

The houses haven't fared so well. Many of the dwellings have been turned into apartments or abandoned all together. The rusted FOR SALE signs bear that out. This is the way with Savannah: You can walk down a beautiful street, marveling at the cornice designs, and the gardens holding secrets behind wrought-iron gates, and then turn a corner and be scared.

I park the car and keep it running with

the music on. Jack Johnson sings "Flake," and Willa opens the passenger side door, swinging her legs out but remaining in the car, leaning forward to stare.

The tree is at least a hundred years old or more, a gnarled live oak with branches that bend and take sharp turns upward and then dive down again. Spanish moss hangs in bearded clumps, and on the ground, moss grows in the shadow of clustered, embracing leaves. Bark clings to the trunk in overlapping and oversized barnacles. Three feet up from the bottom of the tree, a bite mark exposes its inside honey-colored meat.

I glance up for the broken remnants of the branch Brando said could have killed Willa, but I can't find it. Willa leaves the car and stands next to the tree, her oversized sunglasses covering her eyes. "I got nothing." She runs her hand across the smooth wood of the injured and exposed area under the bark. "It's like I was never here. Like this might as well be the Hundred Acre Wood, where Winnie the Piglet lives with Pooh."

I laugh out loud. "God, Willa. You're a mess."

She smiles, but her cheeks don't rise enough to touch the bottom rim of her sunglasses. My sister, touching something that might have taken her life as if it is just another tree, any tree at all. She leans against the bark and looks upward, and I go to her and do the same, wanting to know what she sees, wishing I could feel what she feels. The canopy of moss and leaves hang as lace turned green, a tablecloth crocheted in intricate patterns. Music spills from my car and now the Dixie Chicks sing "Landslide." Their voices are soft, muffled, like they're in one of the dilapidated houses, singing behind the rotted windows and warped doors.

Together, Willa and I rest our backs against the tree, staring up, the scarred gash between us. She reaches her hand down and rests it on the wounded tree as if trying to heal it and her mind with the same touch.

"I know I went out that night to sing. I know it even if I can't remember it. There would be no other reason to go to the Bohemian on open-mike night. And I had my guitar. Benson said I was there and then I was gone — that I left before my set."

"Go on," I say.

"There's nothing to go on about. Next thing is you in the hospital, looking at me. Until I felt the pain, until I woke up completely, you know what I thought?"

"No. What?"

"Why is Eve in my bedroom, staring at me while I sleep? That's creepy."

"I was so scared. . . ."

"And mad."

"Why do you say that?"

"I can read your face. And you were mad as hell. I don't blame you. It was my fault."

"I'm not mad, Willa."

"I know you're not now. You probably didn't want to be even then."

"I don't think I was, but I don't know. I was so confused and worried."

"What could I have possibly been doing that would make Cooper force me to leave?" Willa lifts the sunglasses from her eyes to stare at me now. "What? Did I try to sit on a client's lap? Did I holler or scream, or dance, or kiss him?"

"He just said you were so drunk and that you were headed for his table, and he was nervous about what you would do or say."

The music changes then, and so does Willa. It's a wondrous thing to see the way a cloud passes and the sunlight bursts through the tree's moss and leaf canopy while Willa's eyes widen as if to take in the light and music. Lucinda Williams sings "Can't Let Go" in her sultry man-woman voice, and Willa grabs my hand. "This music. This CD. I made it for you."

"Yes. Last Christmas. All your favorite songs."

"I was going to sing *this* song *that* night."

"Okay."

"I was warming up in the back kitchen, waiting for Marisa to finish her set. Cooper was there. I said something to the waiter, something about not wanting Cooper to hear me play because he makes me nervous with his furrowed brow. I was thinking about not playing at all. About just hanging out."

"Why would Cooper make you so nervous? You've played in front of him before."

She shakes her head. "It wasn't him, Eve. It was something else. I don't know."

I rest my hand on her shoulder. "Maybe his clients?"

She shrugs and touches the tree again. "Do you have to get right back to work?"

"I have a quick meeting with that accountant, and then I'm free. Why?"

"I want to go ask for those pictures. . . ." She turns around and points between the houses. "That's where they found him. You think that's a coincidence?"

"Yes, I do. This isn't the best part of town. Things happen here."

"But what were we doing here? Me and Cooper?"

"This is how he cuts through to get home from downtown," I say, glad to offer this simple explanation.

"Oh."

She looks toward the houses, toward the dark alley. I imagine a tiny seed inside the folds of her brain that holds the memories of that night, hidden and dark. I read once, before the accident — everything's now divided into before and after — that the Hubble telescope once pointed its lens to a vast area of dark, empty sky. "We were just curious," the scientists said. "We just wondered about the blank patch of universe." But what they found in the darkness, in the nothingness, were millions of galaxies. What looked to be empty was anything but.

The design for number eight in the Ten Good Ideas line — *Find Adventure* — waits on the project table. The thick cotton stock is dense with a sketched forest. In the far right corner, there's a figure, a woman in a white dress set against a dark blue night sky, peeking around a tree. On the left side of the card, there's a man — also peeking around a tree. They're facing each another, and yet it's unclear if either sees the other. The night is so dark. The trees are so dense.

Max comes to my side as I look at the

drawing, turning it at different angles. "Like it?" he asks.

"No." I place the sheet down and turn to face him. "I love it."

He waves his hand toward Francie, who's on the phone across the room. "She did most of it."

"But your idea."

"How was Willa's appointment?" he asks.

"Okay. Nothing really new except that what she's experiencing is normal, whatever 'normal' means these days."

A jittery silence quivers between us. We haven't talked about the Kiss. I've done my best not to think about the Kiss. But it's there — sitting between us, smirking. It seems to beg for an answer. I can't give one. I don't have to, either, because the overhead bell rings, signaling another appointment.

"The accountant," I say to Max. "Right?"

"Probably."

Francie opens the door and allows the woman into our space. She stands taking our studio in the way she did the first time she visited, looking for something or some-one she can't seem to find.

"I'm back here," I say.

She sways toward me, her long black pants — wide at the bottom, like a skirt — billow-ing out in a dance. Her white tank top is a fashionable version of a man's undershirt, pulling tight across her breasts. A white bra strap peeks above her collarbone, and a fragile gold necklace hangs on her neck with a peace sign pendant. A woman trying to look like a girl, I think.

"Hello," she says to me, her voice crisp and quick, like she wants to get it over with.

"I have your packet here," I say. "Let's sit down and go through it. I think you'll like what we did with this third concept, incorporating your changes."

She pulls out the metal chair and it scrapes loudly, a screech across the concrete floor. Sitting, she folds her hands in her lap. "Show me."

I open the file and spread the graphic-design sheets across the table. "This is the branding logo we like best, but on this second page are alternates. And this" — I point at a wave pattern with her initials inside — "is a watermark to put on all your stationery or cards." I continue on, explaining the designs and how they can be combined.

"I told you I didn't like the wave at all," she says.

Mary Jo, with her peace sign pendant, has never once mentioned she doesn't like the wave, but arguing with a customer is about as effective as arguing with a cat, so I smile. "I'm sorry."

"I'm not paying you to be sorry. I'm paying you to help me find a brand that echoes my superior accounting services."

"Moving on to this concept, then." I slide the next sheet toward her. "The palmetto leaf and sea oats, and —"

She interrupts me. "Stop. Really the best you can do is a wave and some plants? I could hire a grad student from SCAD who could do better than this."

"There's more than the images; it's the package. We mix them up to find exactly what you feel. . . ."

"I feel like I need to take back my project." She stands and looks down at me. "Find someone who knows what the hell she's doing."

By the time she's reached the end of her obnoxious speech, Max is at the table, standing next to me. Willa has entered the studio and sits in the back corner, strumming her guitar.

"Is there a problem?" Max asks.

The woman looks at Max and her face softens. There she is, the kind of woman who knows how to act differently in front of a man. I've been jealous of these kinds of women. I know how to be one way, and switching personalities for gender has never been in my bag of tricks. It's definitely in hers, I think.

"No real problem. I just don't think that Eve here understands my needs. So I think it's best if I move on."

Here is how something goes for me: A narrative forms in my head, a running dialogue, as if I'm writing a screenplay for the scene, what I *want* to say and what I *do* say hardly matching. My internal dialogue says this: Yes, why don't you move on, and after you do, please stop at a restaurant and eat something to put meat on your bones. It's obvious why I don't say these things out loud, right?

"If you think it's best" is what I do say.

"I do." She begins to gather the papers and place them neatly into the file folder.

Max drops his hand on top of the file. "You can't take that with you."

"It's mine. I paid for it."

"No, you didn't. If you want to finish the process and pay your final installment, then you can take it. Otherwise, no go."

Willa's music and voice gain speed in the back of the studio. Francie joins her with the lyrics, a melody of love: something lost, something needed.

Mary Jo opens her mouth and another

voice comes out, a new and high, screeching voice. "Give me my folder. Give it to me." She opens her mouth again as if she means for more to come out, something else, but nothing at all erupts. Willa and Francie stop singing. I hold my breath, and Max places his hand on my lower back. In the aftermath of the song and the screeching demand, a silence falls over our studio. Far off, that owl again hoots.

A scuffling sound follows, and Willa stands with us, her guitar still in hand, an extension of her arm and voice. "You," she says to Mary Jo.

Mary Jo looks down, digs into her purse until she finds her sunglasses, and shoves them on her face so quickly, it seems she might break the bridge of her nose. "Me," she says in a sarcastic echo of identification.

Willa's face drains of color, and her fingers flutter in the air as if she is still playing the guitar. She stares at Mary Jo, moving closer. "In the booth while I practiced that song."

"What?"

Mary Jo walks backward toward the door, clutching her necklace as a talisman.

Willa hands her guitar to Max and takes two steps toward Mary Jo, who is by now more than halfway across the barn. Willa catches up and places one hand on Mary

Jo's shoulder. "You were there. You were with Cooper. In the booth."

Mary Jo spins around, her mouth twisted. "You're crazy. You know that, right? I don't know why they let a crazy person work here, but maybe that's why the designs suck." She pulls away from Willa and looks toward Max, then at me. "I don't know how y'all were voted the best letterpress in Savannah. Probably because of your husband's rich Morrison family. Because it's not for your work."

"That's enough," Max says.

"I'm not crazy," Willa protests in a monotone voice. "Your voice. It's stuck in my head." Willa takes in a long breath. "You were screaming at Cooper about not leaving you there alone. That terrible voice."

"I have no idea what you're talking about." Mary Jo trips backward, trying to leave, to escape.

"If I'd been Cooper, I'd have left you alone in that booth, too." Willa says this with a hiss behind her voice, a threat.

Mary Jo reaches up, and it all moves slowly, but not slowly enough for me to stop her hand from slapping Willa across the face, lightly, almost a pretense of a slap. The sound — skin on skin — breaks our silence and we run toward Willa and Mary Jo, tripping over chairs and piles of paper, over boxes and bags. I reach Willa first, but she's recovered, holding her hand over her face and glaring directly at Mary Jo.

Max stands between them. "Leave," he says, his low voice vibrating underneath my ribs like thunder.

Mary Jo turns and slides open the barn doors, but she doesn't close them. We don't move. Willa holds her hand over her cheek. I place my hands over my stomach, where I feel an opening begin to form, a cavernous, bottomless opening. Max rests his hand on my shoulder and Francie slumps to a chair. The geo-tagging, I think, the uniting of place and memory.

"Sorry," Willa says, tears rising in her eyes. She bends over as if she is going throw up. "I did it again. I mucked it up again, didn't I?" Sobs tear through Willa the same way they have a few times since her return home. But this holds passion: something true. She looks up while bent over. "Eve."

"Yes," I say, exhaling the breath I've been holding.

"Cooper was with her that night. She was there."

"Okay."

"She didn't want him to leave her alone. There wasn't anyone else there."

"Why was she *here*?" Max asks.

"I don't know." Willa stands up straight, wips at her eyes. "To see who we are? What we do?"

A flood opens inside me. I slide open the barn doors and run up the gravel path toward the house. A hurricane wind blows behind my eardrums as I fling myself into the kitchen. "Cooper," I holler, the screech of my own voice harsh.

Gwen appears in the curved entryway. "What's wrong with you?"

I grind my teeth together, a vain attempt at self-control. "I'm looking for your dad."

"He's upstairs."

I walk slowly, even as my body wants to run up the stairwell. I push away the larger understanding as I notice the smaller things: The frames in the hallway need dusting; the corner of the rug runner is folded over; Gwen's bedroom light is on. These are things I can fix and these are things I notice, ticking them off in my brain to keep from hearing Mary Jo's voice, hear the slithering slap of her hand against Willa's cheek.

Steam flows from the master bath and into the bedroom, where it fogs up the windows. There is my husband, in the steam, a towel wrapped around his waist. This is an ordinary moment, one repeated for years and years, a familiar scene of our married life, and here I am, seeing everything in a new way: What is familiar becomes distorted and peculiar. His wet hair hasn't yet been brushed and he is placing folded shirts in an open suitcase.

"Going somewhere?" I ask.

"Hey, darling." He walks toward me and kisses me.

I am rigid with anger. "Where are you going?"

"I told you. I have to go to Nashville to meet with the music publisher who wants in on the magazine deal."

He did tell me. I'd forgotten. "Is Mary Jo going with you?"

I watch him carefully, the details sharp and holding clues. First his brow drops down and then his eyes open wide. He yawns: a one-two count. He touches his chin, where only moments before he shaved, there must have been stubble. "Who?"

I am silent as I allow her name to settle into the room.

"Eve, I don't know what you're talking about."

"The woman with the long dark hair. Skinny. High-pitched voice."

"Oh, her. The accountant for the Glencoe documents."

"The woman you were with the night you wrecked the car."

Cooper drops a folded shirt into the suitcase and then walks toward me, tightening the towel around his waist. "Let's start over here. I didn't wreck the car. Your sister did. And I wasn't with Mary Jo. That's insane."

"Yes, you were."

"Is that what Willa says?"

My voice doesn't shake, which surprises me, because everything else about me quivers. "Yes, that's what Willa says."

Cooper's face softens and he shakes his head. "Poor thing." He sits on the bed, next to his suitcase.

"What do you mean?"

He holds out his hand for me to take, but I don't move. "You can't do this, love. This has to stop. You can't let your sister come between us. When have I ever, in all our married life, given you reason to distrust me?" He looks directly at me, the way I used to make Gwen do when she was young and I wanted her to understand what I was saying. "When?" he asks again.

"Never." I drop my gaze, unable to hold it any longer. "Until now."

"Why would I start now?" He exhales. "Remember when Willa showed up drunk

282

at our rehearsal dinner? Remember when we visited her in Colorado and she forgot we were coming and she'd gone camping? Remember when Willa slept with my best man? Remember when —"

"I get it. She's screwed up a few times."

"I know things have been bumpy and we're both buried in work. Gwen isn't behaving, but to think . . ." He shakes his head. "I know this is hard for you, but I think you're forgetting what it is for me." He touches his scar, a reminder of his pain. "And to have you not believe in me, it's almost . . ." He closes his eyes and then opens them again, and now they're full of tears. "If you're doubting me, I don't know you as well as I thought."

"What does that mean?"

"How could you think I'd be able to do something like that?"

"Something like what?" My voice rises on the last word. "I didn't say what I thought you were or weren't doing. I am asking if this woman is someone you know. If you were with her that night."

He holds his fingers to his lips. "You're yelling."

I lower my voice. "Do you know her?"

"Yes. I just told you that I think you're talking about the accountant on the Glencoe project."

"Then why in the hell is she fishing around in my studio? None of this makes sense."

He stands up and walks toward the closet. "I told her about your branding and incredible business. She must have decided to use you. I brag about you all the time."

The steam has dissipated and the bathroom is clear; my husband takes socks from his drawer and I sit on the edge of the bed, trying to find something to say.

"Eve, I have a plane to catch. I can't sit here and debate with you about what is real and what isn't."

"What is real, Cooper?"

His voice floats from the closet. "I am." And then he emerges with that smile. "And you are. And this family is."

"So we just pretend that night didn't happen."

He speaks slowly, enunciating each word. "How am I supposed to pretend it didn't happen when I'm paying the outlandish hospital bills for your sister, who doesn't have insurance and needs therapy? And I'm facing at least two surgeries. No, I don't think we can pretend it didn't happen. But we can stop looking for excuses for Willa."

The hollow, floating hope inside me sinks. There is nowhere else to go when the conversation goes here, back to this cul-de-sac.

Cooper returns to the closet, and when he comes out, he's fully dressed, his pale blue tie tight against his Adam's apple. "Are we okay here now? I hate leaving if you're mad at me."

"I'm not mad," I say. "I'm confused."

He bites down hard, teeth on teeth. His jaw clenches on the side. "You're not the one who was hit in the head. I have no idea why you're the one who's confused."

"Who were you with that night, Cooper? Who were the clients you were with?"

"I already told you. Harvey Bern and his wife, the owners of the Anglers, that charter group that does the fishing show on NBC Sunday mornings. They're trying to decide whether to pay a huge sum of money to advertise in my magazine. It's the largest advertising deal we've ever had."

"Mary Jo wasn't there?"

Cooper slams the top of his suitcase down. "No, Eve. Mary Jo, the freelance accountant, was not there."

"Why does Willa think she was?"

"I'm not trying to be a jerk here. I'm just saying what you already know, so don't make me the bad guy. She was unreliable before the accident, so why would you believe her now?"

"It seemed so real; her memory seemed so real. The way she heard that woman's voice and then fell apart."

"What do you mean, 'heard' her voice?"

"Whoever she is, she's a nut job, Cooper. She came to the studio."

"What?"

"When Willa thought she remembered her voice, she went a little nuts."

"Shit, I'll take her off the accounts." Cooper holds out his hand for me and I take it this time. He pulls me close. "I love you. I'm sorry this is so hard for you, but you can't freak out every time Willa freaks out. We'll all go crazy. We have our own family to protect."

He's right. If I go off the tracks every time Willa does, we'll all be in a mess. It just seemed so authentic — the memory rising with the music and the voice, the language of that particular night returning to my sister in full. But it was a ghost, a shadowed memory of another night, another woman, and another place.

"Cooper, I have one more question."

"I have a plane —"

"I know, a plane to catch. This will only take a second. I need to know why you emptied my business account."

"I didn't empty it. I moved things around for a few days. Nothing is missing."

"Okay, but why? And why didn't you say anything to me?"

"Eve, I've always managed the money, and you've always trusted me. I was liquidating a money market account to pay our bills — family bills — and the money hadn't made it to our account yet, so I just . . . switched."

"I don't get it. Why couldn't you pay family bills without liquidating an account? Is there . . . something I don't know?"

"No, it wasn't a big deal. I'd invested in a new stock and didn't have enough cash flow. Nothing to worry about at all."

"That's what Fritz was talking about. . . . Now I get it. You should have told me. That's my company. Our payment to a provider bounced. You can't do that."

"I can't do that?" He squints at me and his scar puckers.

"No, you have to tell me."

"Okay. Next time, I'll tell you."

"No next time. Don't use Fine Line money to pay family bills. Please."

"I have to go, Eve. I'm going to miss my plane." He smiles and holds up his right hand. "I swear never to move things around without telling you."

He hugs me good-bye. A dry kiss to the

side of my lips and he's gone.

I'm as tired as if Cooper and I had run six miles while having that discussion. I want to lie down, sleep a month, when I hear Gwen's voice. "Mom?"

"Hey, Pea."

"I believe Willa," she says.

We're on fragile ground here, mother and daughter. One wrong move or sound and everything will shatter.

"Memory's a strange thing, Gwen." I pat the bed for her to come sit with me, but she stands firm. "It's not something reliable like a photo. Or a video."

"But Aunt Willa would never make something up like that."

"Were you listening to us?"

"How could I help it, Mom? You guys were, like, totally screaming at each other."

"I don't think Willa made it up. But I do think her mind made it up. Does that make sense? I've learned that when there are blank spaces in our memories, we can fill them in with other images, other memories, other dreams."

"Not Willa. She doesn't lie."

"I don't think she's lying. But I don't think she knows the truth, either."

"I don't think *you* know the truth."

"I might not, Gwen. But here's one true

thing: I can't have our family fall apart. I can't. . . . I'm doing what I can to keep it all together, and help Willa."

Gwen rolls her eyes, a skill mastered when young. "So you *just* believe Dad?"

I don't answer; I can't.

"I don't." Gwen shakes her head and her hair falls to the side, and there it is: the dreaded ink on skin.

"Stop," I shout, and shoot from the bed to her side. "What is this?" I hold her shoulder and lift her hair. There on the bottom of her scalp, directly on her hairline, is a half-inch feather, dark and permanent: a tattoo.

She jerks away from me and bolts down the hallway, slamming her bedroom door for emphasis.

"Gwen, open up." I'm at her door, trying to speak through the crack, wanting to crawl under the small space between floor and door.

"No. You'll just lecture me."

"Just let me in."

Silence.

I lift my hand to bang on the door and then think better of it. A small feather at the base of her neck; the slightest rebellion, not meant to be seen. I take a deep breath and walk away, moving down the stairs to the kitchen.

I roll paper into the typewriter and hit the keys to type a note, which I leave on the counter for her to find when she finally emerges.

To the moon and back . . . I love you, Mom.

Seventeen

The phone rings and I hope someone will answer it.

I hope no one answers it.

I'm parked on Preston Street, alone in the car. Somewhere in Charleston, a phone rings in the Anglers' office.

"Hello." The voice is soft, trained to answer the phone.

My finger hovers over the end button. She tries again. "You've reached the Anglers. How may I help you?"

I close my eyes. "Yes, may I please speak to Harvey Bern?"

"May I tell him who is calling?"

"Yes, this is Eve Morrison, from *Southern Tastes* magazine."

"One moment, please."

I've practiced this conversation, how I'll pretend to be the publisher's dutiful wife, asking if a client is happy with his advertising. But my mouth is dry when he comes on the line.

"This is Harvey."

"Hi, Mr. Bern. This is Eve Morrison, Cooper's wife. I'm making some follow-up calls for *Southern Tastes* and want to make sure you're happy with your advertising campaign after your meeting at the Bohemian."

The deceit. I feel nauseous.

"Well, Mrs. Morrison, I'm glad for your call, but we haven't decided on our campaign yet. *Southern Tastes* is one of our favorite online magazines, but we haven't made a decision. And you must have us mixed up with another meeting."

"Another meeting?" I ask.

"We've never met with Cooper in Savannah. Only in Charleston."

"Well, please do forgive me." I throw out my best southern accent.

He laughs, and I imagine an older gentleman with white hair and smile crinkles around his eyes. "No need to forgive. Thanks for following up. I should be back with Cooper soon."

"Thanks for your consideration, and have a lovely day."

"You, too, ma'am."

And there it is. One more lie to add to the equation.

■ ■ ■ ■

The car outside Willa's cottage is beat-up and dusty, a faded blue Corolla missing its bumper. A tuft of Spanish moss sticks out from under the tire on the passenger side, as if the car came straight through the yard instead of the traditional driveway route.

The lights are on inside the cottage, even though the midday sun flares directly toward the windows. I stand at the door for more than a minute before knocking. Somewhere in the back of the house comes Willa's laugh, the same one she's had her entire life, full and throaty, a laugh that could never be called quiet or mysterious. I hear voices, too; their conversation is clear behind the door.

"How many times have you had to visit the morgue?" Willa asks.

A male voice, strong and sounding of cigarettes, replies, "Shit, more than I can count. It's part of the job."

"I don't know if I could do that. I'd like writing the stories, but I don't think I could see . . . that. You know, see death all the time."

Willa opens the door wide and I see a man — tall and rugged, as if he's just driven in from out west and needed to stop for water. His dark hair pokes from all angles and his beard is cut clean and sharp to the edges of his angular face. He holds out his hand. "Hello, Mrs. Morrison. I'm Noah from the *Savannah News.* We spoke on the phone."

"Nice to meet you."

Willa closes the door as I enter. "He was just telling me some stories about our city that we'd never know. . . . It's fascinating and terrible."

Fascinating and terrible. That's the last thing I'm in the mood for.

Willa motions me toward the kitchen but continues talking about Noah, awe in her voice. "Noah has seen murders and overdoses; he's met gang leaders and drug dealers. And here we are, just reading about it in the paper, like it exists somewhere else." She pauses and then hands me a thick manila envelope.

"What's this?" I ask.

"Photos of the man who died on Preston."

"What?" I yank my hand away. "I don't want to see this."

"Neither did I. But it's real."

Noah rubs his hand across the stubble on his cheek. "You should see it. Everyone should. That's why I'm writing this piece. People need to know what's going on in this city aside from fancy horse-drawn carriages and beautiful old buildings."

I hold my hands behind my back, as if handcuffed. "I don't need to see it to know it's true: There's a dead man."

Willa pushes the envelope toward me again. "Sometimes we have to look at it. Really look to understand. It wasn't as real to me until . . . I saw it."

"It's real to me, and seeing it won't change that. Have you found out anything new? I mean, do we know how he died?"

Willa glances at Noah, but then answers me. "Not much, really. The man has been cremated by now and numbered."

"Numbered?"

"Yes, numbered. The guy has a number, Eve, not a name." Willa cringes. "A freaking number. It's too awful to imagine. How do you get so alone that you're only a number?" She closes her eyes against the thought. "Anyway, the photos and autopsy they did showed he died of blunt trauma to the abdomen, where he then bled out internally. I thought maybe if I saw his face, I'd . . . I don't know, maybe recognize him? But there was blunt trauma to his face also."

"Blunt trauma," I repeat.

Noah shuffles his feet as if to move or leave, but he remains in the same spot. "I'll let you two be. I wanted to know if Willa remembered seeing this man that night, but she doesn't. So . . . I'll be getting on."

Willa walks him to the door as I sit at the kitchen table with the unopened envelope in my hand. Do I want to look? Or know? Or see? Without answers, I am still sitting there as Willa returns to the kitchen. "Listen, Willa, I know you want answers. I know you do. So do I. But we have to let this rest. We can't make up a story by piecing together all these dream images. We can't."

"I'm not making up a story out of dreams." Willa speaks in a whisper but forced, like air is being pushed through a furnace full blast. "That man is dead, and that's not a dream. That woman, Mary Jo, and her voice are real."

"Just because they're real doesn't mean they are part of that night."

"I wouldn't believe me, either."

"Willa." I say her name as if it's a quiet offering.

"That reporter wasn't here to involve me. Or Cooper, for that matter. He only wants to know if we saw anything."

"And you believe that?"

"You don't?"

"I don't know what to believe. Nothing is adding up."

"How so?"

I spill it, all of it. I tell her about the money being moved and the cards that have arrived at the studio. I tell her about Harvey Bern and how he denied meeting with Cooper. Words fall out and nothing adds up to a coherent story.

She sits quietly for a long time, and I wonder if she's understood me, if she's absorbed anything I said.

"Something isn't right," she says.

"You think?"

Our laughter comes full force. We're sisters hiding under the bed once more. "Whatever it is," she says, "it will be all right. It will. Whatever happened that night, whatever the hell really happened, isn't just about me, or my injuries. Now it's about you and your marriage. Your life."

"What?"

"All this time, I haven't wanted to bother you with finding out the truth of that night because it was all about me and what I did or didn't do. Now it's about us. It's about Gwen. It's about the truth."

"Yes," I say, because it is all that is left to say.

An hour later and I'm back at work. Only, I'm not really back, because my mind is wandering through the halls of a morgue with a man with no name, and through the halls of a bank with that obsequious manager, and then the bar where my husband claimed to be with clients who weren't there.

I look across the table, which is strewn with design ideas, and see Max working on a rough charcoal sketch for Larry Ford's big party — and I do a 180. My mind is made up. I'm going to do it. I'm going to bring it up — the Kiss. I'm going to make sure Max understands it wasn't what it seemed, but even so, that it was a one off and won't ever happen again. But that's not what comes out.

"Gwen got a tattoo," I say.

"Of what?" he asks.

I drop the chart onto the table. "A feather."

"Where?" He leans back in his chair. His neck cracks and he readjusts to stare at me. Those damn blue-ringed eyes.

"The back of her neck, right under her hairline. You can't see it unless she pulls her hair up."

"Are you going to kill her? And how? I mean, how are you going to get away with this murder?"

"Do you take anything seriously?" I smile at him.

"You could just send her to a convent."

"Or to my in-laws, since they seem to know how to do everything so perfectly."

"Problem solved." He smiles. "Sorry. I just don't know what to say. I'm not sure what I'd do, and I don't have kids, so I don't want to offer advice."

"Please don't offer advice. I have more than enough of that." I turn my chair to face him. "Do you remember when we were at Soapbox and we worked all night on that city project?"

"And we ended up lying flat on the floor, drinking vodka and talking about why we wanted to spend our days and hours with type."

Time was slippery then. It was more than twenty years ago and we were exhausted and lying on a linoleum floor, half-drunk on our way to full drunk. "You said that you liked the way letters looked next to each other, the way they changed and made something new. It wasn't just the words, but the way you could make the words *look.*"

"And you said it was so we could all get "good mail" in our boxes and not just bills. And here we are talking about your daughter. It all moved so . . . quickly."

I take in a breath. "I'm doing that thing you don't like."

"What thing?"

"When I talk about something besides work. Sorry." I rub my eyes. "I'm tired. I said too much."

"I never said I didn't like it. I said you never do it. It's the other way around — I love talking to you, Eve. About everything and anything and all things."

I don't know what to say to such kindness.

"I think Gwen is doing the same thing you did when you made these commandments. She's trying to make sense of things."

"Well then, damn, can't she just hide in a fort and make some new commandments?"

"You know what I think? I think that these new commandments you made were a bigger rebellion than a feather under a hairline. I have a feeling that there is a reason this isn't finished." He taps at the empty number ten. "You are an extraordinary woman. Do you know that? Don't get too mad at Gwen for the tattoo, okay?"

"Thought you weren't going to give me advice."

"I changed my mind." He grins, and it almost turns into a smile before he stands and shoves the chair backward. "I gotta teach that class tomorrow morning. Some sleep in between would be great."

"Thanks for all the help with this." I point to the cards. "We're almost there."

"Almost." He grabs his bag to leave and then hesitates, as if there is something he knows he's forgotten but can't remember what.

"Max."

He does stop and looks over his shoulder. "Yes?"

"About that night . . ."

He holds up his hand. "I know. You didn't mean it. You're sorry. You don't have to tell me again."

"Okay."

With a few steps and the slide of a door, he's gone and I'm alone, Regina Spektor singing that line from "How" — "How could I forget your love?" — over the iPod speakers.

I pick up the pen and write the last commandment; the last of the Ten Good Ideas; the first thing I want: *Love.*

That's all. Just that.

EIGHTEEN

Ford doesn't just give a party; he gives an all-out soirée. The Fine Line, Ink Posters hang off street lanterns and the restaurant banners dangle below. Servers walk around passing out meatballs and salmon puffs off silver trays. Champagne with floating raspberries is served in tall flutes. Max, Francie, Willa, and I stand outside around a bistro table facing the Savannah River.

A wooden sailboat, a 1700s replica, bobs against the current. Jazz music plays from the outdoor speakers and the crescent moon appears ready to take a dive into the river and swim in its own reflected waters. Larry Ford comes to say hello. "Where's that handsome husband of yours?"

"Nashville," I say. "Business."

"I promised him some ad money in his e-magazine. You can tell him it's only because I love you. I'm loyal." He winks and then hollers toward an entering group of friends.

Francie laughs out loud and slaps her hand over her mouth.

"What?" I ask.

"I just think it's funny that Cooper hates the Fine Line but goes after our customers."

I shake my head. "Francie, Cooper does not hate the Fine Line. And he goes after every business in Savannah."

"Okay, maybe *hate* is too strong a word." She blows her bangs off her face with a quick breath. "But he doesn't love it. Is that better?"

I try to smile but can't. It's Willa who answers. "He doesn't like anything that takes Eve away."

For a full minute, there's only the sound of the piped-in jazz music and the overlapping voices of other partyers. "Well," Max finally says, "I wouldn't want anyone to take Eve away, either."

"Good point," Francie agrees.

The conversation takes a hard right into Max's stories. "Okay, you know my friend Mark? The one y'all met last year?"

"He's hilarious," Francie says.

"And a little crazy. Last night, he finally wanted to prove that his girlfriend was cheating on him. He decided to spy on her."

"There has to be an easier way to catch a cheater," Francie says. "These days, it takes nothing less than sneaking a peek at a cell phone."

"Well, Mark can't do things the easy way. His girlfriend lives on the marsh side of the river, so he kayaked out behind her house with binoculars."

"And?" I ask. "What did he find?"

"The tide went out; he was stranded and too proud to get out and slog up to her house. His cell phone didn't have service, and so there he sat, curled up in the bottom of the kayak, trying to sleep until the tide came in."

"Hilarious if it's not you." Willa shakes her head. "Did the girl find out?"

"Well, she'll probably wonder why he has so many mosquito bites that he had to get a steroid shot today."

"And did he prove his theory?" I ask.

"Nope." Max shook his head. "He just sat there watching her watch a movie alone with her cat and a glass of wine."

Laughter flows into the story and we drink another glass of champagne and tell more stories, taking turns trying to top Max's tale but never able to do so.

Finally, I point at a flickering sign down the street — SAVANNAH STYLE. "That's where Gwen works. Let's go embarrass her and say hello."

Walking as a foursome to the small tourist store, Francie comments on how she hasn't ever noticed it.

"That's because there's nothing here you'd like." I stop in front of the plate-glass window, where a glowing peace signs winks at us. A headless mannequin wears a flowing red sundress, and multicolored hookah pipes are displayed on a bright pink shelf surrounded by faux fur pillows. The scent of patchouli greets us at the door.

Gwen stands behind the checkout counter, her hair pulled up in a ponytail. Her tight black T-shirt declares SAVANNAH STYLE inside a neon circle. She looks up and sees us. "Willa, Francie," She waves. "Hey, Max."

No "Hey, Mom" for me.

Willa and Francie walk directly to the counter and I wander to a back aisle to catch my breath, not wanting my hurt to show. Max follows me and silently we browse the shelves that hold mood rings, stringed bracelets, salt rocks, and incense sticks.

A white-painted frame surrounds a burlap board where necklaces hang off small pins. I pretend to be interested in the dangling pendants, but I'm listening to my daughter laugh and talk to Willa as she once spoke to me — kindly and with warmth.

"Aunt Willa, I like totally love that skirt. Where did you find it?"

"I've had it since my first week in Colorado. I found it when I was cleaning out my boxes last week. Bohemian chic never goes out of style."

"Don't come looking in my room if it suddenly disappears from your cottage."

Gwen laughs as my fingers reach for a gold chain; I absently lift the pendant in the air, with the chain still attached to the board. A shiver runs through me, the kind that settles in the back of my neck and reaches around to my throat.

Lying faceup in my open palm is a peace sign, a single symbol, nothing to give me the chills or the shakes that begin in my hand.

But I see the necklace on Mary Jo's throat, the way it bobs up and down, the way she grabs at it as she backs away.

"Max."

"Yeah?" He's next to me, flipping through a novelty joke book.

"Have you seen this before?"

He looks in my palm and then unhooks the necklace from the display. "A peace sign? I think I have seen one before, maybe in the seventies in a tattoo parlor? Or on a T-shirt at a Grateful Dead concert?"

I smile but can't find the laughter this deserves. "No, *this* necklace," I say.

"No, why?"

I take it from his hand and walk to the front of the store. "Willa," I call out.

Willa and Francie turn to me. Gwen falls silent in the middle of a sentence.

"Do you remember seeing this?" I hold the necklace high.

They both stare at the peace sign. Willa's brows bend down over her eyes in concentration, as if I'm giving her a test, and she shakes her head. Francie takes the necklace and her eyes open wide. "Yes."

I step toward the counter. "Gwen," I say quietly, "Do you remember selling this necklace in the last few days?"

"I sell about a million of those necklaces a night."

"A million?" Willa asks in an attempt to ease the tension.

"Well . . ." Gwen tries not to laugh.

Francie hands the jewelry to Gwen. "Was there some skinny crazy lady with dark hair who bought one lately? She's about the size of a Polly Pocket doll."

"Yes." Gwen smiles at Francie. "She was

so weird. She asked me like a gabillion questions about myself. She creeped me out, and she put it on even before she left."

"Mary Jo," Francie says, and turns to me.

A purple lava lamp behind Gwen wavers and burps its misshapen blobs upward. The ground below me does the same. "Gwen, what did she ask you? What did she say?"

"She wanted to know if I liked my school. She wanted to know how long I'd worked here. And she talked about my hair, how pretty it was. Supercreepy."

I glance at the group. "Do not ever let her back in our studio. Ever."

"The studio?" Gwen asks.

"Yes. This same woman came to us for a new logo."

Gwen's gaze jumps from Francie to Willa and then back to me again. "Is she like seriously crazy? Like I should be worried?"

"No," Francie says, and shoots me a look. "Just obsessed with our work. Who wouldn't be?"

Customers wait behind us, and Gwen opens the cash register. "I have to work, okay?" she says with her perfect eye roll.

I leave the store first and take slow, deliberate steps heading to the river for some fresh air.

They all follow, but Francie reaches me

first. "Don't go jumping to conclusions, Eve."

"Really?"

"Okay, jump away."

"Do you believe Cooper?" I ask. "Really believe his story?"

"Don't ask me that, Eve. You're my boss. I love you. I wasn't there. I have no idea."

"Do you believe him?" I ask again.

Silence shimmers between us like silver fog, her answer held back until she takes a deep breath and let out the one word: "No."

I sink to an iron bench and she sits next to me as Willa and Max join us. I look up at my sister and my coworkers. "What the hell is going on?"

"Don't ask me," Willa says. "Apparently, my mind erased all the facts. I can't get any of it straight."

"I don't know, either." Francie places her hand on my leg.

It's Max who's silent and it's Max whom I want to say something, anything. I look up at him. "It' confusing," he says. "But I'm sure there's an explanation."

"An explanation?" I say. "Are you kidding me? Some woman comes to our studio and insults us. She comes here and quizzes my daughter, my only child? Enough is enough. Somebody has to know what happened that night. And I have a feeling that *somebody* is stalking my family."

"Stalking?" We are all startled by Gwen's voice behind us. "Seriously, Mom?"

"Shouldn't you be in the store?" I stand up next to my daughter.

"I came out to see if you were okay. You seem totally freaked-out. Who is this lady?"

"I don't know, Gwen."

"God, Mom. Why don't I believe you?"

The discomfort, the alternating currents of disdain and accusation, keep us silent until Gwen throws a curt "Whatever" over her shoulder and stalks back to the store.

"What am I going to do?' I ask, not to anyone in particular, but to the air where my daughter just stood.

No one answers because no one can.

NINETEEN

No one tells you this — that you can love your child so much that the hurt she feels becomes your own. That the pain rummaging through her soul unpacks your own hidden past and together the aches entwine. That there is a kind of eviscerated pain that makes you feel utterly helpless because you can't take the hurt away from her and claim it for yourself. And no one tells you that the things you fear aren't the things that get you in the end.

"Mrs. Morrison?"

"Yes?"

"It's Dylan. I think you need to come get Gwen. She's not looking so good."

"What do you mean 'not looking so good'?"

"She's been drinking, Mrs. Morrison. She's passed out, and I'm scared."

When I think of all the phone calls I've dreaded — the truancy, the accidents, the

311

broken hearts — this call, the one that ripped me from my sleep, well . . . it didn't even make the top ten. But it should have.

I speed through the streets of Savannah, oblivious to anything but my need to get to Gwen. Dylan's home is downtown, a downtown so far removed from Preston Street that it could be in a different country. This is a manicured street, with sturdy ancient homes surrounded by palmetto trees and solid live oaks. This is an area made of wealth and history and ghosts. The ghosts of the past are always here.

I run up the stairs to the front porch and bang on the door.

"Where is she?" I ask a disheveled Dylan, who opens the door immediately. "And where are your parents?"

"My parents are out of town. Gwen's in the living room." He moves aside to let me in. "She drank whiskey straight from the bottle. I couldn't stop her."

The living room looks like it could be in a magazine spread for chintz — all flowers and vines, all pink and green. My daughter, in her black T-shirt and jeans, is an ink stain in the midst of all this floral clutter. She's lying on the couch, bent over in child's pose, a yoga position for rest. Except she's not resting. Facedown, she's buried in the cushions and her arms are spread before her in surrender. Her legs are bent and her knees are digging into her stomach. I rush to her and now I hold her, attempt to lift her up. "Gwen!"

She doesn't answer and she is too heavy, too limp to lift. I turn her over and prop her head up on a pillow. She's breathing slowly but rhythmically. I say her name again and again without response. I look to Dylan.

"Tell me what happened."

"She came here. I promise. I didn't call her or anything. There was no stopping her. I'm telling you. She was so upset. Like completely undone."

"Go get me a cold washcloth." I point toward what I think might be the kitchen.

"Good idea. Good idea." He hustles to the kitchen.

I brush Gwen's hair back from her face. Black mascara and eyeliner have been smeared to the edges of her hairline and down her cheeks. She's pale, but there's a high red sheen to her cheeks.

Dylan reappears with a towel wrapped around ice, and a cold dishrag. I take both from him without thanks and wash Gwen's face. "Honey, it's Mom. Wake up."

Dylan's voice interrupts. "I swear to God,

I tried to stop her."

"Why was she so 'undone'?" Seeing my girl like this, the word seems perfect, tragically perfect.

"She was going on and on about some woman stalking her. And then she said you'd gone to see her at work and . . ." He pauses and sits on the floor to touch Gwen's knee. "She said you were freaking her out."

"How much did she drink?" I ask.

"I don't know, because she'd started before she got here. She had some girl drop her off. I know you hate me, but I swear I tried to stop her."

"I thought you broke up."

"We did."

My chest, already caving in with the weight of sorrow, is now crushed. My daughter went crawling back to the boy who'd left her. She got drunk enough to pass out.

I wash Gwen's face and lightly shake her shoulders. "Gwen, wake up. Please."

That's when I hear the sirens. Like I need to hear sirens again.

"I called nine one one," Dylan says. "When you were taking too long to get here . . . I called a few minutes ago."

At Dylan's voice, Gwen opens her eyes and bends forward. "Oh God. I'm gonna throw up."

Dylan jumps up and runs toward the kitchen again. "Not on the couch. No!"

The paramedics knock on the door, a loud, authoritative knock.

"Dylan," I holler out, and hold Gwen upright against my chest. I feel her shudder. From maternal instinct, I hold my palms out for . . . well, just in case.

The knock comes again and a deep voice calls something unintelligible. Dylan comes from the kitchen and tosses a porcelain mixing bowl my way. It clatters to the floor and I reach down to pick it up, hold it beneath Gwen's face.

I place my hand under her chin and lift her face to mine. "I'm here."

She covers her mouth with her hand and hiccups with a sob. Tears run down the sides of her face and she wipes at them.

"Don't let her puke on the couch. My mom will kill me," Dylan says.

Gwen looks up at him. "You're sush an assshhole."

Dylan doesn't hear her because he's gone to the front door for the paramedics — a man and a woman in dark blue uniforms — who rush to our side.

"Ma'am," the man says, "please move aside so we can assess the situation."

I hold up my hand. "She's fine. There's no reason for you to be here." My heart is thumping against my chest like a jackhammer. It's a wonder they don't want to treat me.

"Who called nine one one?" the woman asks, and sets a box on the floor, then takes a stethoscope from around her neck.

"I did." Dylan's voice isn't so sure now. "I couldn't get her to wake up. But I guess her mom —"

"She's okay," I say. "You can go."

The woman kneels next to Gwen and asks me again, "Can you please move aside?"

"This is my daughter," I say. "And no, I won't move aside."

"I'm Cathy," she says. "And I need to check out your daughter." She looks at Gwen. "Can you tell me your name?"

"Gwen."

"Do you know what day it is? Do you know where you are?"

Gwen points to the bowl I'm holding and then she throws up nasty brown liquid that smells rancid and sour, like the back alley of a bar. It splashes onto my pants, the collar of my shirt. She heaves two more times and I hold back her hair, use my sleeve to wipe her cheek. "Get a towel, now," I say to Dylan. "A wet one."

"Gross," Dylan says as he moves toward the kitchen.

Gwen closes her eyes and moans before answering Cathy. "It's Thursday and I'm at Dylan's house." Her eyes roll up as she looks at me. "It's still Thursday, right?"

"No," I say. "It's actually Friday morning. It's two A.M."

Cathy puts the ends of the stethoscope in her ears and then bends toward Gwen. She listens to her chest, asks her to breathe in and out. "Deep breaths . . . deeper," she says. When she's finished, she stands and looks down at me. "It's good she threw up. It would be best if we take her in for IVs and hydration, test to see if there's anything else in her system."

Dylan reappears with a dirty dishcloth and a wet paper towel. His face is twisted and sad; I swear he wipes away tears. "Here, Mrs. Morrison."

Cathy now turns her attention to Dylan while the other paramedic steps away to answer his squawking phone. "Did you give her the alcohol?" she asks. "Do you know what she ingested?"

"No way. No." Dylan holds up his hands. "She just showed up like this."

I wipe Gwen's face with the wet towel and twist her hair behind her head. "Did you take anything else?" I ask in a whisper. "Or only the whiskey?"

"It was just the Daniel's." She bends over again, another heave racking her chest. Tears pour down her face, but she doesn't move to wipe them away this time.

"The Daniel's?" I look at Dylan.

"Jack . . . Jack Daniel's," he says. "That's what I think she means."

"That's what I mean," Gwen says, so quietly that only I hear her.

"She hasn't had anything but whiskey," I say to Cathy. "There's no need to take her to the hospital. I'm with her now. . . ."

Cathy stands up and her partner motions that they need to leave, "There's a call two blocks over." They rush out of the house, leaving the front door open.

"We need to go home," I say to Gwen. "Can you stand up?"

She nods, and yet when she stands, she stumbles forward, her shin slamming into the corner of the coffee table. She cries out with a mewling sound, swaying toward me. I grab her shoulder to steady her, wrap my arm around her waist.

The bowl, the porcelain mixing bowl that saved Dylan's mother's couch, sits on the same coffee table. Dylan points at it. "You have to clean that up. . . . I can't."

Gwen lurches forward as if she's going to grab the bowl; I stop her. "I've got it," I say.

She sits in the wing-back chair to the left of the couch and drops her face into her hands. "The room . . . it's upside down, inside out . . . something," she says.

"Sit with her for a minute, Dylan." I pick up the bowl and take it into the bathroom to dump out the bile, the remains of a terrible night. Then I rinse the bowl in the kitchen sink, throw away the towels. My stomach rolls with sickening nausea and I wash my hands twice before returning to the living room, but the smell comes with me, stuck to my shirt. I stop to stare at Dylan and Gwen. She's bent over with her head on his shoulder and he is petting her back like she's a dog. "It's okay. It's okay. It's okay." He's repeating this mantra over and over, as if these are the only words he knows.

"Let's go," I say as I reach their side. I take the porcelain bowl with us — just in case.

Gwen is awake for the twenty-minute car ride, but she doesn't say a word. By the time we pull into our driveway, she needs the bowl again. And I still don't say a word. In some ancient ritual, I find myself making the soothing sounds I'd once used when she was a baby, when her colicky cries echoed through the house, unabated by any effort on my part.

"I'm sorry," she says. "I'm so, so sorry." Her words are put together in a slushy string of apology.

I hug her small body. "I know."

I tuck my drunk daughter into bed and place a cold washcloth on her face. "I'm going to get you some coconut water and ice," I say. "It will help."

She holds up her hand. "Don't tell Dad," she mumbles. "Don't. He'll kill me."

"Not right now. Not yet . . ."

"He's going to kill me." She buries her face in the pillow. "Dead."

I hold her tighter, closer, then even tighter.

All the talking will come later because, thank God, it can come later. There's a difference in what seems to matter and what *really* matters, what loss can be tolerated and what cannot be. I hold what matters, what I cannot lose.

I sleep late, the fatigue like concrete in my veins. Gwen sleeps later. It's four in the afternoon by the time she gets out of bed. And she looks terrible. Her eyes are swollen and her face pale, almost yellow. I've spent the day cleaning the kitchen, making chicken soup, checking on Gwen every thirty minutes to watch her sleep, to listen to her breathe in and out, in and out. She comes straight to me at the stove, where I'm lifting the tea kettle from the flame. Her left cheek is marked with the wrinkled impression of her pillow. "Mom." Her voice cracks as it rises from her parched throat.

I turn to hug her and then pour the boiling water into a mug. "Here, baby." I hand her a cup of chamomile tea. "And I made soup."

She sits on the stool at the island and drops her face into her hands. "This is the worst I've ever felt. I'm so . . . stupid."

I go to her and from behind I wrap my arms around her, drop my chin onto her head. "Let me get a couple Advil for you."

"I'm grounded forever, aren't I?"

"Can we save that discussion for later?" I hug her one more time before opening the cabinet for the medicine. "But we do need to talk, Pea. You've got to talk to me. You can't do these things, or something terrible will finally happen."

"You'll lecture me. Ground me. You don't get it. . . ."

"What don't I get?"

"How awful it all feels."

"Why wouldn't I get that?"

"Because to you, everything is just perfectly perfect." She twists in her seat and looks over her shoulder at me.

"Really? Perfectly perfect?" I ask, setting two Advil in front of her. "That's not true. I want to hear from you what is so awful that you can't tell me."

"Everything. I can't tell you that I almost slept with Dylan and then he broke up with me. I can't tell you that I don't believe Dad. I can't tell you that I want to get stoned so I won't feel so bad. I can't tell you how much I hate you for being so stupid."

I want to know what "almost slept with Dylan" means, but her last words come with such great force, they take my breath away. *I hate you.*

"You hate me?" I stand next to her, touch her face.

"God, I don't know what I'm saying." She buries her face into my shoulder. "I — I don't — hate you," she stutters between breaths. "I just . . . There's so much happening and nothing makes sense. I'm sorry. I'm sorry."

When her tears stop, I hug her again before giving her a bowl of soup. "Try to eat, sweetie. It'll help."

She takes a few sips and looks up to me. "Did you ever do anything wrong, Mom? I mean, get in trouble with your parents?"

"Of course I did. I was anything but perfect." There it is. That word again.

"Did you ever do anything terrible like I just did? I mean . . . really terrible?"

"Gwen, we have to talk through a lot of things — you and I — about boys and love and depression and sadness. But what you did was not terrible. You're not terrible."

She opens her mouth to say something, but we both hear it at the same time; the garage door's gnarled sound. "Dad," she says.

"Sounds like it."

"Don't tell him," she begs, her voice pleading and desperate.

Cooper walks through the back door, and it's clear that I don't have to tell him. His mouth is drawn downward and his lips are thin, white. His brows are drawn so tightly together that the wrinkles above his nose are etched deeply into a V of anger. He knows.

"Dad." Gwen says this in a quiet voice.

"Is there something you two want to tell me?" he asks.

"We had a bad night," I say, trying for understatement, for something resembling equilibrium. "But she's okay." I touch the top of Gwen's head to feel the warmth of her life.

"Thank God," he says, and moves toward Gwen. The air shimmers between them, and I realize that I'm holding my breath. Then all at once, Cooper swoops in and holds his daughter like the child she is. "Oh Gwen." Cooper is crying. Gwen is crying. I thought I didn't have any tears left, but I'm crying, too.

This goes on for a while and the moment is heartbreaking and wet. It's Gwen who looks up first. "Dad." She attempts a smile. "I've got snot all over your shirt."

"And mascara," I add. "Don't forget the mascara."

Cooper smiles a little, but it's strained and I can see him coming back to himself. "Why did I need to hear about this from my assistant, who found it out from her paramedic boyfriend? Why didn't you call me?" He speaks slowly, as if studying each word before setting it down in his voice.

"It wasn't something to discuss on the phone."

"Well, it's something to discuss now." He walks to the sink to wash his hands, splash cold water on his face.

"Okay," I say. "Okay. We can talk, but let Gwen eat first."

We stand there in the kitchen — a family, quiet and still, as if waiting for permission to talk.

Cooper unpacks his suitcase, throwing the dirty clothes into the hamper and putting the things for the dry cleaner's in a separate basket. Gwen is shut in her room, taking a shower, she says. Cooper tosses his Dopp kit onto the bathroom counter next to his sink and stares into the mirror before brushing his teeth and then sitting on the edge of the Jacuzzi tub. "Okay. Tell me what the hell happened."

"We went out last night," I begin.

"Who is 'we'?"

"Me, Willa, Max, and Francie. It was a celebration of Ford's five-year anniversary and he included us. Anyway, we walked down to say hello to Gwen at work and . . ."

"What did Willa do?" His voice is tight, raspy.

"It was me, Cooper. This was my fault."

"How?"

"I saw a necklace and it was the same one that woman, Mary Jo, wore. I was mortified that maybe she had gone to see Gwen at work."

"Seriously? You're getting paranoid, my love. Way paranoid. And now it's affecting our daughter."

I swallow the guilt; it tastes sour and biting. "And then after Gwen got off work, she went after her old boyfriend and guzzled some whiskey. She was sick. She was really sick." The truth of the night, the boldest truth, comes near me then, and so does the fear. A sob rips from the back of my throat and I drop my face into my hands, speaking through the cracks of my fingers. "I think I scared her."

Cooper comes to me and wraps his arms around me. "This is not your fault. Gwen has been on a downward spiral for a while."

His response — it's like expecting the lightning after the thunder and not seeing it. I'm stunned that Cooper hasn't lost his temper. This kindness, unexpected and needed, allows me to cry.

"Shhhh," he murmurs.

"It's been so hard, and I know it's been hard for you, too. I'm sorry. It's all too much, and I don't know what to think or believe, and I made myself and then Gwen crazy."

Cooper sits again and pats the edge of the tub for me to join him. He takes my hand and wipes at my face gently. "I love you. I love Gwen. This family is more important to me than anything else in the world. I would not do anything to harm us. Ever."

"I know" is all I manage to say.

"What are we going to do about Gwen now, though? There has to be some consequence," he says.

"She's talking to me now. And I think she needs a therapist or a professional."

Cooper holds up his hand. "No."

"No?" I'm stunned.

"That's too much. She doesn't need that kind of help. Our family doesn't need a psychiatrist."

"How do you know? I mean, if she's drinking enough to . . ."

"That's what teenagers do."

"That's not what I did."

"You're the exception." He leans in to kiss me. "She's grounded, of course. She needs to go to work with you every day until school starts back up. Find something to keep her busy other than just her job. She's either at home with us or at work with you."

I can only stare up at him. I don't know what to say.

"You agree, right?"

In the bedroom, the phone rings, and we glance at it as if someone has entered the bathroom. Neither of us moves to answer it. Then Cooper asks again, "Right? You agree?"

"I need to think about it, Coop. I've been a mess all night; I'm not sure what I think."

"Mom?" Gwen's voice calls from the hall. "Max is on the house phone. He says he needs to talk to you real quick."

Cooper turns away from me with a noise that is somewhere between a grunt and a groan. I pick up the extension in the bedroom. "Hey, Eve. Hope I'm not disturbing anything, but I need a huge favor."

"Sure."

"My Saturday class tomorrow. Can you teach it? I know you can do it in your sleep. I have to drive to Atlanta to see my brother. Long story, but it's important."

"Sure thing. I've got it."

"Thanks."

"Is everything okay?" I ask.

"Yes, and I'll be back by Saturday night. Promise."

"No problem."

I hang up and I turn to Cooper, who is standing directly in front of me, his face hard and closed. "What was that about?"

"Max needs me to teach that letterpress class tomorrow at SCAD. No big deal."

" 'No big deal'? You'll be gone again all day. What about Gwen? I think right now we need to focus on her, not work."

"Aren't you off tomorrow?"

He stares at me for so long that I think maybe I haven't spoken out loud, merely thought the words. He says nothing, just walks away, leaving me alone.

It's dark now. Night came quickly to a quiet house where Cooper and I have been watching a baseball game I don't care about at all. A hurricane swirls in my chest and stomach. Finally, I go up to Gwen's room, where I find her sitting on the bed with her laptop open. The pale light falls on her face, a spotlight. She looks up. "Hey. I know, I shouldn't be back in bed. I know, but . . ."

"Did you finish the soup?"

She nods. "I feel . . . better."

"We'll keep talking, Gwen, but tomorrow you'll be hanging out with me, okay? I have to teach a class at SCAD and you'll go with me."

"Okay." She leans back into her pillow. "Dylan must hate me even more than he did before. I made such a fool of myself." She presses her fingers into the corners of her eyes. "Such an idiot."

I don't know what to say to my daughter now. There's never a class on what to expect when your daughter gets drunk enough to puke. I make a feeble attempt. "You are *not* an idiot. We all make mistakes."

"I seem to be really good at it lately," she says.

"Yeah, well, this is one subject I'd rather you didn't get an A." I kiss her forehead, wipe back her hair. "Good night, sweetheart."

I turn off her light and shut the door. The hallway is dark and I run my hand down its wallpapered surface, my fingers lightly feathering against the print of roses and urns. Our master bedroom is dark and the ceiling fan whirs on high. In the bathroom, I perform my nightly routine, teeth, face, lotion, and pj's — drawstring pants and a tank top — and crawl into bed. Cooper has come upstairs and is already in bed. His back is to me and I move toward him, curling around him like a shrimp in water, rounded and soft.

His body tenses and I reach up to rub my hand through his hair. "I'm taking Gwen to SCAD with me tomorrow."

He makes a noise, something that sounds like approval, and turns to me, wrapping his leg over mine. I kiss him, but my throat clenches. I feel an awful need to pull away.

I've heard it said that the heart wants what it wants. But there's a counterpart to this: The body wants what it wants, and it doesn't want this. It wants to pull away, to run, to flee. I fight its urges and fold myself around my husband. His hands run across my back and slide my pj bottoms down. I slip one leg out of the cotton pants and I close my eyes as he moves into me, as we move together.

He shudders and whispers, "I love you, Eve. So much." And then he's done.

My tank top is still on, and I slip my one free leg back into my pants. I sidle to the edge of the bed and place my feet on the floor, feeling his warmth slide down my thigh. Soup rises in the back of my throat and I run to the bathroom.

What destroyed my desire for him? For his touch? My chest crushes under the panic.

What the hell is wrong with me?

We made love after Cooper had approved of my choice to take Gwen, after I did exactly what he wanted. And it was just this — the lack of partnership — that killed desire. He's kind when he approves, distant and unkind when he doesn't. And it's this, this not knowing *which* Cooper I'll be getting at any given moment, that's killing us.

I want to go back and find the place where the change started, where our relationship went from crush to boyfriend to lover to boss figure who offered praise and warmth.

I want to go back and yet I know we can't.

I can be the perfect hostess. I can smile and support him and say all the right things. I can be there for the speeches and the family functions. I can keep a perfect house. Damn, I can even close the studio. The Fine Line, Ink if that's what it would take. But what it would take to make my body cling to his, or even want his . . . I don't know.

Who am I without Cooper? Who am I *at all* without a family? Hi, I'm Eve. I'm married, one daughter, one sister, and a letterpress company.

Without a marriage, I would become someone else completely — someone smaller and free-floating. Not part of a family at all.

When my dad threatened to kick me out and then later when he'd quit talking to me because I wouldn't go to the Bible college that had given me a scholarship, it was like small pieces of me were floating off into space. In those days, I came back to myself slowly, waking each day a bit more intact. So yes, I know what it feels like *not* to be part of the family, to be separate, and I'm sure I can't bear it again.

Without our family, who will we be? Who will I be? This is what matters.

Something has to be done.

I slip quietly downstairs and take from my bag the envelope the anonymous someone has sent me this time. In the dim kitchen, I see the disfiguration of idea number one: *Be Kind.* The large oak tree, its arms reaching high, have been colored on with a dark marker, a slicing through the trunk. I open the card, and once again nothing is signed; no words are written, but one sheet of paper falls out: a bank statement for *Southern Tastes,* LLC.

TWENTY

It's Saturday, and Gwen and I are at SCAD's Poetter Hall. I'm setting up to teach a class in the place where I'd once wanted to take a class, wanted it with all my heart.

Every hall or building owned by SCAD was once something else. In the 1880s, this was the National Guard Armory. Before that, it was the site of the Savannah Female Orphyn Asylum. The asylum is a rich part of Savannah's history, an institution once run by the city's "female elite." In a patriarchal age and city, the affluent women did what they could, and what they could do was be fully in charge of the orphaned children here. I imagine those girls, young ones submitting to a strict regimen of twice-a-day worship services and, if needed, a whip. This was a place where girls were trained for "useful and respectable employment" — so maybe things haven't changed so much. But if they could look down, those ghost girls from a hundred years ago, and see the students now, some bleary-eyed and hungover, in their torn jeans and printed T-shirts, playing with iPhones, what would they think?

Gwen is sitting at a desk, reading a novel, completely engrossed in someone else's story. I take the chalk and fill the blackboard with my handwriting — definitions for the simple terms we'll discuss today: font, kerning, leading, polymer plates, case, typeset, and more. I then place a booklet, one Max made to teach the class, on every desk.

One by one, the students settle into their seats. A boy with dreadlocks sits in the front row, alert and ready; two young girls (either best friends or sisters) huddle next to each another, a pile of letterpress books between them; a middle-aged woman arrives, nervous and fingering the buttons on her cardigan. It's a diverse group, but almost everyone seems to arrive with white cups wrapped in brown cardboard. And everyone seems to be checking their cell phones.

"Hi." I smile at the group. "I'm Eve Morrison, and we're in for a really fun day. I know you expected Max, but I'm your sub. So pretend it's middle school and you *want* a substitute teacher."

The students laugh lightly. Gwen rolls her eyes and shakes her head.

I continue. "So Max and I work together at a company called the Fine Line, Ink, where we specialize in letterpress. Our focus is on card lines and invitations, but we also do branding and logos."

A girl on the right, her hair a mash of dark brown curls, raises her hand but speaks before I acknowledge her. "So, so cool. I totally bought my mom a birthday card that y'all made. The one with the balloon . . ."

"Yes," I say. "That's one of ours. And I have some other samples up here when we're ready to use the presses this afternoon." I launch into my speech, the one I give every few months when I sub for Max. I end with my favorite quote: "Typography is to text what voice is to singing."

The boy with the dreadlocks raises his hand. "Really, how long till we use the press?"

That's always the first question. The students don't come here to learn about the letterpress process; they come here to *use* the press. I get it. "Soon," I reassure him. "You have to know a few of the basics before you can use it. Okay?" He's impatient, as they all are. I get that, too.

I open a box and spread cards and invitations, posters, and postcards on top of a long table. "These are examples of letterpress done by my company and by past students. We use three different machines in our shop — The Vandercook cylinder press, the Chandler & Price platen press, and, my favorite, the Heidelberg, which is the most versatile. This up here" — I motion to the machine at the front of the room — "is an Excelsior, a tabletop press we use for teaching."

The student leans forward and I hold up both carved-wood and cut-metal fonts and offer a history. "These are fonts. This is one of my favorites," I say, holding up a placard with the Elegy font. "It was crafted based on only three hand-drawn letters."

A young girl, sitting in the back row, raises her hand and blurts out, "That's my favorite, too, but it's hard to read sometimes. I mean, if it's too squashed up or something." She looks down, hiding from her own proclamations.

"You're right," I say. "Which brings me to this point: Communication is the first thing you need to think about when choosing a font. Some fonts are for illustration, some for communication, and some for design. If you can choose what story you're trying to tell, finding the right typeface will be a whole lot easier." I motion to them. "Come on up here and you can look at the examples."

Chairs scrape across the hardwood floor and the students walk to the front. I'm here with the students and yet underneath the day there is the low-level hum of anxiety and worry about my family, as if I have my own weather system under my ribs. The boy with the dreadlocks picks up a card and rolls his finger across its edges. "This is my favorite," he says.

"Good taste," I tell him.

"Really?" He looks up, happy, like students can be, to know he's just pleased the teacher.

"Yes, really. It's part of a full line of cards called Ten Good Ideas."

The older woman lifts a card with a misspelling — a book signing called a "book singing."

"What do you do when it gets messed up like this? I mean, it's all pressed into the paper."

"We try to make sure that doesn't happen. But if we do mess up in the beginning phases — and who doesn't? — we use something called blackout or black patch."

"Which is?"

"When we place a special tape over the

error and mask an area, leaving a window into which another element can be stripped."

"I'm not sure I understand. Can you explain?" The middle-aged woman — her name is Donna — asks that question.

"Well, I'll give you an example. Last month, we did a wedding invitation, but I messed it up and put the information from another wedding onto the prototype layout. The client was on her way."

"And?" Donna asks, leaning forward.

"I had to do something fast, so I covered the original information. I put tape on the prototype plate and repressed the typecast. She never knew. The final copy was perfect."

I glance up when I've finished explaining and catch Gwen's gaze. Her finger holds a place halfway through her book. Her eyes are wide and knowing, as if I've spoken some secret, opened a magic door. Her face is young and smooth, calm with understanding. We move through the rest of the session, which includes pressing the platen over cotton paper. I help students design their own cards until the time is up.

When the class is over and everyone has filed out, I pick up the cards and my leather books. Evening light — my favorite — waves across the hardwood floors like water, an outgoing tide. I gather my things, click off the light, and lock the door. The hallway echoes with our footsteps.

Outside, the gas lamps flicker into the dusk, glad to take over from the sunlight that has outdone them all day. The brick sidewalks, cracked and crooked, unroll along the side of the road. Live oaks, holding their arms above the street like a protective demigod of tiny coarse green leaves, shadow our slow drive through the Savannah streets.

"Were you bored out of your mind?" I ask Gwen, who is quiet and still next to me.

"No. I actually liked it."

"What? The part where the guy in the back row flirted with you?"

"He was not," she says, but she laughs. "He didn't understand the difference between a platen press and a rotary press, and I needed to explain it to him."

"Explain it, I'm sure."

"Whatever, Mom. Plus, I learned something new." She plays with the automatic window and then she says, "Blackout."

While Alison Krauss sings "Dimming of the Day," music floats up into the studio rafters with Saturday's quiet ending. I wanted to pick up a few loose ends before dinner, and

Gwen came with me. I like to think that she wants to be here, that this isn't just a condition of her "parole," as she calls it. Then again, I like to think a lot of things.

I'm scrolling through my e-mail and she's looking through the latest designs. She lifts number nine: *Forgive.* "You don't have this design yet?"

"Nope," I say.

"What about a heart here? That would be good for someone to send when they want to make up with someone or fix things." She smiles at me a little shyly before continuing. "I don't mean like a Valentine red heart, but something artsy like Francie draws, something with messy edges and . . ." Gwen closes her eyes. "I can see it."

"Here." I hand her a pad of thick cotton paper and a set of colored pencils.

She yanks her ponytail tighter. The small feather peeks out, wavering against her skin. She absently reaches back to touch it, as if she can feel the quill landing gracefully on the arch of her neck. Gwen is left-handed, like my mother once was, and I watch her fingers grip tightly as she moves the pencil across the page, at first lightly and then pressing harder. Her sketch appears from hand and imagination. I sit back and let time slip away without my clocking of it, without giving notice to its existence at all.

I'm not sure how late it is when we hear the crunch of tires on gravel and Max and Willa enter the studio. "Hey," Willa calls out, and comes to us, hugging Gwen first. "What are y'all doing?"

I wave my hand in the air, run it over the table. "Working. And you" — I point to Max — "I thought you were out of town."

"I was. Just got back, and Willa needed a ride to the grocery store."

"God, I hope they let me drive soon," she says.

Max glances at the table. "The heart. Did you do that, Gwen?"

She nods.

"That's really good. It looks like an Ed Hardy tattoo."

She laughs fully. "Tattoo. That's a bad word around here." She feigns a whisper.

Max makes a cute face, somewhere between embarrassed and entertained. "Sorry."

"But thanks. I'm glad you like it." Her smile is wider than I've seen in months.

Gwen yawns, stretches. "Mom, do you mind if I go back to the house? Dad just texted that he's home."

"Go on. I'll be there in a few minutes."

"I'm gone, too." Willa turns to Max.

"Thanks. I owe you."

The silence, which isn't quiet at all, settles between Max and me. Gravel crunches. A horn honks far off. A crow screeches, its call irritating and high-pitched. He sits with me at the table. "So how did class go?"

"It was great. I always sort of dread doing it and then it all works out great, you know? It's nice to talk about the basics again. Always a good reminder."

"You know," Max says, "I think that after a few more sessions at SCAD, we'll be able to hold our classes here."

"Cut out the middleman," I say. "I like it."

"Or in this case," Max says "the middle school."

I roll my eyes. "Yeah, okay, smarty pants."

"This will be great visibility for us, Eve."

"I agree. We'll be able to grow our customer base with our student base. And maybe we could put in a sort of gift shop — a kiosk or something to sell the cards."

"I like the way you think, boss."

We talk this way for a while, back and forth about our grand plans; then we dial it down a little and talk about work and due dates and which machines need repair. That's when Max smiles, shakes his head at me.

"What?" I ask.

"Even when you're sitting here with your hands all prim and folded in your lap, serious and focused, I can see that there is a big laugh in the back of your throat ready to break out at any second. I'm always trying to find a way to get it out of you."

I laugh loudly.

"There, like that." He touches my arm and then pulls back.

"Not much to laugh about lately."

I stare at him and that kiss comes back to me in a rush. It unravels something in me. I turn away. Wanting him isn't just wrong but unethical, ridiculous, and needy, too. A cliché. "I gotta go."

I leave him sitting there at the table. What else am I to do?

Walking back up the pathway, I find myself on Willa's front porch, knocking. She doesn't answer, so I knock again then hear the shuffle of feet, the click of an opening lock, and then she is standing there in her robe, her wet hair dripping onto hardwood floors. "Hey." She smiles. "You should have just come in. I was in the shower."

"Did you and Max have fun today?" I'm surprised by how harsh I sound.

Her face closes in, and she walks away from me toward the kitchen. I follow her in silence as she puts a teakettle on the stove, pulls down two cups, and opens a box of chamomile tea bags. "What's wrong with you, Eve?"

"What?" I settle back onto the counter, my hands behind me, grasping the granite edge.

She turns to me, her face clean and wiped fresh, like the sky after a storm. Her green, green eyes, the ones I'd always wanted as a child, bore into me, hot. "What is wrong with you? I mean, don't you know what you have?"

Tears spring up. "I know. I know. It's like there's something bro—"

"Don't you dare say 'broken.' That's not what I mean at all."

"Sorry . . ."

"You can't see what's in front of you. You can't. I'm the one who's supposed to be having problems seeing the truth, and here you stand, and you can't see what's right in front of you."

"And what, exactly, is that?"

"You have it all, Eve. And you're scared to death of not having anything."

" 'Have it all'?"

"Your work. A beautiful daughter who loves you and doesn't want to disappoint you. A good man in love with you. These are the things we all want, and you stand there, scared to see anything at all."

"I know what I have. I know Cooper is a good man."

"Not Cooper."

"What are you talking about?" I ask. But I know.

"Max. That's what I'm talking about. He's in love with you, Eve. I've been hit in the head, but even I can see that." She rolls her eyes. "God only knows how long he has been, but he's got it bad."

"That's not true," I say. "It's not like that. It's our work."

"Yes, it *is* like that. You don't think I'd want him to look at me the way he looks at you? Don't you think I'd want him to talk to me with that soft voice? He's gone."

I turn away. "Stop."

"And Cooper. You believe his shit. I don't get it."

"What shit?" I bite down hard on the last word just as the teakettle whistles. I jump, knock a mug to the floor, where it shatters. I turn on Willa. "Believe his story? Yes, I do. This situation, Willa, it's nothing new. You said you wanted to get your life together, but really? And your dreams. Should I just tell Cooper that he's a liar because you had a weird dream about a dead man? Because you'd heard a woman's screechy voice before?" I take in a long breath and kick at the remaining pieces of mug on the floor. "Should I break apart an entire family because you can't remember a night when my husband had to take you home?"

She stares at me. "Yes."

"What?"

"Open your eyes."

"I don't understand why you're being so mean." My throat clenches around tears I won't shed now. Not here.

"I'm not being mean. I know that you and Cooper gave me a place to live and you've helped me through this hell. And I will be forever grateful. I will." She turns off the gas stove and then takes a step closer. "I love you, Eve. I'm not being mean."

"You're wrong — about Cooper, about Max. It's not like . . . that."

"Just because you don't want something to be 'like that' doesn't mean it isn't. I know my emotions are all over the place and that something weird happened in my hippopotamus or whatever the hell it's called. I know that these images and songs and dreams are all mixed up in my head." She hollers the next sentence. "I know all of that."

I don't move.

"But," she says, "I also know when a man is lying and when a man is in love. So you might know the facts, but I know the truth."

My sister walks away from me and I'm left to marvel at the role reversal that has just taken place. The earth moves. It shifts. It alters completely.

I was nineteen years old and Max and I were surviving on ramen noodles, caffeine, and cheap boxed wine. We worked through the night on printing projects and laughed about things that were deeply funny then and completely forgettable now. There was only one night when we ended up alone at the studio. We worked until 3:00 A.M. and then collapsed onto the white faux-leather couch, which was covered in greasy spots and ink-stained fingerprints.

"This is a crazy way to live." I flopped down on the pillows.

"I know," he said. "But I guess we could quit anytime."

"I can't."

"Obsession is a terrible thing." He leaned back into the couch, closed his eyes.

"Not in this case," I said as we reclined quietly on opposite sides of the couch, exhausted. Finally, I spoke up. "I'm hungry."

"Let's go get something to eat, then."

"What's open at three A.M.?" I asked.

He smiled, propped himself up on one elbow. "My apartment."

I looked at Max and that smile of his. I saw it all: his messy hair, the two-day stubble and crooked grin, the blue-ringed eyes. And I felt something beneath my ribs, a wanting I'd never felt before. It was something different from merely wanting to touch him. It was different from my adolescent obsession with Caden. It was different from the nervous need with Cooper. It was an open feeling, like water running.

Max slid across the couch and touched my face, his palm on my cheek. Between us, invisibly, stood Cooper and also Max's live-in girlfriend, Amanda. Cooper and I had been dating for a year by then, and I knew where we were headed. We'd talked about marriage, about family and future. But there I was with Max. I leaned into his palm, closed my eyes. I felt his lips then, on my forehead first. I moved closer and crawled into his lap, my legs wrapped around his waist, my head resting on his shoulder. His hand moved to the back of my neck, pulling me closer, tighter. It was my decision, and even in the exhaustion and confusion, I knew it was. I could lift my

349

head from his shoulder for a kiss or stay tightly where we were and let the moment pass away, fall asleep even.

I chose the kiss. And so did he.

It was dark, so dark, in that room with a single window and a moonless night. What happened unfolded like a slow-motion dream, untethered from real life, high above us. It was in that moment that all we needed to say, all that wouldn't and couldn't he spoken, found its expression in our bodies. There was the languid way he removed my T-shirt and how my shorts slid to the floor, the path my hands took under his shirt and then to undo his worn leather belt. Our kisses moved along skin that was warm from the long night of work and the stifling room. We were one in every movement, with every shift of our bodies.

There was nothing else in the world but to make love to him. My body would come undone, disintegrate, if I didn't. A connection between us, something that had tied us together from the moment we met, was finally able to be expressed in something other than words and laughter.

Eventually, we fell asleep, an old cotton drop cloth covering our bodies. As I slipped into sleep, I understood that Max and I would find a way to be together, that we'd both been avoiding the inevitable even as each of us was committed to someone else. I'd never before felt so at peace — ever.

We were awakened by the buzz of the front door alarm as the owner arrived for the morning's opening. We stretched and dressed quickly, tripping over equipment and boxes, over our own feet. We laughed and zipped and smiled when the owner entered the back room. We greeted him as if nothing but work had ever happened in that tiny room.

And later, when we stood outside in the harsh sunlight, our separate car keys in our hands, our separate lives waiting, Max pulled me close and the panic came, something hidden far below the surface of the night's peace. What had I done? I was on the brink of having the life I'd always wanted — Cooper, safety, a house, a home, a normal family. I backed away from Max, from his hand reaching for me.

"Eve," he said, "are you okay?"

"I don't think so. Are you?"

"Yes, I am." He took my hand, kissed the inside of my palm

"I can't do this. I'll ruin everything. . . ." I pulled my hand from his. I know he had more to say; I heard his voice as I ran toward my car, toward the life already set in motion.

I married Cooper. Max lived with Amanda for another few years. Then we worked together again: nothing more, nothing less. Not once have we mentioned that night.

TWENTY-ONE

I've never been in a therapist's office before and I don't know what to do. "Where should we sit?" I ask.

"Wherever you're comfortable." Dr. Parker is a petite blonde with horn-rimmed glasses. She smiled as she answered my question, but nothing can undo the tight knot of nervousness under my breastbone.

Gwen and I sit together on the love seat, each of us scooted close to the armrests, a lavender throw pillow between us. The therapist sits in a chair, a yellow pad on her lap. "It's nice to meet both of you, so please tell me what brings you here. What are your concerns?"

Gwen shrugs, so I speak first. "Gwen had a bad incident with drinking. I'm scared. Something's going on. What should I call it . . . some sort of issue? Some sort of hurt? We need help."

Dr. Parker looks at Gwen. "And what do

you think?"

"I think I did something stupid. That's all. Nothing big that should bring me here." Gwen twists at the fringe on the throw pillow, glances around the office.

"You don't agree with your mom that maybe the drinking episode came from an 'issue,' as she called it."

"Whatever."

That's my daughter.

"So." Dr. Parker looks at me. "What do you believe is the hurt that spurred this?"

"My sister and my husband — her dad — were both injured in a car wreck. My sister, Willa, and Gwen are very close and Willa lives in a cottage on our property. This has been really hard for us. Gwen's boyfriend broke up with her, and her dad and I aren't getting along the best we ever have. And I think" — I take Gwen's hand and speak to her — "you are hurting more than I can help. I didn't bring you here because I think something is wrong with you; I brought you here because I want to help."

"Dad is gonna be so pissed," Gwen says in a hard voice.

"And why is that?" Dr. Parker asks.

"I heard him tell mom not to take me to a therapist."

"Well, here we are," I say. "So let's see if

we can talk about things."

"Like . . . Aunt Willa told me that she's going to move out."

A sinking feeling comes over me; a helpless jolt of electric knowledge. "What?" I ask.

"You have to talk her out of it, Mom."

"We're here to talk about you, about us." I lean forward to place my hand on Gwen's knee, but she pulls back.

"Eve," Dr. Parker says. "Why don't you let Gwen and me talk for a while and I'll come get you in a few minutes."

"Yes."

The waiting room is bland enough to be forgettable. Black-and-white photos of flowers and water and bridges and stones hang on a cream-colored wall. The furniture is taupe — maybe winter wheat, or just plain old beige. Unread magazines are scattered across a chrome coffee table and I shudder once again with the thought that maybe this is a terrible idea. But I don't have another.

I flip through a year-old *Simple Living* magazine and don't see a photo or read a word. I wait. Gwen comes out, and her eyes are puffy. "Are you okay?" I ask.

"I'm fine." Her voice is soft, a whisper almost.

Dr. Parker hands me a slip of paper.

355

"Gwen and I have made an appointment for Friday."

"Do you need to talk to me?" I ask.

Dr. Parker smiles, a practiced effort, I'm sure. "Let's let this be Gwen's session for now, and we can talk next week?"

The drive home is heavy, like humidity. "How did it go?" I finally ask.

"Fine, Mom."

"I'm glad you're going back."

Gwen twists away from me to look out the car window, dragging her finger along its edge. "Yeah, I think maybe it's good." She pauses before taking in a long breath. "Mom?"

"Yes?"

"I'm sorry this is so much trouble. I'm sorry I'm such a mess. I'm just sorry."

"No." I choke on the word. "Do *not* be sorry."

"Okay."

"I love you."

"I know."

Tuesday night and the Bohemian is crowded. People are three deep at the bar. The summer heat presses against the windows and only the most scantily clad girls are on the deck overlooking the river, trying to catch a breeze that doesn't exist. Beers turn warm in the glass mugs.

Cooper talked me into meeting with a group of old friends: the Williamses, the Clayburns, and the Marshalls. "Let's get back to normal," he said. Whatever that is. We're seated at a round table in a corner booth, private. I scoot to the inside to settle into the seat, glad to be out with friends. A glass of Malbec sits in front of me and conversation spills from every corner of the restaurant.

Friendships are born in different moments for different reasons, and these four families — the eight of us — had met when all our kids were in preschool. The women, Clara, Starla, and Baylor, have been friends of mine since Gwen was born. I haven't seen them in months, and it's nice to feel settled, part of a life Cooper and I have been building for years now — all these years of making something real. I reach over and take his hand; he smiles at me and then kisses me.

"Get a room," Starla says, laughing.

Baylor joins in, raising her glass in a toast. "Here's to long-lasting friendships and marriages."

"Seriously," Clara says. "I think the eight of us are the only ones who have made it from that original preschool class." She settles back. "Remember those days? I have never been so tired in all my life."

"That Barney cake we made for Gwen's birthday? Do you remember that?" I ask. "It took us three tries and it tasted like burned flour. I had purple fingers for days from that disgusting frosting."

"God, yes." Baylor groans. "And the playgrounds with the mean moms. And getting up at five A.M. to wait in line for the just-right preschool-class registration. The hours spent singing Disney movie songs in the car."

"Sometimes," Starla says, "I wake up singing the *Arthur* theme song. But I don't know how I would have made it without this group. Why has it been so long since we've gotten together?"

"Busy lives," Cooper replies.

The men, Brad, Taylor, and Cliff, nod. "Damn," Brad says, "I've been in town two days this month."

"Well, I'm not that busy." Carla pokes at her husband. "Except for keeping everything afloat while he gallivants around the country."

"Yeah, if you can call begging for business gallivanting," Brad says.

I laugh. "That was one of my mom's favorite words," I say. " 'Don't *gallivant.*'

What does it even mean?"

The conversations overlap; we order our meals and then, as we're being served, a silence falls over the clink of dueling forks and knives. Cooper is wearing a bandage tonight — although it's no longer needed — to cover his puckered scar.

Lifting her wineglass, Starla leans forward. She teaches yoga downtown and has four thriving kids, the kind you brag about. It would be easy to hate her, but she's as funny as the best stand-up comic. This time, though, she's serious. "Eve, I heard about Gwen's overdose. God, I am so sorry. Our kids, they just kill us, don't they?"

"Overdose?" My fork flips in my hand, clattering to the floor.

Starla looks to her husband, Taylor. "That's what you said."

"That's what Mary Jo told me." He shrugs and takes a long swig of his wine.

"She didn't OD," I say. "She drank too much and . . . I had to go pick her up. It was awful and scary." I smile at Starla because I know she meant no harm.

Baylor, who sits next to me, takes my hand. "We had to send Rusty to a rehab place this summer. After his knee surgery, he couldn't get off the Oxycontin, and it's been terrible."

"I swear," Carla says, "sometimes pre-school feels like the golden days."

Something niggles at me, something in the jumbled conversation, in the tense feeling of Cooper next to me, like a muscle cramp.

That's what Mary Jo told me.

"Taylor." I lean forward with a false calm. "Who's Mary Jo?"

"Our accountant. She does work for all of us." He waves his hand around the table.

Cooper doesn't speak, taking a too-big bite of steak.

"Damn gossip," Starla says.

The topic of conversation switches as Starla tells us about the new yoga studio she's renovating. Then Baylor talks about her art endeavors and going back to school. Cliff says he's learning to kiteboard.

Cooper attempts to take my hand; I refuse. "It's been a long few weeks." He touches his bandage for emphasis. "I have my first surgery on the twelfth."

"It's so awful," Cliff says. "And how's your sister?" Cliff asks me.

"Better every day. Thanks for asking."

"Wait," Starla says, glancing around. "Isn't this where y'all were that night?

"I wasn't here," I say. "It was just Cooper and Willa."

"I never did hear exactly what happened."

Brad lifts his wineglass, as if waiting for someone to tell a really good story. "Thank God you weren't hurt worse, my friend."

I set my fork on the table and settle my gaze on Cooper. "I don't think anyone knows exactly what happened."

Cooper flinches. "I do." He looks around the table and smiles that charming smile. "It's a simple and stupid story. I wish I'd just left her alone and just let her embarrass herself. But hindsight is twenty-twenty."

"No good deed goes unpunished," Starla says.

"Dingle," I say.

"Huh?" she looks at me.

I smile at her and wave my hand in the air. "Nothing."

A few minutes later, I excuse myself to go to the ladies' room. In the tiny bathroom, I stare into the mirror, taking stock of my face, my feelings. I apply lipstick and a quick swipe of mascara. If only my feelings could be so easily glossed over. When I'm through, I make a beeline to the bar, where gorgeous women bartenders juggle orders, demands, and beers while wearing black-laced bustierres. I sidle through the crowd and holler, "Is Benson here?"

"Over there." A girl with long auburn curls points to the far end of the bar.

I walk toward him. He's talking to a crowd of people and soothing what seemed to be an argument about who first had claim to a bar stool. "Hi, Benson."

"Well, hello, Eve." He hugs me. "How are you?"

"Good."

"I saw Willa yesterday." He smiles with such genuine regard. "She's doing so great. I can't wait until she comes back to sing."

"Me, neither. I'll be in the front chair."

He laughs. "Damn, if you'd only been here that night instead." He isn't accusing; he's smiling with his eyes, with his voice.

"You were here, right?"

He nods.

"What happened?" I ask.

"I wish I knew. I was in the back, working with the sound system. I knew she was up next, but when I came out, she was gone. Her guitar was here, but she wasn't."

"Do you remember her acting weird or drunk or anything at all off?"

"No. Not even a little." He exhales. "I mean, I don't know what happened the half hour I was back working on the sound system, but not before."

"Thanks."

I feel it; I feel Cooper staring at me. I glance back to Benson. "Do you remember

Cooper there?"

He shakes his head. "I don't usually notice the dinner crowd. I'm too busy taking care of the crazies at the bar."

I hug him and return to the table. "It's nice to see Benson," I say as Carla and Cooper stand to let me back into the booth.

The check has arrived at the table and the men are playing credit card roulette, where they fold the credit cards in a fan and made the waitress pick one with her eyes closed. Cooper loses, or wins — depending how you looked at it.

We gather our things and wait for the bill to be signed, but when the waitress returns, her eyes drawn together above her reading glasses, she hands the credit card to Cooper. "I'm sorry, sir. There seems to be a problem. It was declined."

Cooper laughs as if she's playing a practical joke. "That's not possible," he says.

"Well, maybe you can call. Sometimes a halt is put on it because they think there is a funny charge. . . ."

"Geeze." Cooper smiles at her and then at us. "Gwen probably bought something at an iffy store. . . ." He reaches into his wallet and then looks at me. "Honey, this is all I brought."

I reach into my purse with a smile, but

my mouth is arid, parched, as I realize I haven't brought a wallet or cash; I always depend on Cooper to cover it all: the dinners, the bills, our life.

"Damn, Cooper." Brad places his hand on the table. "I've got this." He hands the card to the waitress. "But you owe me, Coop. For this dinner, I want a free half-page advertisement."

Cooper laughs, but I know the sound is devoid of anything but unease. He places his card back into his wallet. "Consider it payback for last week, when you kicked my ass on the golf course."

On the drive home, darkness presses onto and into the car. I reach to turn on the radio, but Cooper stops me. "I think it's best if we talk, Eve. I can't live with us like this."

"Like this?" I repeat. My hands are folded in my lap, belying the fast beating heart and the anxiety grip on my throat.

"You doubting me."

"I don't know what to do, Cooper. I don't."

"You might not know what to *do,* but what do you *believe*? Whom do you believe?"

"I don't believe either of you."

"What the hell?" He pulls the car over and

parks on a side street, turns to face me.

I continue, strong. "I don't think your story is wholly true. I don't think Willa's memories are wholly true. I think there's something in the middle — a story in between."

"And what is that?"

"The truth."

"Eve, I'll tell you the truth. If you pursue this, if you go looking for something that's not there, we will lose everything. You'll lose everything."

"What does that mean?"

"Think logically. Just try to do that for me. Okay?"

"What do you mean, Cooper?" My throat tightens and anger fills my chest with hot wind.

"Sometimes you live in la-la land, Eve. You don't even have a college degree. Do you think that the house and your studio and your company just happened? The house we live in, the studio, Willa's cottage — they're all here because of my family's work and reputation through the years. We live on the bedrock of all that came before us: family."

"So," I say, bitterness finding its way into my words, "you're telling me that everything we have is built on a reputation that you can't allow to be ruined. And if your image is ruined, so are we."

"Something like that."

"*That's* the logic you want me to see?"

"Yes. And I don't understand why you're being like this. What is wrong with you?"

"What is *wrong* with me?" I lean my head back on the seat rest, tears springing up quickly. "I keep asking myself that very question."

"Well, you'd better figure it out before you ruin us. Our family. Your business. Everything."

It sounds like a threat.

"Let it be, Eve. It's over."

"Yes," I say. "But to let it go, I have to ask you two questions. And I'll ask them only once and then I won't bring it up again."

"I'll tell you the truth. What do you want to know?"

"Were you at the restaurant with that Mary Jo?"

"No. I already told you."

"Did you hit a man, a homeless man?" It's a dreadful relief to finally ask this question.

"No. And I already told you that. We hit a cursed tree, Eve."

"Okay, Cooper. You hit a tree. I believe

you." Because the alternative is too awful to bear.

"Can we go home now?"

"Yes. Home." He takes my hand and leans over, kissing me deeply, satisfied. He's the only one.

TWENTY-TWO

It's Wednesday morning and already the streets are teeming with tourists in their sun hats. The carriages are lined up for tours; the street vendors are selling hats made from palm leaves and bar owners are passing out flyers for their two-for-one night. I'm on a fool's errand, but then again I have been a fool, so that's appropriate. I don't really know what I expect to accomplish by this confrontation. But I've got to do it. All the years, all the times that I've stepped away from the truth, from seeing what lies below, this time I can't.

I find Mary Jo's office easily. It's above my favorite store — the Paris Market — and this alone seems a personal insult. How could she sit there doing her work and keeping my secrets, stalking my family? It seems a great slap in the face.

I ring the street side doorbell for Mary Jo Hoffman/Accountant. No one answers. I back away, glance up to the windows and see the lights are on. A voice comes from behind me. "Ma'm, can you tell me where the Paula Deen restaurant is?"

I turn, to see an older man, large and sweating, wiping his red face with a stained handkerchief. His white hair is swept to the right in a comb-over to hide his bald pate. "No," I say with a catch in the back of my throat. "I'm not from around here." And in that moment, it doesn't seem like a lie.

It takes two more tries before a voice comes over the intercom. "May I help you?"

"Yes, I'd like to talk to you."

"Do you have an appointment?"

"No." I bite my lip, nervous that this mission might reveal little more than my own insecurities and doubts.

"And your name?"

"Eve Morrison."

A buzzer sounds and I open the heavy wooden door. The foyer is painted stark white. A black-and-white framed photo of the Savannah River hangs over a white demitable against the wall. An elevator is at my left and also a wooden stairway. A sign hangs on the stairwell wall — MARY JO HOFFMAN — and then a red arrow pointing upward.

No need to rush. I climb the stairs. My

heart sinks into my stomach. I'm in free fall. Can I really go through with this? I reach the top of the stairs, so apparently I can. Mary Jo is there, facing me. Her hair is pulled back into a tight ponytail and she wears large hoop earrings. Her neck is bare.

I try to speak first, to say something that will let her know I'm in charge, but she beats me to it.

"What are you doing here?"

"I need to talk to you. I promise it won't take long."

She motions for me to enter her office — a small pink room with a glorious view of Broughton Street. Two slipper chairs face each other on either side of a wrought-iron coffee table. She motions for me to sit, and I do.

"What can I help you with?" She places her hands in her lap, as if she's in church, waiting.

"I know you sent the cards."

"Cards . . . ? I don't know what you're talking about."

"Don't insult me any further, Mary Jo. And don't pretend that there isn't something going on with my husband."

"Your husband?"

"Stop," I say. "Seriously. This is enough. I don't want to bring in lawyers and affidavits and all that destructive business. I just want you to tell me why you were with him on the night of the accident. I want you to tell me what happened."

Her face blanches white. Even her lips lose their color, so now her pink lipstick looks gaudy; a child's drawing of a face.

I sit still, waiting.

She crumbles; the undoing begins on her forehead and moves down in waves, until her lips shake and she drops her head into her hands. "I sent the cards. I did."

"Why?"

"It's hard to explain."

"Try," I say. It's not a suggestion.

"Because I'm an idiot and I believed that if I could make you look closely, you'd leave him and . . ."

"Is this about love?" I ask.

She doesn't look at me, but her words are clear. "Yes, it's about love."

I thought I was prepared for this moment. I thought wrong.

Mary Jo sees the look on my face. "He doesn't love me. I love him. Or I thought I did."

"Are you having an affair with my husband?"

"No," she says. There's not a hint of hesitation in her voice. "I was with him that night, but it was only business. Accounting."

"At dinner?"

"It was an appreciation dinner. Something to thank me for my hard work."

"I don't even a little bit believe you." I stand. "So I guess we'll have to move to the lawyers."

She waves her hand for me to sit again, and I'm taller in my quiet surety. My legs shake and my hands are wet, but my mind is calm and focused on every detail, every motion and word.

"We were not having an affair." Her hands are folded in her lap, knit together.

"Okay, then what *were* you having?"

Her face takes on the look of a woman who's been caught. "I fell in love with him. I didn't want to." She bites her lower lip and turns away, continuing. "He's so charming and he treated me so kindly. . . . I thought he felt something, too. Always complimenting me. Always asking about my life and my family. He . . . got me to do things I knew I shouldn't. But then I realized that he'd never leave you or your family. I was ridiculous that night at the Bohemian, begging him to see how much better we'd be together than what he had."

"Why the cards, then?"

"I wanted you to see the truth, so you would leave him. It was wrong. . . . I know that now."

"What truth?"

"That he was moving money around. That he used your business money to finance his own company and never told you. Family money, too. I thought you'd . . . leave." She stares at me for a long while. "I'm sorry."

"So, let me get this straight, okay? You've been doing some accounting work for him and some of that accounting work has been tricky enough to cause concern. And you loved him, but he didn't love you? And so you wanted me to know that he was doing something borderline unethical to finance his failing company?"

She nods, and this time her face is calm, as if releasing truth soothes her. "He loves you. He loves his daughter and his family. He loves all of you so much." She chokes on the last word. "That's true, too." She unravels her hands to hold them up, pleading. "Don't tell him I told you all this. He'll hate me." Then her head drops to her chest, deflated. "Forget it; he already hates me."

I walk out alone, and when I stand on the street, I stare into the window of the Paris Market with its vintage antiques and the oyster-shell chandelier I've been coveting for months. A round white marble café table sits outside, and I plop down into one of the chairs at its side. Relief, a waterfall of relief, spreads through me, so warm and calm that I wonder if I've ever felt it before. This is what truth feels like. I smile with such gratitude that when an older gentleman passes me with his cane, he smiles in return, nods and tips his hat.

There wasn't a perfect place or time to tell Cooper what I believe, what I plan. But the kitchen counter, each of us on a bar stool, going through the mail, becomes the place and the time.

His scar has puckered now, pulling his left eye upward, as though he's looking down at me from a far corner. He reaches his hand up to touch its edges, to feel the damage once again.

"Cooper."

"Yes?" he mumbles, tossing a pile of solicitations in the trash.

I take the paper out of the trash and place it in the recycle bin. "I need to talk to you."

"I don't need a recycling lecture."

"What?"

He points to the papers without looking up.

"No, that's not it."

He's distracted and his finger traces the scar, as if to remind both of us of the damage already done. His hair has started growing back and it stands out in different directions, the far corners of the world, unkempt in its new growth.

"The night of the wreck," I say.

He holds up his hand. "My God, Eve. Can we please stop this? Just stop."

"Then you don't have to talk about it. I will."

He walks to the wine refrigerator and pulls out a bottle of Pinot Grigio, pouring himself a glass and taking a long swallow before turning to me. "I can't debate this anymore."

This is what happens when people talk to me this way: I can't find words. My body tingles. My mind focuses on small, insignificant details, like the color of the counter, a dirty towel hanging on the sink's edge, the petals falling off the daisies in the vase. But this time, I draw from some deeper well of belief. "Here is what I think happened," I say.

He holds up his hand. "I told you what happened. You've never been obsessive before. What is wrong with you?"

"I've been asking myself that question for so long, Cooper. You have no idea how many times I've asked that in the middle of the night. What is wrong with *me*?"

"I don't know," he says, quietly now. "There's been a lot of stress here. But it will be okay."

"No. You don't get it. I answered the question and I found that nothing is wrong with me. Only with my beliefs."

"What?" He takes a long — too long — swallow of wine.

"Here is what I believe. You went out that night with Mary Jo and —"

He lifts his wineglass. "Stop it now. This is absurd."

"Yes, you were." I take a breath, betraying the woman who begged me not to reveal the source. "She told me."

"Bullshit."

"I'll start over. So, you were out with Mary Jo when I thought you were in Charleston. You were trying to calm her because she was upset about two things — her so-called relationship with you and some risky accounting. You saw Willa and you were already in panic mode about trying to fix things with the erratic Mary Jo. You took Willa outside, maybe not to take her home, but to try to explain yourself. Willa got upset, and you got in the car to take her home. It was raining and you were fighting. I don't think she grabbed the wheel. I think you were upset and didn't keep your eye on the road and that my sister was a convenient scapegoat. Either way, you hit that homeless man and killed him before you slammed into the tree. You dragged him into an alley while your OnStar called nine one one, and lucky for you, my sister was unconscious."

He's finished his wine during my recitation and he pours another glassful. "You've gone insane."

"Great answer." I stand.

"You have no idea how this all works. You need to listen to me."

"How what works?"

"If you really think that story is true, Eve, do you understand what that means?"

"Yes." I turn to walk away.

"Don't walk away from me, Eve."

I do.

"I'm serious. Do. Not. Walk. Away. You will regret this."

My body floats as if above the floor, above the house, above the earth. The fragile dream breaks like one of my Waterford wedding flutes crashing to a tile floor, unmendable pieces splintered and irretrievable.

I stay at Willa's that night and we are on the

couch at 2:00 A.M. Gwen is asleep beside us, and the movie we watched — *Love Actually* — is still playing, but the sound is off. Willa nods toward the kitchen and I follow her. On the table is the *Savannah News,* open to an article entitled "Finding Home" by Noah Parker. "Read it," Willa says.

It's a long article, the first in a three-part series about Savannah, but the part Willa wanted me to read, the part I needed to know was this: The man who'd been found on Preston Street had been claimed by his family. His name was Skipper Linton and he'd been in and out of rehab; he was seventy-two years old. When the police, under pressure, investigated his death, other homeless witnesses came forth to say they saw Skipper get beaten up over a fifth of vodka.

"Oh, wow." I fold the newspaper over and sit at Willa's table.

She sits next to me. "I don't want you to leave . . . Cooper because of me." She covers her mouth with her hand and tears quickly fill her eyes. "You cannot break up your marriage or life because I had a bad dream about a dead man on the car. You were right about that."

I shake my head. "It's more than this man. It's more than you or your dream! I'm doing this for me. And for Gwen. And for the truth."

"You know what everyone will say, right?"

"Yes, they'll say he's a good man and I'm a terrible person for never having appreciated being part of the Morrison family and that my studio success is owed to their name. They'll say I left him when he needed me most. They'll say I was nothing but white trash from the beginning. That's what they'll say. Well, let them."

My sister smiles at me.

"But," I say, "there's more than one way to be unfaithful, and he's been lying about everything. Where he was. Who he was with. Our money."

"*Your* money," Gwen says, correcting me.

"And the worst part — he used you, Willa, to cover up his lies. I cannot . . . I will not . . . I won't live with him knowing this."

"This is my fault. If I hadn't shown up here, if . . ."

"You walked into a mess that night and not one bit of this is your fault." I hold out my hand. "Don't kid yourself. If you hadn't shown up, it would have been something else."

"I'm sorry," she says.

"No. *I'm* sorry. I've spent so much time making sure we all look good that it took me too long to see it isn't good at all. Our family was an image wavering like that game we had as kids when we'd imagine that the clouds were animals or castles or anything real at all. It was once real; I know that. But somewhere along the way — I don't know where or when — it came undone and I pretended it was all okay when it wasn't. I can't unsee or unknow the truth now." I take a breath.

She reaches across the table and takes my hand. "We'll be okay, Eve. Whatever happens, whatever you do, we will be fine."

"Let's get some sleep," I say, and stand to hug her, motioning to the living room.

My heart is hollow and my insides swept clean. I'm afraid I won't ever feel anything like real love again until I see my daughter asleep on the couch. I cover Gwen with a blanket and kiss her forehead. "I love you, Pea."

"I know," she replies, and rolls over, burrowing her face into the couch pillows.

I'm answering e-mails at the studio the next morning, faking normalcy, when Gwen and Willa show up with coffee and croissants, and smiles — big smiles. "Morning," they say in unison.

They approach the table and I grab a

chocolate croissant. "Thanks for the nutri-
tious breakfast."

They sit next to each other but face me.
"What are you working on?" Gwen asks.

"The last commandment: *Love.*"

The last ideas are almost done, lined up
at one end of the table. Pantone color charts
and finished sketches lie about; font choices
and sizes have been chosen. The polymer
plates and font blocks will come next.

"*Love,*" Gwen says. "I didn't know you'd
picked the last one."

"Just two days ago," I say.

"I love the Love." She looks up at me,
those eyes of Cooper's staring at me. "I have
an idea, but you might get mad."

"Why would I get mad?"

"Because it's almost the same as my tattoo." She cringes. "Sorry."

"A feather?" I ask.

"No." She touches the word *Love.*
"Wings."

"Yes," I say.

"Yes," Willa agrees.

Max's voice comes from the still-open
barn doors. "Perfect."

We all look up. Willa and Gwen laugh; I
smile. He walks toward us in his jeans and
crumpled soft blue button-down shirt.
"Remind me why you don't work for us,"

he says to Gwen, a smile in his voice.

"Because I'm too cool."

"True that," Max says, imitating her lingo.

Francie arrives with her earbuds in, singing to the Civil Wars' "Falling." "I can't help falling/Out of love with you. . . ." Then she looks toward us and quickly releases her buds.

"Keep going," Gwen says. "It's so pretty the way you sing."

Francie waves her hand toward us and comes to our side, points at the card line. "This all came together so beautifully."

Max drops his backpack and sits with us. "Gwen suggested wings for the *Love* idea. I think it's brilliant. You?"

Francie sits next to Max and lifts a thick piece of cotton paper from the torn pile, drawing in silence. Max turns on the music; Gwen nibbles on a croissant; and Willa stares at me with a cautious eye because, without knowing I'd done so, without anyone else noticing, tears have puddled under my eyes.

I wipe at my eyes furiously and mouth the words, *I'm fine.* I'm telling the truth, because although I know that a storm is coming, at that moment I'm with everyone I love and the world, for that minute, has settled into its place.

TWENTY-THREE

Cooper's scar is flaming red and I can't stop looking at it as I avoid his eyes. He's crying, and I know it's real; he's scared and hurt and wants to mend it all.

"I want to take it all back. I'm sorry. I should never have lied about that night. I did it to protect you. To protect us. I didn't want you to know my business was failing. I didn't want my parents to know."

God, how I loved this man once.

"So you wanted me to think that my sister was drunk. That you were having an affair, that you would lie about meetings and places, that you would shift money around — all these things were better for me to believe than that the company was failing?"

"I didn't think about it that way. I just wanted to protect you and Gwen from something that would make you worry, when I knew I could fix it."

"Can you tell the truth about anything at all?"

He reaches behind his chair and pulls out the *Savannah News,* slamming it onto the coffee table. "Did you read this?" He points to the article "Finding Home."

"Yes."

"I didn't kill anyone, Eve. I didn't hit anyone or lie about it."

"I know that now."

"Did you really believe I'd hit a man and leave him?"

"I didn't know where your truth ended and the lies started. I didn't." I look up to Cooper and see a slight smile.

"See? What I did wasn't that bad."

"But . . . you threw my sister under the bus. You were willing to blame her, to lie about her to save face? My sister: For God's sake."

He touches his bandage and attempts humor. "I didn't really get to save face, did I?"

There he is, the charming, smart man I fell in love with — my husband. But I feel nothing. The anxiety is gone and a windless empty space remains.

He pushes on. "All the stuff you were worried about had nothing to do with me. I didn't kill anyone. I didn't sleep with anyone. You are making this so much bigger than it is."

"All those lies — all of them about money and who you were with and why — are no different from cheating. How can you separate them?"

"I'm sorry. It was wrong. But I don't have a mistress. I didn't hit a man and walk away. I just. . . . It was for us. For our family."

"No, it wasn't. It was for you." I can see by the look on Cooper's face that he doesn't get it. "It was for *you,* Cooper. Your image. Your gratification. Your ridiculous pride."

The air shifts and Cooper leans back in his seat to cross one leg over the other. His face is altered, and not just by the scar and the pulled skin but also by the wave of anger that comes, immediate and flaming. "And you want to talk about image? It's what you do for a living. It's all you've ever been about."

"Maybe. But if that's true, I'm lying to myself, not to you. I'm not dragging your family into chaos, or hiding where I am, or shuffling money, or moving people around to make it seem better. You're right: I've been trying to save an image of a family. But now I'm going to save my family." My voice isn't my own; it belongs to someone stronger, braver than I am. I stand to look down at his anger, at his impotent rage to fix what is now shattered.

"Really? Saving your family?" he shouts, and I stumble backward with the force. "Because Mary Jo told me that you and Max seemed a little too cozy at work. You want to tell me about that?"

"About *that*?"

"Yes. I've always wondered about you two." He's gaining momentum now. "About your *friendship*." He spits out the word.

I can't believe how calm I am. "Friend-ship — yes. Love, kindness, all the good things."

The curse words that come out of his mouth are in a string so long and so jumbled, I am impressed by the creativity. I'm in the room and completely discon-nected from it; staring out onto the porch as I can do in dreams when I see myself as another, as someone doing and saying what I only imagine. It's only now that I can walk away, and I do.

It's Cooper who files the divorce papers, a preemptive strike. I stay at Willa's cottage, going home for clothes and mail and neces-sities when I know he isn't home. It's a floating feeling, an untethered peace, like bopping around in space, knowing that soon

I'll run out of oxygen in my tank, but don't. There are lawyer visits and Cooper's texts reminding me that I will lose everything if I continued to "blaspheme" him with my random accusations. It is true: His lawyers, his family lawyers, all of them are better and stronger than anyone I could find.

But who is to blame? This is what my lawyer, Betsy Rusk, wants to know, and I can't answer. Slowly, I tell her, the unseen was seen; the invisible became visible. Nothing was as it appeared. Cooper had become his own fictional version of himself: the stage our house, the players being Gwen and me, the backdrop his job. Meanwhile, the real Cooper was another man entirely, and the double sidedness of the man and family life were both familiar and disturbing.

And I had done the same, I admit, I'd pretended. I needed to believe in the facade, in the Family with a capital *F*. I desired the *family* and the man and the love. I desperately needed it all and refused to see I didn't have it. I'd been holding on to something that wasn't even there, like an old photograph that fades because it wasn't living at all, just a captured shadow.

Cooper created the man he wanted to be and acted it out, and I'd cheered him on, colored inside the lines of his drawn character. In a way, he was telling the truth: The accident wasn't his fault; the dead man's life wasn't relevant. In the end, it was the fictional version that had become true.

You really think I'm that guy? You really believe I could do that?

Yes, I do.

Yes.

I told Gwen, in the presence of her therapist, about the divorce. We'd have to move and close the studio, I said. She cried but looked straight at me, tears running down her cheeks like silver scars, and said, "I know, Mom. It sucks, but still . . . I know."

Late one night, a week later, all the *Ten Good Ideas* cards are complete, lined up in their beauty as stones on an artful walkway. Francie, Max, Gwen, Willa, and I stand over them like a parent at the nursery window, admiring in bleary-eyed exhaustion the red-faced newborns. We know what this finishing means. It is not only a new card line but also an ending.

We are silent for a long while, no one knowing what to say. Some endings are wordless. Then together, we walk outside into the dark night. It's Gwen who looks up and says, "Full moon."

As everyone wanders away, Max and I are left standing side by side, and I try to speak first, but it's his proclamation that overrides mine. "I took a full-time job at SCAD."

"What? I thought we were going to try to teach classes at the studio. Expand things."

He turns and faces the studio, the barn that has become home. "I know you'll have to give this up and find a new place. It's the right time for me to move on, too."

"No." I take one step toward him and place my hand on his chest. "Please don't."

"I took the job." He waves toward the barn doors. "I'll never forget any of this. And I know it won't be here anymore, which maybe makes it easier to leave."

" 'Easier to leave'?"

He touches my cheek. "No, not easier to leave. Just thought it sounded better."

"I'll find a new place for the studio and —"

He places his finger over my lips. "Stop." He reaches into his pocket and pulls out a small box.

"What is this?"

His answer is a smile.

I unwrap the tight knot of paper and find a vintage Paragon letter *T* — the one we've been searching for all these years. "Oh, wow." I look at Max. "How did you find this?"

"I was looking for something else in Cameron's store, and there it was."

"All those years when I looked on purpose, and you find it without trying."

He wraps his arms around me and pulls me to him. With my head on his shoulder and his hands on the back of my neck, he says, "Please be well. You have so much ahead of you."

"I want you ahead of me," I say before I know the words have formed in my mind at all.

He pulls back and looks at me. "It's too late for all that. It is. We had all those other chances and we didn't take them. We were either too early or too late. I know this is a terrible time for you, with Cooper leaving, but I'm not your plan B. You can't, after all this time, say 'I want you now that everything else has fallen apart.'"

"You are not a plan B. That's not it at all."

"You're in the middle of a firestorm that will demand all of you. I can't make it better, and we'll both end up hurting if I'm in the middle of it all."

I take a step back and then another.

"Us." He waves his hand in the space

between. "We've never had our timing right."

He is right. I have — again — been trying to save my family, but this time in a different way, in a parting way. I've let go of everything in order to know the truth, and I won't grab hold of Max, pull him back from the life he wants and needs to make.

"I know you've always wanted to teach. I was hoping it would be . . . with us."

He hugs me one more time, then leaves. Truck tires crunch across the gravel and taillights fade as he makes the sharp right onto the paved driveway.

A swirl of static electricity wraps around my stomach. The free fall of losing him; the painful shock of loss again and again in the middle of my body, and I see that, yes, there's more to lose than a house and a studio and the image of a family.

Minutes pass as I stare at the empty driveway. It isn't fair to grab hold of Max him as my life comes undone, as the waters rise and the storm thunders again. I am still staring down the driveway when I hear the growl of a grunting truck. Headlights appear where taillights have just receded. I grip the fence, my smile rising as hope takes flight.

The full moon spreads its reflected light

onto the drive, and with a sinking, a dropping of the heaviest stone, I see the truck. It is dark green and larger, not Max's at all. The vehicle pulls into the parking lot and a tall man with a handlebar mustache, dressed in a black suit, gets out. He holds a large manila envelope in his hand as he steps onto the gravel. "Are you Eve Morrison?"

I nod.

Without another word, he hands me the envelope. Of course I don't need to open it to know what's inside. Another ending.

Francie walks outside then and glances at the envelope with the lawyer's logo stamped in dark black ink. "Divorce papers?" she asks in a whisper.

"Yes."

"I'm sorry, Eve. So sorry."

"Don't be. I'm the one who's sorry," I wave toward the studio. "We're going to lose all of this." They come now — the tears hidden somewhere beneath the frenzy of finishing our card line, below the bobbing-in-space peace and denial.

"This is not ending," she counters quickly. "I know a warehouse we can rent. I've been looking. We can do this. I know we can."

I try to smile. "A warehouse."

"It's the best I can do so far. But I'll keep looking."

"No, it sounds great. I'll go look with you. But I'll understand if you want to move . . . on."

"Move on? You're not getting rid of me. This is what I do."

"The cards," I say. "They're good."

"No," she says. "They're great."

From inside the barn, a watery light spills out the window and onto the ground, the washed-up remains of all we've been and done here. The last two Ten Good Ideas sit ready to enter the world. Once again, the false commandments are breaking apart what has been: a beginning built into an ending.

Twenty-Four

The loft isn't big, but the tall windows on either side of the corner unit offer us both a sunrise and sunset of such varying hues and contrasts that Gwen and I decide to put up plain white linen curtains, allowing nature to offer all the color it can and will. This morning, three months after I moved out, Gwen is late for school.

I pour another cup of coffee and toss a glance at the typewriter — my Remington — on the counter. Gwen is reading *Ulysses* in her senior Advanced English class and has taken to leaving me quotes from the book. There is a note propped on the typewriter's platen roller in a Lanston Monotype font, stating "Love loves to love love."

I holler down the hallway of our two-bedroom place. "You're late."

"I know. I know. Relax, Mom. I have study hall first." Gwen emerges from her bedroom, which we have designed to look so exactly opposite of her old bedroom that even the sheets aren't the same. Her backpack hangs off her right shoulder. Her hair is loose and she wears only mascara as makeup. Her beauty still stuns me.

In this new life, there are things I thought I'd miss that I don't miss at all, and things I didn't know I would come to appreciate: the simple mornings in a sunlit space; a daughter across the hall who isn't angry or tangled with anxiety; a peace that is free from the desperate need to please someone who can't be pleased. That approval I sought with such desperate busyness, well, I don't need it anymore.

I pour another cup of coffee and look through my cell phone for the name of the man Cameron recommended to fix two of my presses that were damaged in the move. I can't remember the repairman's name and a small spark of anger flicks, like biting a Life Saver in the dark when we were kids — the spark gone before I'm sure it was there at all: anger at Max.

Francie and I now run the Fine Line, Ink from an empty garage warehouse in downtown Savannah, walking distance from my loft, but not quite the short walking distance it was from my house to the barn. We've done what we can to make the studio look the same, to set it up almost exactly as it had been, but with Max gone, emptiness looms. I want to blame the fact that there aren't open beams and stall doors, that there aren't painted concrete floors and the sweet aroma of ghost hay, but the real reason the garage feels wrong is that there is no Max.

The Ten Good Ideas card line entered the world with its own heart and life, becoming the most successful and mass-ordered line we've ever done. From high-end department stores to boutique stationery stores, the orders are overwhelming us. Yet Francie and I have found our way, working long hours, with Gwen coming after school to help. Both Oprah and goop chose the full collection as a "must have."

There was a melancholy heartbreak in seeing this creation enter the world just as my own world came undone.

"Gwen," I say without looking up. "Do you remember the name of the repair guy? I put him in my phone yesterday at Cam's store."

"Van," she says.

"Yes! That's it. Thanks, sweetie." I tap my forehead. "Things are falling out."

"Don't lose your mind on me now, Mom."

I laugh and look up, kissing her cheek as she walks out the door for school. "I love you, Pea. Have a great day. Good luck on the math test."

"I love you, too." She's gone and I walk over to a floor-to-ceiling window divided by iron mullions to watch her. She doesn't know, but every morning when she leaves, I stand here and watch her turn right out of the parking deck and onto Drayton Street. I spy on her car until it disappears around the bend.

Standing at the window, I search again for the repairman's number and tap it out on the phone's keyboard, leaving a message when he doesn't answer. Francie is meeting me at work in an hour, and before then I need to sift through the pile of documents on the kitchen table. I've learned a term I wish I'd never known: *financial infidelity.* Uneasiness fills my gut, making me feel seasick, as if I'm tossed on the divorce's storm-battered waves. No matter how many forms I sign or read or review, there always seem to be more, like Cooper is attempting to drown me in paper so I'll give up. I won't.

He stayed in the house, but why wouldn't he? It's his family estate. While I wait on my "equitable share," I review affidavits and documents. It will take a long while to untangle the mess he's made. I still don't fully understand where all the money is or was, and I've come to understand that *equitable share* is a term I never want to hear again. How can a marriage or a love ever be divided into anything equitable at all? Truth? Belief? Not one of these is divisible by anything else, like an algebra equation without an integer. And because, like the baby in Solomon's law, something living — a marriage or love — can't be split, I lose all the intangibles, gaining only material goods, wondering if that is really all that remains. Dividing money that Cooper is hiding is the trick; he's mastered the art of monetary shifting (a term I made up in complete frustration one harrowing afternoon with my lawyer).

I take blame, too: I was part of the image making, complicit in the act of family design without heart. Now there is a great calm, a tremendous relief, as if those things were mirages in front of a smaller world that holds larger good. It's a much more ordinary life I lead now, one without backstage passes and front-row seats, and yet somehow it is a much more extraordinary life. Every day there is a new wonder. The emptiness isn't as empty as I'd imagined.

Willa is still healing, losing words and

mixing facts, but writing songs and singing with Francie on the weekends at local venues. It's there, in her songwriting and singing that her mind becomes whole and heals itself a little every day. She moved in with Benson, and his love for her is an umbrella that protects her more than I ever had been able to do while soaked in my own rainstorm.

Cooper's scarred face and severed scalp have undergone two surgeries. I tried to visit him after the second, but his mother, Louise, turned me away at the door, announcing — as she must have practiced in her living room for hours — "You are dead to us." She stood tall and upright, smiling with her proclamation.

Sometimes I feel dead to myself, I'd wanted to tell her all those months ago when I was as numb as if my body had been injected with novocaine.

I am still standing at the window as Gwen's car turns, leaving my sight. I hear a shuffling outside the door: the neighbor's dog. The tiny, yappy poodle named Tinkerbell often makes a yellow puddle outside my doorway before her owner, Shawn, gets to the elevator. I glance down at my phone, impatient for the repairman to call me back. I hear a knock on the door and I walk toward it, ready to face Shawn while he apologizes for his dog's mess. I prepare to smile and hand over some paper towels.

And it is Shawn standing there, but he's holding a silver envelope, one I recognize from our Ten Good Ideas card line. He smiles and hands it to me without saying a word, then walks away. TinkerBell glances over her shoulder as if to say, "I'll get you next time."

The metal door clicks shut and I sit on the oversize white couch, which Gwen and I chose from a catalog. My finger slips beneath the envelope fold and I pull out the card I know so well, the one Gwen designed with the ragged heart: *Forgive,* number nine. I think how nice Shawn is to apologize with my own card line. I didn't realize that he knew what I did at all. I smile at the unexpected generosity. A lot different from the last cards sent to me from my own business.

I open it slowly, but inside is a note from Mary Jo, not Shawn.

"Please forgive me," it says.

This is all that's written inside, except for her slanted signature. I place it on the table. I will write her back and maybe I will tell her that there is nothing to forgive, neither the car accident nor the cards, that the truth would have come out with or without her. Cooper misrepresented himself to her as he did to me. Endings. They come over and over, and with each one there is also a new beginning. Cooper was right: Everything was lost. But what Cooper didn't know, could never know, is that it is here in the loss that I finally believe in kindness, in truth, and, mostly, in love.

The autumn sun is warm, but cold air is pushing in behind and will be arriving soon. Savannah feels, on days like this, to hold me in the palm of its hand. The river pulses toward its destination as if somewhere that I can't see a heart is pumping these waters. Palmetto tree branches shudder against one another with the faux sound of rain. Light is cradled in the leaves, as if the sun needs rest also.

I walk slowly to the garage studio this late afternoon, soaking in what feels holy and good. Tonight, Francie and Willa are singing together at a songwriter's showcase downtown. Max will be there, and this knowledge walks next to me like a companion. I've seen him a couple of times since the night he said good-bye — at Cameron's shop, at the farmers' market, and at Larry Ford's restaurant one night.

Willa, Gwen, and Francie are waiting for me as I walk in. Today, we're wrapping boxes of the Ten Good Ideas card line for shipping. It will take all week.

"Hey, Mom." Gwen doesn't look up as she tapes Kraft paper around a box. She's come here straight from school.

"You excited about tonight?" I ask Willa and Francie.

Their guitars are propped in the far corner, waiting, and Willa points to them. "Nervous. Mostly nervous."

"We're singing our new song, the one we wrote together." Francie drops a pile of envelopes into a box and then looks up at me. "The one inspired by you, actually."

"You mean the one you won't let me hear yet?" They've told me about how they wrote this song it after I moved out, after they saw the quiet change in me.

"Yep, that one," Francie says. "We hope you won't hate it."

"I won't," I say, sure as I can be that I won't hate anything they've written.

"Mom . . ." Gwen says my name with a long groan built into it. "You didn't bring my college app folder?"

"No, because you don't need to work on it here. Go home. Work on it. You do not need to be doing this." I spread my hands out across the cluttered table, the same project table we took from the old barn. "College is more important. Go, Pea."

"I'm almost done. I thought I could just do the last bit here. With you and Willa."

I love this about her, this willingness and need to be near us, when only months before she'd cringed at being in the same room with me. My fear, my greatest one during the divorce, had been that I was doing harm to Gwen, but now I see that we both understand that although things aren't exactly the way we want them, at least they're honest and real.

"You can run home and get it," I say. "Bring it back here."

Willa looks up from her work, and even now, although I see her every day, I am immersed in her beautiful healing. The tiny scar has almost disappeared and her mind is now mostly clear. The empty spaces and damaged synapses are finding new ways to function — neuroplasticity, they call it. I haven't told her that I actually love the way she mixes up her words and finds new pathways in her lyrics — it might not be the traditional way, but now it's her way.

"You aren't wearing that tonight, are you?" Willa points at my jeans and white

T-shirt. "There will be lots of . . . people there."

There's this, too — her newfound honesty. She blurts out whatever she thinks whenever she thinks it. I open my eyes wide and lift my forehead: our silent sign language of amusement. I know that by "people there," she means Max. She knows how I feel about him; we've talked about it since the divorce. I've admitted that I always felt a deep connection with him, that I always fought off the desire, and that I wish things were different now. But they aren't different, and I want him to be the happiest he's ever been. He deserves great, wide, beautiful happiness.

Willa acknowledges my sign and we work for a couple hours, the garage doors wide open, breezes ruffling our piles and making Gwen scramble for the envelopes she hasn't yet packed. One by one, Willa, Francie, and Gwen leave. I stay and work silently without music or distraction. I file through our Ten Good Ideas cards, and with each one I remember working with Max as we found the right image, the correlating font, our hands touching, our talk overlapping and tangential even as we found our way back to the center of our conversation. His stories — myths he knew and ones he made up on the spot. His blue-rimmed eyes when he listened to me. His shoulder, the way I rested on it, leaned into the solidness of him.

The memories don't stop. They come one after the other and I can't do anything but watch them pass by. I want to let go, but the desire just won't let go of me.

Francie and Willa are on the makeshift stage, blushing at the standing ovation. Their song — how could they have ever believed that I'd hate a song titled "Stories We Tell"? It's a melody about lies and heartbreak, a song with the lyrics "The beginning inside the end" — a turn of phrase for the way I'd described the last day I lived in the Morrison home.

I'm standing, clapping also, and looking for Max. He isn't here — believe me, I've checked a hundred times, scanning the room for him. I sit again and take a long swallow of Malbec. The next pair of songwriters walks on the stage while Francie and Willa pack up their guitars. Gwen sits up in the front row and turns to wave at me. I wave in return and then blow her a kiss.

"Stories we tell," a voice behind me says, Max's voice.

Before I turn to see him, look in his eyes, I take in a long breath. I stand to face him, holding my wineglass. I don't know whether to hug him or shake his hand, whether to stand there or leave gracefully. "Wasn't that a great song?"

"Yes," he says. "It was really beautiful. Who knew getting hit in the head could lead to such great lyrics?" He has a sly grin that falls quickly. "That wasn't funny, was it? I was trying and failed."

"It was sort of funny," I say. "A good try."

But we don't laugh, and he takes my wineglass out of my hand and places it on the table so he can hug me. He holds me longer than a hug. The room is so quiet between song sets, the clattering of glasses, the soft murmur of conversation, and then the screech of the microphone being re-adjusted. I hear it all, but my eyes are closed as I rest against his chest.

Max releases me and I take half a step back. "How are you?" I ask. "How's teaching and . . ." I trail off, not asking all the things I need to know about him: How's your heart? Do you miss me? Are you happy?

"I'm good, really good. The job is great, and so are the students."

The emcee for the night announces a fifteen-minute break, and Max nods at my small café table. "Can I sit with you?"

"Of course . . ."

We sit so close that I have to twist my head to face him. He doesn't look at me as he speaks, but toward the stage. "Have I ever told you the myth about the skeleton woman?"

"No."

"Want to hear it?" He takes a sip from my wineglass and then hands it to me.

I want to hear a lot of things, but I tell him that, yes, now, I'd love to hear his story. I always love to hear his stories.

"There was a fisherman and he went out into the sea. He was wishing for the best catch of his life, when there was a large pull on his line — something big; maybe everything he wanted." He pauses and his hands stretch along the two chair backs on either side. "But when he pulls up the catch, it's a skeleton he's caught by the ribs." Max leans forward and contorts his face in faux horror. "Agghhh!" He lunges forward.

I startle and then burst into laughter, a sweet release that is too loud, and I clap my hand over my mouth. "Gross," I say. "Greek myth?"

"No, this is Inuit. . . ."

I settle back, smiling. "Why was she at the bottom of the ocean anyway? I presume it was a 'she.' "

"Yes indeed. Well, her father — as is the way of these things — her father disapproved of something she'd done and cast her into the sea."

"Okay . . ." I feel that roll, that motion sickness of a father's casting out, and then I look directly into Max's eyes and I'm centered, buoyant in the current of the tale.

"Now the fisherman runs and runs, but he's already caught her and she bumps along behind him on the fishing line. He finally jumps into his tent, exhaling, breathing deeply, and trying to ignore the skeleton he's brought home. But as he sleeps, as he tries to escape the tangled bones in his tent, she becomes real."

"How?" I ask, quiet and curious, over the sound of someone tuning their guitar.

"His tear. She steals his tear while he's sleeping and quenches her thirst to become real. And she also steals his heart — she takes it right out of his chest. When he wakes, they're tangled together for good. For love."

"Ah!" I exhale. "Finally one of your tales has a happy ending."

"There's more to it. But I'm giving you the parts that matter."

"That matter?"

"To us."

He takes my hands in his, each one folded into a palm. "Even if I've never read it anywhere, I bet that skeleton woman had brown eyes that turned green while she stole his heart."

"Us?" I ask quietly.

"It's always been you, Eve. I love you. I can't run far enough or ignore you long enough, because when I wake up every day, you're always right there, waiting for me."

"I'm right here."

The music begins again at the front of the room and Max leans forward to kiss me. I don't close my eyes. I want to see and know it all, everything there is to know about him, about love.

"This," he says. "This is a happy story."

TEN GOOD IDEAS CARD LINE

1. *Be Kind* — live oak

2. *Tell Good Stories* — stacked books

3. *Always Say Good-bye* —
profiles facing each other

4. *Search for the True* — world in the sky

5. *Help Others* — hands holding

6. *Create* — crayon box

7. *Be Patient* — river over boulders

8. *Find Adventure* — forest and river with
two figures peeking around trees

9. *Forgive* — scraggled heart

10. *Love* — wings

ACKNOWLEDGMENTS

Inspiration doesn't always lead to a story, but when it does, it's great fun to write. This novel was initially inspired by my curiosity and admiration for letterpress — a handmade product in a manufactured world. This book would be a different novel altogether without the people in my life that either supported me or contributed to the words. We don't get to choose when life gets tangled and even comes undone, but we do get to choose how we move forward. And I couldn't have finished this book or moved forward without the love, kindness, and deliciously surprising support of the following people:

To my editor, Brenda Copeland, for her patience, keen eye, wit, and desperate love for story and editing. You push me when I need it and make me laugh when I think I can't. To the publishing team at St. Martin's Press: Sally Richardson and Jennifer

413

Enderlin, I am grateful beyond measure for your support. You are treasures. To Laura Chasen, Nick Small, Marie Estrada, Kerry McMahon, Jean-Marie Hudson, Paul Hochman, and all the sales staff and support staff that make St. Martin's Press the excellent place that it is.

To Carol Fitzgerald of Bookreporter.com, What would I do without your energy, imagination, and keen eye?

To my agent, Kimberly Whalen, who from the very beginning believed and still does.

To my friends: Kerry Madden (and her astounding daughter, Norah), who showed up just when needed and asked all the right questions that made the story more complete. To Lanier Isom, your heart is wide and beautiful and I can't remember what it was like without you. To Cleo O'Neal and Kate Phillips, I don't have room to list what you've done or who you've been for me these past months and how profoundly grateful I am for you both. For the friends who have been there for me in ways I would have never understood until I needed it: Cate and Mark Sommer; Kenneith and Glenn Donald; Brooke and Tyler Wahl; Alison Gorrie; Karen Spears Zacharias; Dorothea Benton Frank, Mary Alice Monroe, Summer Anderson (Oh! Those flowers!!), and Beth Fidler, a sister as much as a friend! To Tara Mahoney, I love you as if you were my own. To Kathy Trocheck, we met all those years ago and still we are here and still you lift me up, make me laugh, and bring me along for the fun. To Diane Chamberlain, for her early words of praise, I am humbled and grateful. To Jamie Allen and Tom Bell, for showing up as if in a dream and taking me away for the day just when I needed it most. I am so lucky to have you in my life. To Susan Rebecca White and Joshilyn Jackson, you are both like some magical apparition turned real — I adore you; your work both inspires me and carries me away.

To Sandee O. Bartkowski, for everything and all things creative, you influence my work. You know you've saved me more times than we'll ever be able to count and I love you more each time. Also, both you and Sara Weinberger infected me with the love for letterpress when you opened a store, 3226, as "Purveyors of Imaginative and Beautiful Things."

And to Scott Fisk, at Samford University, who offered his time and expertise when I showed up at his office with a list of questions about the art and craft of letterpress, thank you!

To the readers who make this all possible: I wish I could thank every one of you in person, so consider this my personal hug. You come to events; you buy the books; you write to me and you make me want to write a better book every single time. Thank you.

To the bookstores, bloggers, book clubs, reviewers, and Web sites that have supported my work, I am incredibly grateful. What would I do without you? Not much.

Always to my family, all of you: my sisters, Jeannie and Barbi, and their families and kids, life would be so bland and lonesome without you. You fill up my heart to its very edges. You showed up when I didn't ask, surrounded me, and held me up. To Anna, Kirk, Kirk and Sofia, I love you. To Serena Henry, this year has been soaked with your love and support, and I don't know what I would have done without you; it's as if I've known you forever, my whole life. To my parents, George and Bonnie Callahan, who could ask for anything more than you? To Gwen and Chuck Henry, who have treated me as their daughter and loved me the same.

To Pat, Meagan Steele, Patrick Thomas, and George Rusk — You are my heart. It's all for you.